IN COLD BLOOD

CAROLINE MITCHELL

PRAISE FOR THE AUTHOR

'For me, this book had everything - an excellent police procedural with tension, pace and a compelling storyline. With the added psychological element, there was nothing more I could have asked for.'
- Angela Marsons, author of Hidden Scars

'Caroline Mitchell at her dark and twisty best' - Teresa Driscoll, author of I Am Watching You

'Will keep you on the edge of your seat' - Alice Hunter, author of The Serial Killer's Wife

The writer's conflicted heroine and twisted villain are superb characters.'
- The Sunday Express magazine

'The tension built up and up...I devoured every page'
- Mel Sherratt, author of Twisted Lives

'A tense and deliciously creepy read' - D.S. Butler, author of On Cold Ground

'With her police officer experience, Caroline Mitchell is a thriller writer who knows how to deliver on plot, character, and most importantly, emotion in any book she writes. I can't wait to read more.'
- My Weekly magazine

ALSO BY CAROLINE MITCHELL

The DC Jennifer Knight Series

Don't Turn Around

Time To Die

The Silent Twin

The DI Amy Winter Series

Truth And Lies

The Secret Child

Left For Dead

Flesh And Blood

The DS Ruby Preston Series

Death Note

Sleep Tight

Murder Game

The Slayton Series

The Midnight Man

The Night Whispers

Individual Works

Paranormal Intruder

Witness

Silent Victim

The Perfect Mother

The Village

Copyright © 2022 by Caroline Mitchell

All rights reserved.

No part of this book may be reproduced in any form or by any electronic or mechanical means, including information storage and retrieval systems, without written permission from the author, except for the use of brief quotations in a book review.

This is a work of fiction. Names, characters, organisations, places, events, and incidents are either products of the author's imagination or are used fictitiously. Any resemblance to actual persons, living or dead, or actual events is purely coincidental.

For my readers

We wear the mask that grins and lies,
It hides our cheeks and shades our eyes
This debt we pay to human guile;
With torn and bleeding hearts we smile,
And mouth with myriad subtleties.

PAUL LAURENCE DUNBAR

CHAPTER ONE

Yasmin had never experienced real fear until now. Fear was the smell of dried-in sweat. Of crusted blood. Of the knowing...the terrifying knowing that she may never see her family again. There was no reasoning with the couple who'd taken her. They were killing machines, devoid of empathy. They fed on fear. At least two people had died at their hands, and now they were after her. She blinked back her tears, the October wind stinging her eyes and cooling the sweat on her back. She had to keep it together. It was her only chance of escape. On she ran, struggling for breath, her heart galloping. She couldn't think about the lacerations on her feet or the gaping wound in her arm. But she *was* thinking of her sprained ankle, because it was holding her back. She wasn't running, she was lurching, fiery pain shooting up her left foot. They were coming, she could almost feel their breath on the back of her neck. They were near.

A flock of birds exploded above her, sending a signal to her captors. The forest was a labyrinth, and she was deep inside it. *One two three, one two three,* she paced her steps. She didn't know where she was going, but she had to keep moving. She felt like a zombie, her limbs heavy, her head woozy. A shot of adrenaline flooded her body, masking the pain of her injuries. It felt like she'd been running forever. She'd never got this far before. Then she heard it. The tantalising sound of safety: traffic on a nearby road. Evening was closing in, but people were still out, getting food in for their tea or picking up a takeaway – all part of the mundane world she was desperate to return to. *Oh God, could it be true? Could she really escape her living hell?* She was so close. She just needed to get clear of the woods. But they were bordered by wide hedgerows. She couldn't go over. She had to go through. How had she ended up here? She'd been so stupid, leaving herself vulnerable to attack. She was a mother, she should have known better. She had more than herself to think of. Thoughts of her daughter forced her onwards. She could not give up now.

The thick briars seemed to go on forever as they tore the surface of her skin. Another car passed. Another flare of hope. But there was something else in the distance. Two scrambler bikes. She had developed a keen ear for the distinctive rev of their engines as they roared through the forest trail. It was followed by excited high-pitched whoops – to Yasmin, a barbaric sound. Her pursuers were armed and vicious, and now they were after her. All the odds were in their favour, but she had to fight. If not for her, then her child. A gurgle escaped Yasmin's throat as she came out the other side of the brambles and landed with a thud on the unforgiving ground. Her ankle was shot. She could barely support her own weight. *Keep going* her inner voice screamed. She crawled on all fours, warm blood trickling down her leg. Old wounds were reopening. Her muscles begged for rest. But she could not stop now. Ahead of her was the road. A car was approaching, but who was the driver? Perhaps it was a trick. Had one of her captives doubled back and taken the car out to find her? Dare she come out of the shadows and make herself known? All she had to do was climb the embankment and she'd be fully visible on the road. But with her torn clothes and bloodied skin, would they stop for her? Back and forth, thoughts raced through Yasmin's mind. She jerked at the sudden movement beside her. A hare, with big, unblinking eyes, stared. Its nose twitched before it disappeared into the brambles. The creature was safe, but she was not.

She dug her fingernails into the earth, trying to propel herself forward. If she could flag down the car, she might stand a chance. Creeping up the embankment, she watched a blue Vauxhall estate approach. She squinted as harsh headlights filled the air. Should she flag the driver down or keep going until she found a house? She had no idea where she was, or what, if anything, was nearby. She tried to swallow, her throat dry from an unquenchable thirst. Her limbs were shaking from adrenaline, hunger, and pain. But she was here and she was alive. Her family would be looking for her. But where in God's name was she? She remembered the last time she'd run. The agonising pain of the arrow slicing through the sinew and flesh of her arm. Her predators weren't just cruel, they were sadists.

The car was almost upon her now, and through a fog of fear, she thought of her baby, Chloe, almost one year of age. She could not leave her motherless. Riding a white wave of pain, she forced herself to her feet.

'Help!' she waved her arms over her head. 'Please, stop!' The car was approaching, slowing but not stopping. 'Please! Help me!' Yasmin cried, catching sight of the female driver, who glared at her as she passed. She was her age. Why wasn't she stopping? Yasmin fell to her knees, her vision blurred. Today was day four. She was going to die. She buried her head in her hands, crying as she brought up an image of Chloe's face. There was movement behind her. Footsteps approached. Spent, Yasmin looked up.

CHAPTER TWO

'Are you OK?' The voice came from Donovan as Amy stood in the bathroom, taking a few breaths.

'I'm fine,' she whispered. 'Quit fussing.'

They spoke in low tones, not wanting to wake Amy's mother, Flora, who was asleep upstairs. It was gone two a.m., and she and Donovan had just finished a gruelling Sunday night shift. The case they were investigating was taking its toll. Between them, they had come up with a plethora of leads. When it came to their killers, two things stood out. Firstly, they were a couple. Secondly, they were sadistic, putting their victims through unspeakable ordeals. Their campaign of violence was escalating.

'I thought morning sickness was supposed to stop after three months,' Donovan said softly, from the other side of the door.

'It is,' Amy replied, washing her hands. 'But lucky me, I get five whole months of feeling like I'm about to throw up.'

'They say it's a sign of a strong pregnancy. Must be quite a fighter in there.' A smile carried in Donovan's voice. Once he'd recovered from the initial shock, he'd been thrilled at the prospect of becoming a father again.

Amy wasn't sure how she felt about that. After getting to grips with finding herself pregnant, she had no clear sense of direction about how she was going to cope. So far, all she'd done was get her hair cut into a wavy, shoulder-length style and bought some stretchy clothes to accommodate for her waistline. Then she carried on, hoping she would come to love the baby inside her. Had she been born into a normal family, her pregnancy might not have been such an issue, but her bloodlines made her turn cold. Her parents were serial killers. What hope was there for her baby? She imagined its little face. Black hair, with piercing blue eyes. The eyes of her grandmother, Lillian. Or worse still, Jack Grimes. What if it was born a psychopath? If its brain was wired wrong?

'How about I make you some peppermint tea?' Donovan suggested, oblivious to the internal monologue which kept her awake at night.

'That would be lovely, thanks.' She followed him into the kitchen, waiting for the lecture to come – the same way it did every night when she felt rough. She recited his words in her head as she pre-empted what he was about to say. *I think you're working too hard.*

'You're working too many shifts...' he poured the tea.

Almost right, Amy thought, watching him intently. *Isn't it time we told everyone about the baby?* She knew that was coming next.

'And it's time we told the team,' Donovan continued, reinforcing her attempt at mind reading.

He was wearing that stupid grin again, the one he always wore when talking about his forthcoming son. She cast an eye over him, appreciating the way his biceps tightened his shirt sleeves, which were rolled up to the crease of his elbow. Despite his nagging, she was grateful to have him. She'd never cared about anyone as much as she did Donovan, not even her ex-fiancé, Adam, who'd jilted her at the altar. There was no fear of being jilted by Donovan, especially not now.

'We'll tell your mum first, of course,' Donovan added. 'It's only a matter of time until she notices.'

'Tell me about it.' Amy rolled her eyes. 'She keeps dropping hints about Slimming World because she thinks I've put on a few extra pounds.'

Amy had always made it clear that children didn't feature in her future plans, so Flora, her adoptive mother, never came to the conclusion that she could be expecting now. Amy was obsessively organised, with her lists, diaries, and journals. She could never be so stupid as to fall pregnant by accident. But she'd been so wrapped up in work that one morning she'd forgotten to take her pill. Now she was pregnant with a boyfriend who she was completely infatuated with. A boyfriend who happened to be her DCI, with a daughter in her early twenties. The very thought stole the breath from Amy's lungs. He slipped his arm around her, and she welcomed the contact, which was afforded to very few.

'Marry me,' he said, his blue eyes filled with sincerity.

Amy opened her mouth to speak, but Donovan carried on. It wasn't the first time he'd proposed, but here, in the early hours of a new day, he seemed determined to continue.

'Not just because of the baby,' he continued. 'But because it's right. *We're* right, and I can't imagine spending my life with anyone else.'

'A proposal over peppermint tea.' Amy smiled. 'Cute.' But she was already turning away.

'I take it that's a no, then?' Donovan's smile faded.

'It's a not right now. Come to bed.' Her thoughts were returning to the case. Without sleep they had no chance of focusing on work the next day. She picked up her pug, Dotty, from her basket in the hall.

'I'll be up in a minute.' Donovan stood in the doorway, disappointment clouding his features. 'But you can't put things off forever.'

His voice trailed behind her as she walked upstairs, cuddling a sleepy Dotty close to her chest. But it was all too much. Work, the pregnancy, and Donovan's marriage proposals. It felt wrong, concentrating on herself with such a big case on the go. Crime didn't stop because of her personal life, although deep down she knew her team would gush over the news. It was why she had hidden her morning sickness, along with doctor's appointments and scan dates. It had been more of a challenge getting Donovan to curb his enthusiasm. Every day, he begged her to share the news. *Why is life so complicated?* she thought. Yet there was something about the way Donovan couldn't take his eyes off her. That pure, unadulterated love that made everything OK. After all, the baby would share his DNA, too. The chink of crockery rose while he filled the dishwasher, no doubt also lost in thought.

Within minutes, Amy was pulling back her Laura Ashley duvet and slipping into bed, while Dotty settled on top. Later, her pet would settle into the basket on the floor. She was glad Donovan was here, and appreciative of his support.

She would tell her mum about the baby, but only when she was ready to share her news with the team. Flora wouldn't be able to hold it in. She'd tell Craig, and then he'd let it slip at work. She pictured the scenario of her brother blurting the news. Then everything would fall apart. She needed all their focus on the case. As soon as they caught the killer, she would go public with the news. But the case only served to worry Amy more. Even if her baby swerved his grandparents' killer instincts, what sort of a world was she bringing him into?

CHAPTER THREE

Damo watched Lucy stomp around the cottage, unable to contain her anger. He could almost hear her ticking. She was an unexploded bomb. The air was stifling as they packed up their things. With all the windows and doors sealed, they'd been breathing in their own air, tobacco fumes and sweat.

'Fuck!' Lucy screamed. 'You shouldn't have given her so much time.'

'It's no fun if they don't stand a chance. No risk, no reward.' Damo grabbed her around the waist. 'It'll be OK.'

But Lucy planted both hands on her boyfriend's chest and pushed him hard. 'You're going soft, that's what it is. You fell for her sob story about her kid. *That's* why you waited so long to hunt her down.' Her red talons flashed as she raised a finger in the air, fury streaked across her face. 'Whereas I would have planted an arrow in them both!'

She was screaming at a pitch that was making Damo's ears ring. His jaw clenched. He wasn't being spoken to like this.

'Don't you fucking push me.' Damo grabbed a fistful of her blonde hair. 'Are you forgetting who you're talking to?'

Another piercing scream filled the air. 'Ow! OK! Let me go!' But as soon as he did, she drew back her hand and slapped his face.

He touched the blood trickling from his mouth from where her nail had caught him. His dark smile spread as Lucy touched his face before licking his blood off the tip of her finger.

'We don't have time for this,' Damo said, his breathing growing heavy while Lucy undid the buttons of his shirt.

'No risk, no reward,' she said, wearing a dirty grin.

It had always been this way. From the moment they'd met, electricity sparked between them. They weren't a vanilla couple. They got off on violence and sex. Damo had given up trying to fight his genes years ago. But while he had shades of grey, Lucy's thoughts were solid black. Nothing could come between them when they were like this. They tugged at each other's clothing. They would have to make this quick.

They'd met on the dark web, in a forum which shared violence too graphic for regular channels. The moment Damo had opened up to her, Lucy's attraction was instant.

'My food's alive.' That's the first thing Lucy had said to him when they'd got together in the flesh. 'Look at it,' she'd said, prodding the rice on her plate. 'It's alive.'

It wasn't alive. Her spaced-out eyes suggested something else was giving her food the extra dimension. Most women would have walked out of the restaurant after he turned up forty minutes late. But not Lucy. He'd texted his apologies, saying he was on his way. She'd texted a reply that she'd ordered her food and didn't care if he joined her or not. He had almost blown the date off, but his curiosity got the better of him. He'd turned up, palms sweating as he'd joined her at the table. It was her who had insisted on meeting at a restaurant. He usually met women in pubs or clubs. He'd liked her enough to invest in a new shirt and black jeans, topping it off with a jacket he'd bought in Next. But then he'd missed the train and had to wait an hour for the next one before he could get home to change.

He'd sat at her table, hoping the meal wouldn't cost him an arm and a leg. He'd blown most of his money on the outfit, and now here he was, feeling like an idiot as he tried to work out which fork was which. 'I didn't think you'd wait,' he'd said. It was as near as he would get to an apology. Damo didn't say sorry. Either people took him the way he was or they could sod off.

A waiter approached, and he shook his head. He hated social situations at the best of times, but this was another level of discomfort. The people around him were well dressed, glancing at him with curiosity as he took in his surroundings. He knew what they were thinking: what was Lucy doing with someone like him?

Lucy had reached out to touch his face. 'You're in 3D,' she'd said, amazed. 'Everything's in 3D.'

He'd grabbed her by the wrist and pushed it onto the table. She'd drawn in a sudden breath.

'And you're off your tits,' he'd said in a sharp whisper. 'Pay your bill, we're getting out of here.'

She'd blinked four times in succession, her big blue cartoon eyes fixing on him. Dutifully, she pulled her purse from her designer bag and paid. He'd brought her back to his flat that night and sobered her up. It wasn't until the next day that they'd had sex. She was a rich kid, ripe for the picking. He could have easily taken advantage but the last thing he needed with his record was some bird running from his flat screaming rape.

He would have packed her off into a taxi, but she wouldn't give him her address. So he'd plonked her on the sofa, with a pillow under her head and a bucket on the floor. He'd half expected her to be gone the next day. Instead, he'd got up to the smell of bacon cooking on the pan. She'd stood in her knickers and bra and given him a sheepish look. For a second, he'd thought he was the one tripping. He'd regarded her warily as he'd sat down to eat. Cups clinked as coffee was poured, and a bacon sandwich was placed before him.

'None for you?' he'd said.

'I didn't get this figure from eating carbs.'

'I guess you couldn't take the chance...' he'd grinned, 'in case it came alive.'

Then her face had creased, but she still looked pretty as memories of the evening before came in. 'Oh God,' she'd said, touching her hand to her face. 'I really need to change dealers.'

Everything about her captivated him, and it seemed the feeling was mutual. He had never told her he loved her. His vocabulary didn't include words like that. She had been raised by her father who couldn't relate to her after her mother had walked out on them. She didn't want to hear of love. So she'd turned off her phone, and they'd spent the next four days in bed, coming out only for steak, salads, and takeaways. Damo didn't expect their relationship to progress, and if Lucy was honest, neither did she. But she hadn't met anyone like him. The plan had been to parade him before her father as an act of rebellion, but after their week together, she'd decided to keep him to herself. They'd talked long into the night, just as they had online. They had grown so close so fast, it had taken them both by surprise.

He made her feel alive. She made him feel like a king. Not like those jobsworths down the dole office who looked at him like he was dog shit on their shoes. It wasn't Damo's fault he was unemployed. With his history, nobody wanted to know. He would not hide from his past. He could handle himself when things got tough. But thanks to a recent windfall, he was doing OK. Good enough to access firearms, rent some accommodation, and buy an array of fun weapons to play with. Lucy gave as good as she got during their power plays. The fact he didn't trust her only served to spice things up. But it was when she'd asked him to hurt her – seriously hurt her – that things had changed. That night, he'd traced the silver scars on her body as she'd told him what caused her to self-harm. Each injury relayed a story, much like his own. But he'd refused to take a blade to her skin. She was the only woman in the world who had ever loved him – if that's what love was.

The memory of that night made him pull her closer. Lucy was his whole life. She nibbled on his ear after he slammed her against the wall. They were panting now, getting off on the danger as she wrapped her legs around him and held on tight.

Over the last few months, Damo deflected her need to self-harm towards violence against others while he recanted stories of his wicked past. It was only a matter of time before she'd wanted to try it for herself. He made her want to walk the path chosen by the special few. The mixture of sex, drugs, and violence had made them feel like gods.

'C'mon.' Damo buttoned his trousers, breathless from their impulse sex. 'We can't waste no more time.'

Lucy licked her lips. 'Didn't feel like a waste to me.'

Her muscles taut, she threw her suitcase in the back of the van while Damo set the cottage alight. A plume of smoke rose behind her, the accelerant taking care of any forensics left behind. Another rental cottage awaited them under their recently purchased identities. Another excuse to play with their weaponised 'toys'. Yasmin may have escaped the hunt, but she was a worm on the hook to reel the big fish in. Nothing would compare to the high that awaited them. He and Lucy were going one better. Because out of all the crimes they had committed, they had never killed a cop.

CHAPTER FOUR

Donovan watched his team through his office windows, resting his elbows on his desk. He shared this space with Amy, and while her desk was set out in a regimented fashion, his was littered with incident print-outs, old coffee cups, and files. Not that he'd had much of a chance to sit down with a brew. Operation Monsoon was gaining momentum in the press, and his team was busy chasing leads. His morning had consisted of a meeting with the command team followed by briefings with the media department, CSI, and the divisional intelligence unit. A family liaison officer had been allocated to the victims, and they were diligently gathering evidence as well as explaining the process so the victims and their families didn't get overwhelmed. Not once had his officers complained about the demands placed upon them. The trend of violence against women on the streets of London was growing, and this recent case was the most worrying of all.

Their first victim was a tourist, snatched on her way home from a club. Drunk, alone, and vulnerable, twenty-five-year-old Abbie Lynn was enjoying everything London had to offer until she was scooped off the streets. She'd turned up four days later, bruised and dazed with little memory of recent events. Traces of Rohypnol were found in her bloodstream, and she'd described being thrown into a silver van. Through a haze of confusion, she'd relayed her four-day ordeal of sexual violence from a masked couple who'd callously dumped her back on the streets. It was believed to be a one-off attack until they'd struck a week later. But nobody predicted just how bad things would get.

Shocked witnesses reported the second victim, twenty-nine-year-old Londoner, Mallory Whitstable, being dragged into a silver van. CCTV captured from a nearby Tesco Express displayed a set of stolen licence plates. But Mallory had not escaped with her life. Her body had been found by joggers in Epping Forest, a map of the bruising and injuries she had endured over four days. The fatal blow was a shot in the back at close range by a flare gun. The presence of a firearm brought the investigation to a whole new level. Donovan hoped Mallory's death would not be in vain. Her body could provide the key to unlocking the killers' identities from the clues police had gleaned. Clues that had not found their way to the press. This time, his team was tight. The couple had used a variety of weapons against their victim, who had numerous lacerations, both semi-healed and fresh on her feet, hands, and arms. A crossbow arrow had speared her thigh, and cuffs had been used on her wrists. She had been beaten at one point and subjected to sexual abuse. Donovan had spoken to the Whitstable family personally, to convey his sorrow and answer any questions before their FLO got involved. This was the worst violence he'd encountered from a criminal couple since researching Jack and Lillian Grimes.

He stared at his computer until the words merged into a blur. There were so many updates to oversee, and the overtime costs were spiralling. He had his officers' welfare to look out for, too. Then there were the briefings, taskings, and media appeals. Not to mention Amy...stubborn, obstinate, fiercely loyal, and compulsively obsessed with her job. The resemblances to her own serial killer parents weighed heavy on her mind. Her pregnancy scan should have been joyous, but instead she had been quiet, staring at the screen. Most parents would be thrilled to discover the sex of their baby. But she was searching for something beneath the surface. Something that couldn't be captured on a grainy black-and-white image. Could serial killer genes be passed on? He blinked, clicking on the images of the victims which had been uploaded to Athena, the case management software. If this job had taught him anything, it was that you should grasp life with both hands. But Amy had turned down his marriage proposal with all the interest of someone who had been asked to put out the bins.

Sighing, he checked the number written on his notepad and dialled his desk phone. After five rings, he was about to give up when a response came.

'Bryn Jones here, who's this?'

Donovan smiled at the sound of his Welsh accent. He always answered the phone in the same way.

'It's DI Donovan, from the Met. I was wondering if you had the chance to study those files I sent you?'

Bryn was a forensic psychologist, who'd had some successes in the past. He was working in Brentford but could be outsourced for a big case – providing they had the budget to cover it. It was Donovan's job to ensure that their money was spent in all the right places, and he needed a quick result. Victimology was a key line of enquiry that could not be ignored.

'Sorry, I've been up to my eyes in it,' Bryn replied. 'I've got as far as printing them off. I'll study them in depth today.'

'Can you quickly go over them, while I have you on the phone?' Donovan didn't want to let him go just yet. He couldn't wait for a detailed report.

'Bear with me.' Bryn paused, the sounds of pages turning in the background as he scanned each one. 'Nothing's jumping out at me so far. Physically, the victims don't appear that much alike, although they were around the same age. Their jobs and financial statuses don't seem to have any bearing on why they were picked.'

Another page turned. Donovan knew he would be poring over the victim's backgrounds, finances, relationships, social lives, and routines – anything which could link them to their suspect. Police spent so much time focusing on the perpetrators, but each victim held a unique point of view of the crime.

After a few minutes, Bryn took a breath. 'Judging by their statements, I'd say Abbie was a practice run. It's why she was drugged to make her forget. The killers hadn't yet built up the courage or justification to go through with a kill.'

Donovan listened intently as Bryn turned another page.

'When they took Mallory, they had no intention of letting her go.'

Donovan nodded into the phone. According to the toxicology report, no drugs had been found in Mallory's system. 'Why keep them for four days?' Donovan's gaze returned to the victims' images on screen. Abbie, with her dark hair, long black lashes, and kohl-lined eyes. Mallory, in contrast, wore wide-rimmed glasses and had cropped brunette hair. But Donovan already knew the answer. Her body was a map of events. By the discolouration of her bruising, the pathologist had documented that she'd been injured every day.

'It's a game. A wicked game…' Bryn's words faded as he paused. 'I see they were both tattooed. They're branding the women as their property.'

This was the evidence Donovan's team kept close to their chests. A fresh inking of a small arrow was on each victim's body, over their belly buttons. It linked them together, and should anyone come forward, it was proof of involvement – as long as the press didn't get hold of it. He tuned back in to Bryn's narrative.

'The belly button has significance. The umbilical cord is our link to life, our first breaths in this world when it's cut. The arrow is similar to Cupid's bow. The couple are branding her and showing the world they're in love. That's my take on it anyway. They're the givers and takers of life. They're getting off on the control.'

Donovan's brows drew together in a frown. 'Are they likely to continue?'

'They're not going to stop until you catch them. The thrill of the chase is like a drug. Any new reports of missing women since Abbie was found?'

'Yes,' Donovan replied, 'but people go missing in the city all the time. Without any specifics, it's difficult to narrow it down.'

'Leave it with me. I'll have a detailed report to you by tonight.'

'Thanks,' Donovan said, glancing up as Amy entered the office. 'I appreciate it.'

By the look on Amy's face, something had come in. Her blazer was open, the cream blouse beneath it baggy to conceal her blooming pregnancy.

'We've had a result.' Her eyes were bright as he hung up. 'Last night, Yasmin Cook was found in Epping Forest.'

Yasmin was on their shortlist of missing people. Donovan groaned, but his concerns were dispelled as Amy smiled.

'She's alive. And get this – she was picked up last night, running from a couple who held her captive for four days.'

'Why are we only hearing about this now?' As interesting as the development was, every second counted.

'She had no ID and she was in a bad way. I guess they were too busy trying to save her life.' Amy grabbed her bag from the floor next to her desk. 'She's been taken to the Royal London Hospital. I'm heading over to speak to her.'

'Wait!' Donovan pushed back his chair. 'Send one of the team. I need you here.' This was a major development. A detective constable could be assigned in the first instance. It was Amy's job to oversee the team.

But she wasn't having any of it as she turned to leave. 'I'll keep you updated!' she said cheerily, before walking out the door. Donovan stood, hands on hips as he watched her leave. He may be her DCI but she took no instruction from him. He only hoped her visit would be worthwhile.

CHAPTER FIVE

Amy gripped the steering wheel of the old Ford Focus. The sky was grey and gloomy as dark clouds rolled overhead. All her attention was on speaking to Yasmin Cook, who had been found injured at the side of the road. Amy negotiated a junction and worked through what she knew so far. Twenty-three-year-old Yasmin had been visiting Shoreditch to see a friend. She was a single mum, and her parents had babysat overnight to enable her to have a break. But when her friend had disappeared with a random fella from the bar, Yasmin was left to make her own way back. CCTV traced her walking through an underpass near Shoreditch, but the camera wasn't working on the other side. Amy's frown deepened. She was maddened by thoughts of Yasmin being left on her own. Her friend's behaviour went against every rule of sisterhood. Never, ever did you leave a girl-friend alone in a city they were unfamiliar with.

Amy inched her foot on the accelerator as her satnav guided her route. Cases involving killer couples were mercifully rare. But this had echoes of Jack and Lillian Grimes. According to initial reports, Yasmin had not been dumped. She'd escaped. Hope flared. Could she identify her kidnappers?

Amy's footsteps echoed down the bustling corridor. She felt ill at ease in hospitals as memories of her dad's sudden demise returned. Not a day passed that she didn't miss the man who'd adopted her as a child. The world was a lesser place since the death of Robert Winter, and she worked hard to fill his shoes. But what would the ex-superintendent think of this case? She squirted her hands with anti-bacterial fluid as adrenaline pulsed in her veins. Every second counted today. She paused for breath, bringing herself to ground. There was a victim at the end of this, and a young woman had died. Amy followed the signs to the correct ward. Each one carried the scent of disinfectant, with hand sanitisers at every turn.

She caught sight of the uniformed officer at the end of the corridor. She was standing holding her police bowler hat, glancing up and down. It was nice to see an older woman in a uniformed role. Judging by her age, she wasn't far from retirement. As a local officer, PC Beth King was the first to attend when the call had come in.

'Thanks for waiting,' Amy continued as she introduced herself to the stout, freckle-faced woman. Not wanting to waste a second, she guided Beth to a quieter section of the corridor.

'I finished my shift hours ago, ma'am.' Beth smiled. 'But the poor lamb was in such a state when she first came in, I wasn't leaving until her mum got here.'

'I'm glad you stayed,' Amy replied, warming to the officer before her. 'How is she now?'

'She's had surgery on her tendon and stitches for her cuts. Looks like she's been to hell and back.' Beth shook her head, her fingers pinching the felt tip of her police hat. 'Her parents live in Kent, they were minding her daughter while she visited her friend for a night out.' She grimaced. 'Some friend she turned out to be, dumping her for a bunk-up.'

Amy nodded, but she was well aware of Yasmin's backstory

and was anxious to get to the point. 'Has she identified the suspects? Given any descriptions?'

A group of visitors passed them in the corridor, clutching teddies, balloons, and cards. Amy blinked, focusing on Beth's voice.

'She was jumped from behind and had a cloth bag pulled over her head. There were two assailants, a man and a woman, and they drove for at least half an hour in what felt like a van.' Beth lowered her voice as an elderly patient in a dressing gown walked past. 'She said the man sounded older than the woman, who was more well-spoken. She didn't see their faces but described the man as sounding rough. They kept her blindfolded in a cottage in the woods and released her every day.'

'Released her?' Amy replied. Perhaps the similarities between this and the Grimes' case weren't as apparent as she thought.

'Yeah. They hunted her down in the woods. Each day, her injuries became more severe.' Beth turned down her police radio as a voice buzzed from her earpiece. 'Animals, the pair of them.'

Amy frowned. 'You don't think she could have got it wrong? The first victim was drugged...it messes with your memory.' She thought of the victim's statement. Of the test results they had gleaned. She hadn't expected this.

'If you saw the state of her, you wouldn't say that. Her feet are in bits. They shot a crossbow through her arm, and the last time they let her go, they had a gun.'

Amy nodded solemnly. A flare gun had killed their previous victim, tearing a hole through her chest, but the post-mortem had revealed both fresh and ageing injuries. Now she thought of it, Yasmin's story made sense.

Beth checked her watch and fixed her police hat on. 'I've

emailed her statement to your team. She's desperate to see her daughter, but her mum wants her to rest.'

'Do you think she'll speak to me?'

'I don't know, ma'am.' Beth shrugged. 'Her mother's protective, and who can blame her? I got as much as I could out of Yasmin until she turned up.'

'Were you able to check for a tattoo?'

Beth nodded, her expression grim. 'It's red and scabbed over, but it's there.'

The inking was their calling card. The symbol of their victim's first unaided breath now marked with a threat of their last. 'OK,' Amy said, sensing Beth was itching to leave. 'We'll take it from here.' Thanks to technology, her team was equipped with details of the crime. She imagined Donovan poring over the statement, a fresh set of taskings underway. It bought her some breathing space. She only hoped she could persuade Yasmin to tell her a little more.

CHAPTER SIX

Yasmin appeared pitifully small in the centre of the hospital bed. Her arms were a crisscross of scratches, her brunette hair scraped back, revealing every bruise on her face. She was in a shared room, with visitors gathered around each bed, oblivious to Amy's presence or the reason why she was here. Amy's gaze went to the woman next to her. Such was their resemblance that no introductions were needed. The woman was heavier than her daughter, but her long nose and arched brows were a mirror image. She hovered protectively, her eyes focusing on Amy as she entered the room.

'I'm DI Winter of the priority crime team.' Amy raised her warrant card as she approached the hospital bed.

Mrs Cook appeared unimpressed. 'She's already spoken to a police officer. Can't you let her rest?'

Amy didn't blame her for being so defensive. 'I won't make Yasmin do or say anything she doesn't want to,' she began, her voice low. 'But I do need to see her while things are fresh in her mind.' In a way, it was a blessing that it was visiting time. Visitors were too busy chatting to notice Amy pull the curtain around Yasmin's bed.

'She doesn't owe you anything.' Mrs Cook's words were sharp. 'The police didn't save her. She got out of there herself.'

'Mum.' Yasmin spoke in a croaky voice. 'I'm OK. Why don't you get yourself a cup of tea in the canteen?'

'Sorry, love, I didn't mean to wake you.' Her mother smoothed a hand over her daughter's forehead. What part of her body wasn't bruised was encased in bandages.

'I'm fine.' Yasmin delivered a weak smile. 'Nothing chocolate won't fix.'

Mrs Cook gave Amy a daggered look before leaving her alone with her daughter. It was easier when it came to such offences if the victim could speak frankly, although it was difficult in a shared space. At least the beds were well spaced out, with Yasmin situated in the farthest corner.

'Thanks.' Amy pulled a seat close, grateful for the opportunity to rest her feet. 'I'll try to make this brief.'

'Mum's right.' Yasmin scooted up on the bed, wincing in pain. 'I've told the officer everything I know. I can't describe them, and my wrists were tied, apart from when they let me go.'

Amy nodded. 'I know it's not easy, going over it all again. But you're a strong, brave young woman, and we're going after the people who've done this to you.' She flipped open her police-issue notebook and clicked her pen. She knew she was pushing her, but every second of a fresh memory was precious. 'You mentioned that they hunted you down. Could you see their faces then?'

Yasmin shook her head. Tears were not far away. 'Sometimes they blindfolded me. Other times they wore masks, like clear plastic, but of someone else's face.' She sighed, every word an effort. 'Sometimes she goaded him, and he'd hit her. One minute she'd act all meek, and the next...' Another shuddering sigh. 'They had sex all the time.' Her face was haunted with the memory of her ordeal.

Amy could see Yasmin was struggling, but she had to ask the question. 'Are you sure there were just two people? You didn't sense any more in the room?'

Yasmin swiped away an errant tear. 'No. There were definitely two. But she acted like different people, whereas he was always the same. It's all in my...'

'Statement, yes, I know,' Amy finished her sentence. 'And I'm really sorry to push. But look what you've done, Yasmin. You fought off two armed suspects. You survived four days in their company and lived. I know you have it in you to tell me a little more.'

A sad smile rose to Yasmin's face as she picked at the threads of her blanket. 'I kept thinking of my little girl. She got me through.'

'I'm glad.' Amy realised she was resting a hand on her stomach and quickly moved it away. 'Can you talk about what they did? There's not a lot of detail in your statement.'

Given the circumstances of Yasmin's kidnap, sexual assault was probable, but this may not be the place to discuss it. The visitors at the next bed chatted, and a television from another bed played a music video. It granted them a level of privacy, but Yasmin was shaking her head.

'No...no...no. I can't...I won't...I...' She raised her good arm and drew her knees to her chest, rocking slightly.

'Hey, it's OK,' Amy said softly. 'We're on your side.' She slid her card onto the hospital table. 'Here's my mobile number. I'm here when you're ready to talk.'

'What is wrong with you? Can't you see she's upset?' Mrs Cook swiped back the curtain and placed a box of Lindt chocolates on top of Amy's business card.

Amy was about to say she was leaving when Yasmin spoke.

'The man chewed gum. Spearmint. I could smell it on his breath.' Yasmin winced, as if the memory was inflicting physical pain. 'The rest of the time they smelt of booze. Sometimes she would blow smoke in my face.' She drew a forced breath. Her hand rested on her chest. 'She said it meant she wanted to... she wanted to...' She looked at Amy, raw fear in her eyes. 'I can't...I can't...breathe.'

'I'll get a doctor!' Mrs Cook shrieked. Amy knew what was wrong.

'It's OK.' She laid a firm hand on Yasmin's shoulder and squeezed. 'You're having a panic attack. Focus on my voice.' She needed to drag her out of her trauma and into the present day. Her mother was right. It was too soon. 'Count with me. Now inhale...' She counted to four before asking her to hold her breath. 'Hold it...now release, nice and slow.'

Amy did it with her until her breathing regulated.

'If you feel an attack coming on, do these exercises. It will pass quicker.'

Yasmin sank back into her pillow and spoke between jagged breaths. 'Find them.'

Amy wanted to guarantee a swift resolution, but such a promise that was impossible to make. The attendance of a doctor was enough for Amy to take the hint to leave. 'Leave it with us. Take care, Yasmin. We'll be in touch.'

Amy swallowed back her frustration as she walked through the double doors. If only she'd been able to see through Yasmin's eyes. She had been gone for four whole days. She must have known more. But her mind was repressing the trauma in order to help her heal. Amy understood that more than anyone. One day, Yasmin may be able to help, but not today.

CHAPTER SEVEN

The tinny hum of electronica reverberated from the flat next door through the walls of Damo's flat. His Shoreditch home was nothing more than a bolthole now. He hadn't missed it in the least. Only now did he realise that the place reeked of damp and weed. Everything seemed so small, so constricted. It made him feel like a battery hen. His time in the countryside with Lucy had opened his eyes. He'd planned to tidy his flat before she came around, but she'd been needy and insecure and hadn't left his side. Her family were stinking rich, but she hadn't been put off. If anything, she seemed to like his cesspit of a flat.

'This is cute!' she'd said, wandering into his tiny bedroom and peeking through his yellowed blinds. There were no en suites here, no fancy roll-top baths. Nothing but some curled-up slices of ham in the fridge and a carton of out-of-date milk. He'd seen Lucy's Instagram pictures. Her house was a mansion. Her bedroom alone was bigger than his entire flat. Her upmarket friends were dripping in jewellery and designer clothes. Then there were the photos of Lucy's luxury holidays to the Seychelles. Up until recently, Damo could barely afford a weekend in Bognor Regis. Why the hell did Lucy want to stay here? She'd ignored the cigarette craters in the carpet, the yellow nicotine stains on the walls. Now he'd been away, the place disgusted him. He'd already given notice. His recent windfall would see him right.

Lucy picked at her manicured nails while she stared through the blinds. She had barely eaten today. She was living on her nerves. He knew a part of her got off on the thrill, but there was another side to her, wild and unpredictable, satisfied only by violence and sex. Then there was his kitten, meek and desperate to please. But their relationship was threatened by lingering mistrust and doubt. People like Lucy didn't stick with blokes like him. Was she playing him or just messed up in the head? She stood, in her camisole, arms mottled from the cold. Her jeans hung loose on her hips, some designer brand that cost more than he made from benefits for the month. It was risky, coming back here. But his family would ask questions if he didn't show his face every now and again. He also needed to see his dealer and put some feelers out, find out if anyone was looking for him. So far, it seemed nobody had linked them to the kidnappings, much less murder. As long as he carried on as normal, they might get off scot-free.

He placed a hand on Lucy's arm. 'Why don't you shoot off home for a few hours? Won't your old man be wondering where you are?' He wanted some time to himself, but Lucy wouldn't let him out of her sight.

'I've texted Daddy.' She chewed the pink lipstick from her bottom lip. 'Said I'm staying with a friend. Are you sure we're safe here?'

Tightening his grip on her arm, he steered her towards the sofa. 'We will be if you stay away from the bloody window.'

His flat was on the fourth floor in the high-rise, with a view onto a courtyard below. Nobody knew about his relationship with Lucy, and for now, they needed to keep it that way. Scowling, she sank into the worn leather sofa. He couldn't talk to her when she was like this. Each hunt was followed by an anticlimax when it came to an end. Lucy stared at the blank television screen. The silence was punctuated by her constant sniffing – a side effect of her love of blow. He liked a bump as much as she did, but he was careful not to make it a habit, and at least weed didn't rot your nose. Soon she would be bugging him for a fix to take the edge off things.

When they'd met, she'd wanted to know everything, and they'd talk all through the night. He'd told her some wild stories of his past, and from then, she'd seemed hooked. She lived her life on social media. Up until he'd met her, that was as exciting as it got. Twitter, TikTok, Instagram, Facebook, she used them all. But her online profile was yet another side of her. There, she was Lucina Baron-Hart, who'd attended boarding school in Stamford in Lincolnshire, before graduating from Lincoln University. To her eighteen hundred followers, she was a successful businesswoman. But in reality she wasn't interested in her family horse racing empire. Since her parents' divorce, her lifestyle was funded by Daddy, of course.

A dog barked in the flat upstairs, and a muffled voice yelled at it to shut up.

His gaze fell on Lucy, who was pacing the room once more. She was raking her nails against her lengthy gold necklace, and her fidgeting was getting on his nerves.

'Sit the fuck down will ya? You're doing me head in.' There was no point in being nice or asking what was wrong. Kindness was weakness in Lucy's eyes. He ground his back molars as he fixed her with a glare.

'What if Yasmin tells the cops too much?' she whined, doing what she was told. 'We shouldn't have let her go.'

Damo's eyes narrowed. He'd been over it a million times.

'Listen.' He grabbed her jaw. 'You knew what we were getting into when we started this. Don't chicken out on me now.'

'I'm not.' She blinked her long lashes. 'I'll do whatever you want.' She fumbled with his belt, so eager to please. But lately, this side of her felt more and more like an act.

'Get off me.' Damo slapped her hands away. His head was too full of thoughts to consider sex.

What happened in the countryside had changed him. There was more to life than inner-city London, and he didn't want to get caught now. All his life, he'd been an underdog, even when he tried to toe the line. He could drive all his life under the limit and the cops would fine him for speeding the second he went a mile over the limit. It felt good to have a purpose, to give authority the one-fingered salute. But was he some kind of messed-up adventure to Lucy or was she ready to commit? He imagined her with her toffee-nosed friends, all taking the piss out of him. If she tried to leave...he had enough dirt to blackmail her for years. He dry-washed his face as paranoia seeped in. He couldn't sit in this flat any more. It was time to move to the next stage of their plan.

'We need to liven things up,' Lucy said.

Damo blinked. He'd been so immersed in his concerns that he'd almost forgotten she was there. He was about to snap in response, but she was only mirroring his thoughts.

'All right, what are you thinking?' He sat on the arm of the sofa, watching her smile grow. Despite his earlier thoughts of betrayal, he was excited to hear what she was going to say.

'We're not getting enough coverage on social media.' She picked up her phone from the sideboard. 'But I can put that right. Soon, the whole world will know our names.'

CHAPTER EIGHT

Amy dealt with violence on a daily basis, but this case had got under her skin. It carried an undercurrent of sadism that felt too close to home. The couple humiliated their victims sexually, in a way that ensured their silence should they ever manage to escape. Her biological parents, Jack and Lillian Grimes, had done the same. She recalled women leaving their home in tears, clutching their clothes to their chests as Lillian's harsh laughter filled the air. In the early days, it wasn't about murder. It was all about sex and control.

As she walked down the police station corridor, Amy shook the memory away. Only now, could her adult memory make sense of what she'd encountered as a child. But as much as she tried to stamp out such violence, it grew like poisonous weeds, even infiltrating the police. Amy made a silent vow. She would go to any lengths to catch Yasmin's abductors before they struck again.

She pressed her security tag against the panel, and the door clicked open just in time for her to hear DC Molly Baxter, kneeling next to the open office fridge.

'Don't sell-by dates mean anything to you lot?' she declared, wafting her hand before her face as she removed out-of-date food. Given the hours they were working, sustenance was important, and Molly had taken it upon herself to run the tea club.

'There's nothing wrong with that lasagne,' DC Steve Moss protested. 'It's a Joe Wicks recipe.'

'Mate, this isn't a freezer.' Molly unceremoniously threw it in the bin. 'You can't keep your grub here indefinitely. And that goes for the rest of you...' She turned around, her gaze resting on Amy. 'Oh, hullo, boss, I didn't hear you come in.' Standing, she brushed the carpet fibres from her trouser leg.

'Here, get something nice for the tea club,' Amy slipped her hand into her wallet and fished out a twenty-pound note. 'You deserve it.'

'Ma'am? You need to see this.' The newest member of their team, DC Daneil Negussie Aberra, drew their attention to his computer screen. Denny's calm, methodical demeanour balanced Molly's high-spirited personality, but today, he seemed concerned.

Molly peered over his shoulder at the Instagram broadcast. 'Oh my God, look at this. They're calling themselves The Hunters.'

The office fell into hushed silence as the Instagram reel played. A heavily filtered man and woman were on screen. The masks beneath the filters were the same as Yasmin had described. The woman was facing forward, sitting on the man's lap. Amy cast an eye over her shiny PVC suit. What the hell was this all about?

'Look at all you lovely people,' the woman purred. 'Who knew murder could be so interesting? Stick around. You won't be disappointed.' She raised her hands over her head, curling her fingers through the man's hair as his hands roamed over her waist.

'Bloody hell,' Steve murmured behind them, in a somewhat appreciative tone.

'Turn up the volume,' Amy snapped, in no mood for it. 'Are you getting this?' They had to cover all the bases just in case.

'I'm recording the screen,' Denny confirmed. The team listened in.

Amy had so many questions. How did he know they were going to be online? Could they be traced? Were they genuine or a wind-up? The fact they had another potential lead was an exciting leap forward. Did Donovan know? She glanced at the office, where Paddy seemed to be informing him. The on-screen couple were rapidly gaining hundreds of likes.

'Is it live?' Amy asked. Dozens of comments were coming through.

Denny nodded. 'It went on minutes ago. They tagged our team in.'

'Damn,' Molly said. 'I take five minutes off to clean the bloody fridge...' Thanks to Molly, the team had its own dedicated social media account, which they used to appeal for help from the public. It had quite the following, due to their recent appearance on a television documentary.

'What's this about a reel?' Donovan joined them.

Unlike Amy, he knew all the social media terms. But then, given her family history, Amy didn't spend a lot of time online.

Rain tapped against the office window. Outside, the skies clouded over, and the temperature in the office dropped as the radiators turned cold.

'I'll forward the screen recording to your phones when it's finished.' Denny clicked his mouse.

Amy could sense Molly's annoyance as she frowned at the

screen. Until Denny came along, she'd been the IT queen. They crowded around the computer. Amy noticed the couple's use of the hashtag 'The Hunters' and peered at their background for clues. But their appearance was made against the backdrop of what looked like a grubby black sheet thrown over a door.

The woman straightened as she returned her attention to the camera. 'Listen up, world. We are The Hunters, soon to be the most famous serial killers in history.' The camera was held up to their faces, but between their masks and the camera's glitch effect, it was almost impossible to make them out. But she could see the woman's PVC outfit and the generous cleavage in view.

She squirmed seductively for the camera, her tongue protruding through red lipstick barely visible behind the mask. 'We take, we release, we hunt,' she said in sultry tones, her eyes flicking up to the man behind her before returning to the screen. 'Could you survive four whole days with us?'

The camera followed the man's hand as he began to tug on the zip of her figure-hugging catsuit. Slowly, the zip parted. The woman gasped as it stopped at her navel, revealing a small tattoo of a crossbow.

'Follow our hashtag for more.' The woman delivered a sharp intake of breath as the man produced a knife and caressed her stomach with the blade.

The office fell into stony silence as the feed was cut off. Amy and her team absorbed the message.

'Blimey,' Molly said, going to her desk. 'I wasn't expecting that.'

'It's a good thing I recorded it,' Denny said. 'It's only a matter of time before the video is taken down.'

'How many views has that had?' Donovan replied.

'It's gone viral,' Molly butted in, 'although it'll be removed because of the content...' She was already clicking different social media channels as she searched for them online. 'Some influencers will jump on the back of this and reproduce censored copies. Anything that will get them a few thousand hits.'

'And you can bet the news channels will get a hold of this, too.' Amy shook her head.

'And the true crime YouTubers,' Molly added. 'Some of them get millions of views.'

'Shit.' Amy groaned. 'Did you see the tattoo? They're either genuine or copycats who know about the case.'

'Then what can we take from this?' Donovan wheeled over a whiteboard, in investigation mode. 'First, we make the tech team aware.'

'Already done,' Denny said. 'I'm sending an intel report in now.'

'What have these hunters to gain?' Donovan continued, not missing a beat.

'Notoriety,' Molly replied. 'Plus the added bonus of playing with us. They wouldn't have tagged the team otherwise.'

'What use is short-lived notoriety?' DC Moss pulled the swivel chair out from his desk. 'Any channel they use to promote violence will be shut down.'

'Which is why they told readers to use the hashtag instead of a user name,' Molly said.

Amy watched her team bounce off each other, all competing for attention. A level of healthy competition was good. It made them work harder for the case.

'But why?' Donovan countered. 'If they're not making money from social media then why risk getting caught? They've given us so much. What are they getting in return?'

'They could be a sex ring of some sort. I mean...she got my attention.' DC Moss glanced around the room. 'What? I'm only saying what every red-blooded male...' He looked at Molly pointedly 'Or female is thinking. She's hot.'

The sight of her partially exposed breasts had brought a new aspect to the investigation.

'He's right,' Molly agreed. 'She knew what she was doing. People are always quickest to click on videos with adult content. It's not good for the victims, though. Everyone will be talking about The Hunters as if they're some sort of celebs.' She began reading through some of the comments.

I wouldn't mind being kidnapped by her #TheHunters

Take me now! #TheHunters

Can we make it ten days? #TheHunters

OMG those sickos – what about the victims? #TheHunters

'It goes on and on,' she said. 'If they wanted to make an impact, they have.'

'A modern-day Bonnie and Clyde,' Paddy said.

Amy jumped. She hadn't realised he'd come in.

'Sally-Ann sent it to me. What's the betting it'll be in tomorrow's morning newspapers, too.'

Amy caught the faint aroma of cigarettes from his crumpled jacket, despite his efforts at giving them up.

One by one, the phones rang. Donovan returned to his office as his desk phone joined in. It was most likely Superintendent Jones, who'd been keeping a close eye on the case. Amy picked up the marker pen where Donovan had left it. She wrote: height, weight, estimated ages, accent, hair colour, identifiers, brand of knife, clothing, backdrop, location? Hashtags, background sounds, digital footprint.

'These are all things we can analyse. But her tattoo is the biggest giveaway. I want clear photographic stills pinned to this board.' She turned to Molly. 'And I mean, of everything.'

'Well, that should brighten the place up.' Steve chuckled.

Amy let him off with the comment. When you witnessed as

much violence and brutality as they did, gallows humour was a way of keeping their spirits up.

Amy delegated each task. 'Molly, analyse every hash-tagged comment. Who were the quickest to get the ball rolling? Which accounts were the first ones to share? Don't get too bogged down with it, just pick out the interesting ones and keep an eye on them.' She turned to Steve. 'Speak to as many tattoo parlours as you can. Start locally and spread your net out as time allows.'

Denny was sitting at his desk, legs crossed, watching and waiting for instruction.

'Speak to the media team. See what spin we can put on this. Have a word with the victims' family liaison officers, too. Make sure they're aware and ask if the families need any extra support.'

Denny nodded in response. Amy's pulse quickened. This was the part of the investigation she enjoyed the most. Leads were the lifeblood of any investigation – although they didn't always produce results.

Paddy stood beside her, two mugs of coffee in hand. 'I'll draft in some extra help in monitoring social media. Specials or PCSOs should be up for it if there's no uniformed officers about.'

'Good idea.' Amy nodded, taking a coffee from his outstretched hand. It was in her favourite James Bond mug, a nod to her father, Robert Winter, whose presence was missed every day. He'd taught her so much about policing. She had big shoes to fill.

The team got to work, and Amy pushed in her earphones and listened to the message again. Why had this woman exposed herself like this? She watched the glint of the knife as the man pressed it against her flesh. Saw her stomach tighten in response. She replayed the last scene. Heard the woman gasp. But it wasn't a gasp of pleasure. It was the quick inward breath of fear. Then she realised that the man was behind her the whole time, taking the dominant role. He was holding a knife to her body as she spoke. *He* pulled down the zipper. *She* had been branded with a tattoo. Just like the other victims. What sort of game were they playing? Was she a victim or accomplice?

CHAPTER NINE

Paddy methodically chewed his pizza. He could almost feel his wife's disapproval from across the miles as he savoured the taste. For the last few weeks, he'd been fed on a diet of rabbit food to bring his cholesterol down. It was bad enough that Sally-Ann guilt-tripped him into giving up cigarettes. What was next, booze? He shuddered at the thought. Dabbing a napkin to his mouth, he watched his DI cross the room. She was restless today, and it was cause for concern. Her appetite had dwindled, and her focus seemed elsewhere. She couldn't be pregnant – she was too ambitious for babies to factor into her plans. But he knew that Donovan had taken her to the hospital more than once in the last month.

He hadn't mentioned his suspicions to Sally-Ann. If Amy was seriously unwell, she'd tell them in her own good time. He'd grown close to her over the years and couldn't stand to think of anything bringing her down. At least Donovan was keeping an eye on things. It was interesting, watching the dynamics between them over the last few months. When Donovan had first taken on the role as DCI, a power struggle had taken place, but then they'd fallen into something deeper.

They hid their relationship well, but Paddy had always known they were cut from the same cloth. He understood the need for privacy. Work was hard enough, without personal feelings getting in the way.

His gaze swept across the dimly lit room. In the old days he'd be sitting in a cloud of cigarette smoke, a bottle of the finest malt whiskey nestled in a drawer somewhere. Something to take the edge off when times got tough. But not today, not anymore. The printer hummed in the corner of the room, and his colleagues finished the last of their pizzas while they balanced sustenance and work. His team were proficient at multi-tasking and had sat through many briefings to bring them to this point. The phones had finally silenced. There was little more they could do tonight. Now Amy was coming back from the toilets, her face ashen, her movements slow. His colleagues didn't notice the wobble in her step, but he did. He wasn't as quick as Donovan, who strode out of his office to join her, talking about the case but discreetly guiding her inside. Amy was a trojan who found balance in work. But this case had shades of Jack and Lillian Grimes. Was it taking too much out of her?

CHAPTER TEN

Donovan pinched the bridge of his nose. He wasn't very good at following his own advice about going home. The office lights had been dimmed, but there were a couple of officers still working, despite him telling them to go home and get some shut-eye. They'd ordered pizza to fuel the extra hours, and the smell of cheesy feasts and garlic bread lingered in the air. Denny was diligently tidying his workspace. Molly was frowning as she made notes with her unicorn novelty pen. Paddy, their sergeant, was mumbling into the phone. They'd been making the most of the recent leads. They'd built up a profile of the perpetrators on the whiteboard, but Donovan was cautious of being blinkered by the recent Instagram post. They'd spent hours contacting tattoo artists, and it was eating into their time.

He clicked his mouse, closed down his tabs, logged off the system, and shut off his computer. Weariness had seeped through to his bones. At least he didn't have to make a fresh press appeal. Their media team had been guarded, warning him not to acknowledge the Instagram reel. He agreed not to feed the beast, but it wasn't like the old days, when you could persuade local media to have a news blackout. Social media had catapulted the story around the globe. Donovan's focus was on the victims. He sat at his desk, putting his thoughts in order as he rubbed his stubbled cheek.

Donovan sighed. Yasmin's escape was a testament of her determination to see her daughter again. In the majority of murder cases, victim and killer were previously acquainted. Apart from drug-related killings, most murders stemmed from domestics which had escalated out of control. But the suspects in this case were a different breed. These killers were arrogant, scooping random women off the street. They got off on power, bullying the women into submission as they forced them to play their games. Yasmin was a living, breathing crime scene, but she'd refused to allow CSI to harvest swabs of her skin. A more thorough examination was off the cards. According to attending officers, as soon as she'd been able to stand, she had showered until her flesh was pink. She wouldn't go into details about the sexual assaults, but the fallout was obvious. Frustratingly, the suspects had not left a trace of themselves on her clothes. The tracksuit Yasmin was wearing had been fresh from the wrapper that day. The couple may have been arrogant, but it seemed they were forensically aware. Securing the scene where Yasmin had been found was a challenge in itself. It wasn't as if they could cordon off the whole of the Epping Forest. Police dogs had been drafted in, as well as drones and a helicopter. There would be more boots on the ground tomorrow as POLSA continued their search. Donovan checked his watch. For now, there was nothing more he could do but go home and get some much-needed sleep. He'd sent Amy home an hour ago, after she'd had a dizzy turn. She couldn't keep working these hours. Something had to give.

His desk phone rang. It was most likely Amy, wondering where he was.

'Call for DI Winter, sir,' Elaine from reception said. 'Some woman, insists on speaking to her about the case.'

It had to be Lillian. Donovan grimaced at the thought of the spiteful woman. What was Amy's biological mother coming out of the woodwork for now? No doubt she'd heard that Amy was overseeing the case and just wanted to yank her chain. Or perhaps she was hoping to make some more money by selling yet another story to the press.

'I'll take it,' he said firmly. He could at least spare Amy the stress of having to deal with it.

'H...hello? Can I speak to DI Winter, please?'

Donovan straightened in his chair at the sound of the young woman's voice. This wasn't Lillian. 'DI Winter is off duty. I'm DCI Donovan. What can I do for you?' He softened his voice, trying to put what sounded like a shaken woman at ease. There had to be other victims. Not everyone came forward straight away.

'Yasmin didn't escape. Not really. I let her go.'

Now she had his attention. In the half-light of his office, Donovan listened for background sounds. All he could hear was the woman's trembling breath. 'OK,' he said assuredly. 'Who am I speaking to?'

'I can't tell you.' The woman whimpered. 'Not yet. 'I...I need to speak to DI Winter. She knows what it's like to be dragged into something against your will. She'll understand.'

'And what *is* it like?' Donovan gesticulated at his colleagues through the office window. Was this the PVC-clad woman he'd seen on Instagram earlier? She was well-spoken, just as Yasmin had described. He had to keep her talking.

Molly snapped to attention. Donovan pressed his finger against his lips in a warning to be quiet.

'I didn't want to hurt those girls…he made me.' The woman whined. 'I didn't want to make the video. Exposing myself like that…' She sniffled. 'I had to make it convincing or he'd kill me.'

Donovan scribbled on a notepad and held it up to Molly. Her eyes widened at the message. *Female suspect.* She turned back to Denny and whispered. Donovan sat on the edge of his desk, knowing one of them would alert control. But they hadn't been expecting the call. It was doubtful they could trace it now.

'He's taking another one.' The woman continued sobbing. 'Every day he lets them go, then he drags them back here again.' She paused for breath. 'He took me first, but I told him I liked it. That I wanted to be like him.' More tearful sobs followed. 'He was going to kill me. I…I had no choice. But now I'm way in over my head.'

Molly crept through Donovan's office door.

His grip tightened on the phone. 'Tell us where you are and we'll get you to safety.' He half expected her to laugh and say it was a wind-up.

Molly stood, pen in hand, preparing to make notes.

The woman's breath billowed down the line.

'Tell Yasmin… I'm sorry I messed up her tattoo. My hand was shaking so much, but I… I had to make it seem like I was with him all the way.'

That was all the proof Donovan needed. The tattooed arrow either side of Yasmin's belly button hadn't been straight. He exchanged a look with Molly. One half of the killer duo was on the phone.

'But now I know too much.' The woman exhaled. 'And it looks like it's all my fault.'

'Then come in and talk to DI Winter. Explain what it's really like.' Donovan imagined calling Amy with the news. She'd be thrilled at the prospect of getting their caller in.

'She *would* understand.' The woman seemed to be trying to

convince herself. 'She's lived with serial killers. She knows how controlling they are.'

Amy was only four years old when police had plucked her from the Grimes' family home. She'd lived with bodies in the basement and the stench of death in the walls. She had experienced unspeakable horrors and came out the other side. Now it seemed she inspired the woman on the other end.

'I'll meet her, but not at the station. And it has to be tonight. It's the only time I can get away.' She reeled off an address. 'But nobody else. If I see a police car, I'm off.'

Donovan was about to speak when the line went quiet. A dead tone followed. She was gone. He turned to Molly, whose brow was furrowed as she scribbled some notes.

'Control are aware,' Denny said as he joined them. 'No trace, I'm afraid. I've spoken to front desk, but the caller blocked their number.'

'I need to organise a team,' Donovan said after filling him in.

'Would you like me to call DI Winter?' Molly piped up.

'God, no,' Donovan said, a little more forcefully than he'd meant. 'I'm not dragging her into this.'

'But she said...'

Donovan didn't have time for this. 'I know exactly what she said, and that's the reason Winter's not getting involved. These people are killers. It's too dangerous. This could be an ambush for all we know.'

Molly seemed to have a thought. 'Sir, I can be a decoy, I've been undercover before.'

Donovan managed to stop himself from barking a laugh. Molly was talking about their last high-profile case. Having a stroll on Clacton Pier and talking to some teenagers was a world away from this. She was a conscientious officer, but sometimes her inexperience shone through. Even if he agreed, Molly's pear-shaped figure would be a dead giveaway. But none of these answers would be satisfactory to the young woman desperate to emulate her boss.

'This needs to be handled by a dedicated team. And not a word to Winter until this is over. Do you hear? Not one word.' He could imagine Amy's reaction. She'd be hotfooting it over there without a thought for herself or the baby she choose to ignore. He knew what he had to do: assemble a team and bring this woman in. Then Amy could talk to her when she was safely ensconced within their four walls.

CHAPTER ELEVEN

Amy begrudgingly returned to her home in Royal Crescent, where she lived with her mum. The curved terrace home was in Holland Park, an exclusive part of London that came with a hefty price tag to match. It had seemed like a castle when Amy had come to live there as a child. It was an adjustment, coming from her stinking terrace house to a four-floor townhouse with huge sash windows and deep-pile carpets on every floor.

Yawning, she climbed up the steps and shoved her key in her front door. Moving home was meant to be temporary, but she had matured since her adoptive father, Robert Winter, had died. She was getting on better with Flora, her mum, these days. She shrugged off her coat and hung it on the hook on the wall. Dotty, her pug, came bounding downstairs, bright-eyed and delivering a whole body wiggle as Amy bent to stroke her fur.

'Hello, Miss Dotty, have you been keeping my bed warm?' Amy accepted her slobbery kisses as she petted her. She shrugged off her coat before hanging it with her bag on a hook on the wall.

Given the nature of her job, it was hardly surprising that

Amy preferred the company of her dog over most of the people she encountered at work. Her tongue lolling, Dotty followed her into the living room. Amy admired their new bookcase, and the fat porcelain lamps which cast the room in a soft, warm glow. Flora's evening was evident; her bi-focal glasses rested on the coffee table next to an open book. A half-eaten packet of chocolate digestives and a furry throw rested on the edge of the sofa. Amy smiled. It could be a hundred degrees in the room, and Flora would still drape a throw over her legs.

Amy slipped her ankle boots off and enjoyed the soft carpet underfoot. Her stomach rumbled in complaint. Nausea had taken hold, and she'd barely eaten all day. She pressed her fists into the small of her back before strolling into the kitchen. Tea, cheese and crackers were the order of the day while she waited for Donovan to come home. He spent a lot of time at her place now, and Flora enjoyed having a male presence around.

As she sat at the table and nibbled her crackers, Amy's thoughts returned to Yasmin. She had read and reread her statement until she knew it off by heart. Her abductors had clearly dragged her into the pits of hell. Why did some people get off on other's pain? She thought of the euphoric feeling she got when she brought offenders to justice. Were the killer couple experiencing the same thrill on the opposite side of the coin? It was the same with her biological parents, Jack and Lillian. Were their brains wired wrong, or were they born evil? She thought about her older siblings and the things they'd seen. Yet her biological sister, Sally-Ann, had just left her job in private healthcare to return to the NHS. The money was nowhere near as good, but she gained satisfaction from helping regular people in different ways.

Amy sighed, clearing the dryness in her throat with a mouthful of tea. She'd work every hour if she could. But nothing would ever repay the debt for the pain her biological parents had inflicted upon the world. The burden felt constant, and the remnants of her parents' evil acts still lingered on. The only way Amy could be relieved of that burden was if Lillian was imprisoned or dead.

She stemmed her darkening thoughts, conscious of the growing life inside her. Could her unborn baby sense her anger? Hormones were running wild, and the case was getting to her.

'They won't stop,' Yasmin had said. 'Not until they're caught.'

That much was true. But was Amy the right person to catch them?

CHAPTER TWELVE

'Babe, you ready?' Damo gave one last glance around his flat as he waited for Lucy to hurry up. If everything went to plan, he wouldn't step foot in here again. He'd first rented the place five years ago in an effort to straighten himself out. As if he could live a normal life. Whatever job he got, it didn't last. He'd tried to rein in his temper, but his bosses always wound him up, and then all the old feelings would kick in. Feelings that made this world a very hard place to live in.

'Just a minute!' Lucy called from the bathroom.

She had braved the wonky showerhead that had a life of its own, spraying everywhere except where you needed it. All the times he'd stood under it, hot tears of frustration running down his face. Weed and booze only got you so far in the day. But the more time he spent with Lucy, the less he relied on the old crutches. He'd lived in this area for years, feeling adrift from the world. Now every hour in Lucy's company made him feel alive. Sure, she got on his nerves. But he liked the unpredictability of it all. He never knew who he was going to get. Fate had brought them together. Women like Lucy were in short supply.

. . .

Right now, she was sexy and determined. He never would have gone on Instagram if she hadn't suggested it. At times he doubted just how genuine she was, and earlier today, she'd looked at him like she was scared. But then she'd poured herself into her PVC suit and pulled out the camera. He didn't want to talk. It was too dodgy for people to hear his voice. But Lucy spoke in a sultry voice that made her sound like a porn star. Nobody would recognise her from that. She'd even worn a fake nipple piercing. Just a glimpse was enough to drive her followers wild. They hadn't been privy to her real piercing of three coloured studs on the back of her neck. Of course, there was the usual reaction from the do-gooders to their video online. But the Bible-bashers and internet freaks were secretly lapping it up. Death was just part of life. It was a lesson he'd learned from an early age. And now he was getting ready to do it all over again. Except this time it was different. This was the biggest catch of all. He wasn't there when she made the call to the police helpline, but from what she'd said, she had put on a good show. It was strange to hang out with someone even more devious than him.

Before Damo had met Lucy, he'd lived life robotically. He was never fully there, because he was still stuck in the past. His time in the here and now had been so mind-numbing. Get up, go to work, come home, go for a run. Lift weights. Make food. Get stoned. Eat shit, watch TV, and go to bed. He thought things were bad then, but that was before he'd lost his job. That's when things really went downhill. He didn't need to get up – there was nothing to get up for. He didn't need to wash – he didn't see anyone, apart from his dealer. Then there were the trips to the dole office to claim unemployment benefits. They hated him down there and treated him like something they'd scraped off their shoe. So he'd plod home, wondering if he'd been happier in prison than he was in the real world. He was no stranger to the big house, but now he was with Lucy, and every day meant something. He didn't know where things were heading, but he'd enjoy it while he could.

'Ready!' Lucy threw back the door, her face pink from the shower. Her damp blonde hair was pulled back in a ponytail and her eyes were bright with mischief.

Even in jeans and his hoodie, she still looked too good for the likes of him. Sometimes he wondered what it must be like to be in a normal relationship. To watch TV and cuddle on the sofa, or to go out for a pub lunch. Maybe even have kids one day. He'd always wanted to be a father, but there wasn't much chance of that. He wouldn't know how to act normal. He had nothing to base it on. He looked around his grubby flat. He wouldn't come here again.

'C'mon then,' he said, grabbing his things.

The car was ready to go. Lucy virtually bounced out of the door. The next challenge wasn't going to be easy. It could end them both. But they were ready for this. They had big plans.

CHAPTER THIRTEEN

Donovan stood around the corner from the target house on Claverdale Road. The Brixton three-bedroom semi was on the market and hadn't been lived in for months. The house was in the hands of the bank, having been recently repossessed. Judging by the images on Rightmove, the place was falling apart inside. Yet even here, such places could fetch up to a million pounds. He had gone out on a limb, assembling a team to attend on the strength of a phone call, and their police carrier was parked nearby. It was a miracle that he'd managed it in such a short space of time. The brief was for the decoy officer to enter the building. She was an experienced officer, and even though it was meant to be her day off, she was happy to be involved. Specialist trained officers would closely monitor her while others covered all exits.

The back garden was mostly cemented over, surrounded by a rotting wooden fence. Given the boards had been removed from the windows, it wouldn't be too difficult for someone to break inside. At least there were no concerns of an unsuspecting family opening the door, and the streets were mercifully quiet at this time of the night. Most of the homes were in darkness, with orange and black ribbons flapping lazily from Halloween wreaths in preparation for the end of the month. It certainly felt like a ghoulish night.

Donovan held his breath as the Amy lookalike walked down the short garden path. She was a couple of inches taller than the woman he'd come to love, but her hair was similar enough, and he'd given her one of Amy's coats which she'd left behind. Her stride was confident as she reached the end of the path. Beneath the glow of the streetlamp, she appeared convincing. She paused at the door. Officers were nearby, barely discernible in their black clothing and black baseball caps. Donovan's police stab vest felt constrictive over his shirt, reminding him of his time in uniform when he'd worn it every day. It felt good to go on operations like this and be physically present, rather than sitting in his office listening in to police airwaves and worrying about overtime budgets. He crouched low behind the car, his colleagues behind him. Radio communication was being kept to a minimum as they relied upon hand signals. Nearby CCTV was being checked, as well as ANPR, which would flag the licence plate numbers of any known offenders in the area.

Donovan's pulse quickened and he pushed his radio earpiece farther in. He could not afford to miss a second should an update come through. Three loud knocks echoed down the empty street as the decoy stood at the door. Her hood was shielding her face, a scarf wrapped around her chin. But there was no sign of life from within the house. DS Daniels, the covert sergeant, relayed that officers were in place. His whispered instructions came over the police airwave channel dedicated to the operation alone.

Keeping their heads low, Donovan's colleagues followed him as he crept along the side wall of the house. Neighbouring homes had their curtains and blinds shut, the blue-white glow of televisions within. A dog barked in the distance, but the house before them remained in darkness. No light of a torch. No flicker of a candle. Nothing. Was anyone inside? He watched the decoy knock for a second time before peering into the letterbox and calling out. Silence fell heavy as he waited for a response. Officers were at the rear, guarding each exit. The address had been checked and double-checked. Donovan crouched, with a clear view of the door. A Toyota Yaris drove past, it's occupant elderly – certainly not the person who had made the call.

'There's no answer,' the decoy eventually said, covertly updating her radio.

'Take it,' Donovan instructed officers. 'Go, go, go!' He leapt from his hiding place. Adrenaline pumping, he followed them down the garden path.

One swift battering with the ram nicknamed 'the big red key', and they were in. One by one, they cleared each room. But all he was left with was a sick feeling in his stomach as he realised that he had been played. Had the presence of police spooked his caller? But they had arrived early, their attendance concealed. The caller had seemed so convincing. He glanced through the window across the street. She could be watching them right now. Perhaps she hadn't been able to get away. The house was declared safe and Donovan shook his head in defeat.

'Thanks, guys,' he said. 'We'll call this a wrap.' A short post-briefing would follow, and the system would need updating. He wouldn't be home before midnight, and then he had Amy to face. It was of small comfort that she had missed nothing. At least she was safe.

CHAPTER FOURTEEN

Amy felt the stirrings of discontentment as she checked her watch for the third time. Donovan should have been home by now, and he wasn't answering his phone.

She gasped as something fluttered in her abdomen. She'd felt the faintest of sensations previously, like tiny butterfly wings. 'Oh my God,' she said softly. She thought she'd imagined it before, but there was no denying this. Her baby was moving inside her. She rested her hand on her stomach, as frightened by the enormity of the situation as she was in awe.

She jumped as her mobile phone rang from its resting place on the coffee table. She quickly grabbed it before her mother woke up. Flora had returned home tipsy from her friend Winifred's birthday bash and was now snoring like a foghorn upstairs.

Amy glanced at the screen before answering the call. It was the office.

'Hello?' she said quietly, one hand back resting on her stomach. She expected to hear Donovan's voice. But it wasn't Donovan. It was Molly, her DC. 'Sorry to bother you, Ma'am, but…'

Dotty awoke from her slumber on the sofa as Amy sat up

straight. If Molly was calling her ma'am, something was up. 'What's wrong?'

'A lead has come in. A strong one. The DCI told me not to say anything, but...' She exhaled a breath. 'I thought you should know.'

'Spit it out then,' Amy said ungraciously.

She and Molly trusted each other. She wouldn't take it the wrong way.

'A woman called the police helpline asking for you. She was really upset. She told the DCI that she and her fella took Yasmin and the others, but she had no choice but to go along with it. She said she'd only speak to you because you'd understand what it's like, being forced into something like that.'

Amy stood so quickly that little pinpricks of white lights floated in her vision. She leaned against the sofa arm as she caught her breath. 'Are you sure she's not a crank?'

'She knew about the tattoos, down to the squiggle on Yasmin's arrow. Donovan's convinced it's her.' She continued to bring her up to speed on the latest call.

'I'm coming in,' Amy said, scouting the room for her boots.

They'd kept details of the victims' tattoos watertight. Dotty looked at Amy from the comfort of the sofa before resting her chin on her paws. She was used to her owner's unsociable hours.

'You can't,' Molly blurted, 'at least, not because of me. But if you, um...happened to ring the office and find out...'

'Thanks, Molly, you are my eyes and ears.'

Amy had softened towards Molly since their last big case in Clacton-on-Sea. She'd found out a lot about her background and admired her loyalty and strength. Amy's inner circle was small, but those within it had her loyalty and respect. Donovan, however, would be a different story. How could he keep her at bay from such an important call? She disguised her annoyance as she rang his mobile once more.

'I thought you'd be home by now. Everything OK?'

But Donovan's words were clipped. 'I'm heading for debriefing, I'll call you when I'm done.'

Amy's lips thinned. Debriefing meant something had taken place – without her. There was no way he was shutting her out. 'Sounds interesting. How about I come back into the office, we can travel back together. I've got a few bits I need to do.' She rested her phone in the crook of her shoulder and put on her shoes.

'Don't do that.' Donovan said, with an edge to his voice. 'I mean... I'm wrapping things up now. You may as well stay put.'

'You've had a lead, haven't you?' Amy grabbed her jacket from the hook next to the front door. She wouldn't give away her source. 'I can tell by your voice. Something's up. I'm coming in.'

She heard him excuse himself in the background before a door creaked closed.

'I had a call from a potential suspect who gave me a meeting place in Brixton. I organised a team. The caller didn't turn up. End of story.'

Amy scowled. No mention of the tattoo or that their caller was female. 'Then why can't I come back to work? I'm not going to sleep a wink with all of this going on.'

Donovan spoke in hushed tones. 'Because the caller asked for you by name. This could be dangerous. I'm not having you involved. We're skating on thin ice as it is, not declaring our relationship or your... condition. I used a decoy.'

'You did what?' A string of expletives left Amy's lips as she vented her frustration.

Donovan sighed down the phone. 'The command team

would never allow you to take such a big risk. And if you come in, I'll tell them why.'

'I'm sick of this,' Amy fumed. 'How come you get to do your job and I don't?'

'You know why,' Donovan said softly. 'Look, I know it's frustrating but this is about more than you. We have someone else's safety to keep in mind.' A pause. 'You're not coming in now, are you? Because I meant what I said. Stay put. I'll be back soon. I'll tell you all about it then.'

'I'm not coming in.' Amy was downcast, feeling like an errant child.

'Good. Love you.'

Amy gripped the phone tightly as she fumed. She didn't trust herself to speak.

'Try to get some sleep,' he said before ending the call.

Amy sat on the stairs, threading her hands through her hair. It was so unfair. All she wanted was to be able to do her job. Without it, she was nothing. Her work kept her sane. Why had she decided to keep this baby? This was only the start. What if she couldn't love it? What if it split her and Donovan up? Around and around her thoughts whirled, each one filled with regret. She wasn't cut out to be a mother. This case could collapse because she hadn't been consulted on the development. The suspect must have seen the decoy and left. But what if they called again? She rose, grabbing her bag and coat from the hook on the wall. She would sleep in the office tonight if it came to it, or divert the office phone to her mobile number so she received the call direct. If Donovan thought she was playing house while he followed up a lead, then he didn't know her at all.

CHAPTER FIFTEEN

Staring at the starless sky, Amy stood on the pavement, planning her next move. Normally, she'd cycle into work and use the journey time to think, but her balance wasn't what it was, and she couldn't afford to delay. *The cheek of it*, she thought, *leaving me out of my own investigation*. It was the very reason she hadn't informed the team of her pregnancy. Had Molly known, would she have called?

Walking down the street, Amy fumbled with her leather handbag, searching for the car keys she'd deposited there minutes before. The road was unusually quiet, although she could hear sirens in the distance, and most of the well-to-do dwellers on her street had their curtains and blinds closed. It was a cool but dry night, and she had only brought her coat because the extra layers helped cover her small bump. Head down, she rooted in her bag, grumbling beneath her breath as her phone began to ring. It was probably Donovan, checking up on her again. She did not hear the silver van drive up behind her, and by the time its masked occupants jumped out, it was too late.

The assault came swiftly. She barely had time to catch her breath. A pair of strong hands wrenched her arms behind her back and another pulled a black cloth bag over her head. She was blinded and barely had time to cry out before a bolt of electricity shot into her thigh. Amy crumpled to the unforgiving ground like a marionette whose strings had been cut. Her bag fell, her phone skittering across the pavement. The pain was excruciating as every muscle in her body convulsed. It felt like fire was running through her veins. As she recovered her breath, she threw a couple of punches, but she was drunkenly lashing out in the dark. Her captors moved silently and quickly. Soon Amy was immobilised, cable ties slicing into her ankles and wrists. She was in a van, her face slammed against hard metal.

She lay in the cramped space, adrenaline pulsing as she recovered from the sudden bolt of electricity which had been pumped into her thigh. The door had been slid shut with force, but not before her pockets were searched. Breathing hard, Amy tried to focus her thoughts. The case. Yasmin. The Hunters. It carried the same trademarks. Amy's pulse quickened as the pieces fell into place. The exposure of her identity had brought unwanted attention. She had received plenty of crank calls and abusive communications alongside the fan mail. Everyone knew who she was now, thanks to the TV documentaries and stories in the press. But she had faced it head-on, and now she was paying the price. She tried to calm her thoughts. A taser. They'd used a taser to stun her. Then she thought she'd caught a glimpse of a silver van. It had to be the same kidnappers who'd taken Yasmin.

Fury grew as the truth dawned. The call to Donovan had been a diversion. But how did they know where she'd be? These people had turned up outside her home. She went through the incident while the van bumped along the road. They were waiting for her, but how? Movement came from beside her. She tried to scuttle away, but a strong hand clamped her arm.

'Get the hell off me!' Amy roared. It was an automatic reaction.

She was yanked to one side, the cold, hard prongs of a taser pressed against her neck. Amy froze as the van sped down the city road. The attacker's grip relaxed, and the taser was withdrawn. It was a warning to stay silent. All Amy could do now was wait. She utilised her senses as her police training kicked in. A heavy metal channel played on the radio, but neither party spoke. The van smelled of damp cloths and petrol, with the hint of something sweet – her captor's perfume? They were moving at speed, but not fast enough to be pulled over by police.

It felt like she'd been travelling for hours when the van came to a juddering halt. Her mind raced with possibilities as she was blindly forced outside. The transfer was quick, another warning jab of the taser buying her compliance. All she could think about was her baby and pray that he would be OK. She'd heard of cases in the past, where pregnant women had been tasered by the police in the US. Such actions disgusted her. But she took comfort from knowing that their babies had survived.

The silver van was known to the police, now Yasmin had escaped. The fact they'd bundled her into the boot of a car gave Amy more to worry about. It wasn't a random kidnapping. Her colleagues would pull out all the stops to find her. She lay in the cramped space, fighting to calm her breathing and focusing on what she knew. If anyone had witnessed her abduction, officers would be looking for a silver van, but now it seemed they had transferred her to a car. She cried out, overcome by the sinking feeling that she was screaming into the void. What did they want with her? If this was the work of The Hunters, Amy didn't fit the pattern. Their victims were young and vulnerable, walking alone in isolated streets. Amy was older, a capable police detective, who barely left the confines of her home to go anywhere other than work. She thought about Donovan. If the call he'd received was a diversion, then what was going on?

She immersed herself in her surroundings, drawing on her senses. Muffled voices rose, their radio drowning out her screams. Where were they taking her? Not Epping Forest. There were too many officers on the ground there now. Their presence would be enough to keep her attackers at bay. Were they heading to another forest? Perhaps a warehouse or an isolated house? She inhaled deeply through her nostrils. She could smell diesel fumes, oil and dirty rags. She scratched around in the darkness, rubbing her head against the rough lining of her compartment. She pressed her face against the material, trying to spit through the cloth bag. If these bastards were going to kill her, she would leave as much of herself as she could. She rubbed her hands against the rough lining, kicked out with her feet. She jolted as the car hit a pothole, the sudden bump almost winding her. If she could smash the rear lights, it might alert someone driving behind.

She wasn't giving up without a fight. She clawed around in the darkness, her bound limbs almost numb. There was nothing she could use as a weapon, apart from her own body. But even if she managed to headbutt her captors, how would she run? She thought ahead. Had they picked up her handbag after it had fallen on the ground? Surely someone had witnessed what happened and called it in? But what good would that do, now they'd dumped the silver van? There were no police sirens on the road, no sound of chopper blades in the air.

Amy had heard the sudden whoosh of fire as the van burst into flames. But it wouldn't go unreported. It had been abandoned close to where she lived too. It was obvious they'd set it alight to destroy any forensics. Her team would be on the trail. Amy taught them everything she knew. But it was terrifying, being the person that they were looking for. She sucked in a breath, trying to calm the hell down. Donovan would do everything in his power to find her. Her life couldn't end like this.

CHAPTER SIXTEEN

Donovan shoved his key in the door, half expecting a stony-faced Amy to open it for him, but darkness folded in as he walked into the hall.

'Hello, Dotty,' he said. The pug danced in delight. 'Am I in the doghouse?' He stroked her soft fawn fur before entering the living room. He took in the evidence of Amy's night-time snack as he looked for her on the ground floor. 'Where is she?' he said to Dotty. 'Asleep?'

He approached the wide stairwell, reminding himself to keep the noise down. Dotty followed him up, taking each step in turn, her pink tongue lolling out the side of her mouth. At this hour of the night, she was usually curled up on Amy's bed. After opening the bedroom door, Donovan was surprised to see the light on. He glanced around the empty room. The bed was still made, the plump cushions perfectly aligned. Something about this scene was all wrong.

'Amy?' he called, coming out onto the landing.

He checked each room in turn. Nothing. He glanced at Flora's door, his hand hovering mid-air. The last thing he wanted was to frighten her half to death. But the decision was taken from him as the bedroom door opened and Flora appeared.

'Oh!' she said, a hand planted on her chest. She tightened her white dressing gown around her ample waist.

'Sorry,' Donovan said. 'I was looking for Amy...'

'Well, she's not in my room, dearie.' Flora looked pointedly at the bathroom door.

Flora's bedroom was the biggest in the house, but it did not contain an en suite, and he guessed she'd got up because she was dying for the loo.

'Isn't she home yet?' she said as he stepped aside.

'It's nothing to worry about. I'll give her a ring.' Donovan smiled. 'We had a bit of a work-related tiff. She's probably gone to Sally-Ann's.'

'You two.' Flora chuckled as she passed. 'You're like a couple of teenagers. You need to put a ring on her finger and settle down.' Her words followed her into the bathroom.

If only she knew that Donovan had popped the question countless times. Would Amy ever settle down? The last thing he wanted was for her to resent him – just like she was now. They would both have to make sacrifices to give their baby a home. He only hoped they survived it as a couple. Amy was his whole world.

His hand glided over the stairwell as he tried ringing Sally-Ann's mobile phone. He told himself there was no need to panic. Amy was teaching him a lesson, that's all. She was miffed that he'd left her out. He couldn't blame her for that. As for her sister... it was hardly any wonder that Sally-Ann wasn't answering, given the late hour. But a fearful heaviness settled over him. Amy wouldn't just take off, not without telling her mother.

Flora returned to her room, bringing Dotty with her. Donovan stood at the bottom of the stairwell, willing Amy to walk in the door. He fished his car keys from his pocket. Something was wrong. If Sally-Ann wouldn't answer her phone, then he would knock on her door.

CHAPTER SEVENTEEN

'Is everything OK?' Paddy stood aside to let a worried-looking Donovan in.

The home he shared with Elaine was a modest but comfortable respite from work. But as Donovan barged into his living room, it seemed work wasn't done with him yet.

'Is Amy here?' He glanced around.

The television was turned off, the curtains drawn. A newspaper rested on the coffee table, a cup of hot chocolate next to it. One cup. Not two, or three. Only then did Donovan seem to notice that Paddy was wearing his dressing gown.

Miffed at the intrusion, Paddy wanted to say he wasn't much of a detective if he couldn't figure out that Amy wasn't there. 'No, she's not here, why?' he replied instead. 'Should she be?'

'What's wrong?' Sally-Ann joined them, looking Donovan up and down.

Her blonde hair was sleep-tousled, and Donovan apologised for waking her up.

'I'm worried about Amy. She's not at home.' His gaze

roamed the room, as if he was half expecting her to pop up from behind the sofa. 'Something's not right.'

'She *should* be back by now.' Paddy frowned, checking his watch. 'She left before me.'

'That's the thing,' Donovan continued. 'She was at home, but then she left. But she went on foot because her bike is still there and her bag has gone.' He was breathless with worry and unable to stand still.

'Let me get my phone.' Sally-Ann turned to leave. 'I'm charging it in the kitchen. I'm reading this book by Mel Robbins. She said you shouldn't have your phone next to your bed.' She spoke brightly about blue lights, not at all concerned as her slippers slapped against the hall tiles.

But Paddy could see concern in Donovan's eyes. Amy had a temper at times, and lately he'd heard her complain to Sally-Ann that Donovan was smothering her. But he'd never struck Paddy as the overprotective type, and if he was honest, he was glad there was someone else watching out for her.

'Her mobile's switched off.' Donovan tapped the redial button on his phone.

Paddy pushed his hands into his dressing gown pockets. 'She didn't go out for a takeaway? Called in to see a neighbour, maybe?'

Donovan shook his head, recalling the evidence of Amy's presence in the kitchen. He told them about the leftover plate of crackers and crumbles of cheese on the plate. 'The neighbours keep to themselves,' he added. 'And even if they didn't, she wouldn't bother them at this hour of the night.'

Paddy sensed his growing discomfort. He was about to ask about Amy's earlier wobble when Sally-Ann walked in.

'I'm sure there's nothing to worry about,' she said, phone in hand. 'Sit down, I'll give her a ring. She always answers for me.'

She was beginning to sound more like his mum than Amy's sister. 'Did we have a little row?'

Paddy watched Donovan's frown deepen.

'She went straight home from the office. She rang me at work, and I told her I wouldn't be long. She never would have left without letting me know.'

The smile faded from Sally-Ann's face. 'Her phone's switched off. That's not like her at all.' She swiftly typed a text. 'I wouldn't usually ring Mandy this late because the kids will be in bed, but I'll check just in case.'

Mandy was their biological sibling. She and Amy were hardly the best of friends.

A text was returned, and Sally-Ann peered at the screen. 'Nope, she's not with Mandy.' She tore her eyes away from her phone. 'And you're sure she didn't go back to work?'

'Positive.' Donovan ran a hand through his hair. 'I already checked.'

'It's all right love.' Paddy rested a hand on the curve of Sally-Ann's back. She was growing more worried by the second as she tried and retried Amy's phone. 'Maybe she popped out to the shops. Or took Dotty out for a walk?

Donovan shook his head. 'Dotty's at home. Amy wouldn't go out for a walk without her.'

'Keep trying,' Paddy urged Sally-Ann. 'Her phone's probably on silent. She might not be able to hear it.'

'I am!' Sally Ann flapped. A flush rose to her cheeks, and her head bowed as she tried to make the call.

Paddy walked to the window and peeped between their curtains onto the streets outside. The path shimmered beneath a streetlight, empty apart from some moths bumping against the lamp. He looked at the clock on the wall. It was almost one a.m.

'I have a bad feeling about this,' Donovan spoke behind him. 'What if we were sent on a wild goose chase on purpose?' He told Paddy about the call he'd received and subsequent operation that had followed as they'd sent a decoy officer in Amy's place.

'You think the call was a diversion?' Paddy thought it over. 'But they were expecting to see Amy. And how would they know where she lived?'

'Not everyone is out to get her.' Sally-Ann sank mournfully onto the sofa, phone in hand. 'Have you not stopped to think there might be another answer to this?' She looked up at them both as they turned. 'Do I need to spell it out?'

Paddy sat heavy on the arm of the sofa. He was tired, and the ache in his lower back was screaming for his bed. 'You're going to have to.'

'They've had an argument,' Sally-Ann glanced at Donovan. 'That, I can tell for myself. Amy's been feeling...stifled lately. She's told me as much.' She raised her hand as Donovan took a breath to protest. 'It's not your fault. Just give her some space, and she'll come back.'

'I don't think it's our place to get involved...' Paddy began to say as the lines between work and family blurred.

'Come back?' Donovan interrupted. 'From where?'

'It's obvious.' Sally-Ann didn't take her eyes off her phone as she redialled Amy's number. 'She's probably taken herself off to a hotel. But I'll be having words. She should at least answer her phone to me.' Taz, Sally-Ann's small grey cat, wandered into the room and jumped up on her lap.

Sally-Ann wanted to see the best in her sister, but Paddy had a feeling there was more to it than that. He was about to ask about Amy's earlier wobble when Donovan spoke up.

'Amy's pregnant,' he blurted. 'She's five months gone.'

'Feck. Off.' It was all Paddy could think to say. Yet it made sense. Her odd behaviour, the doctor's appointments, and Donovan's protectiveness.'

Sally-Ann laughed in disbelief. 'She's not pregnant. No way! You're barking up the wrong tree there. Amy doesn't want kids, and she's certainly not five months...'

'I don't know...' Paddy reasoned. 'She's been out sick a lot. And she *has* put on a few pounds. Come to think of it...I've not seen her with a drink in her hand for months.'

'She's in denial.' Donovan heaved a sigh. 'Amy will kill me for breaking the news, but I can't keep it to myself. Not now.'

Sally-Ann stared at the wall, her face ashen, her voice low. 'She can't be. She would have said.'

'Sorry.' Donovan slipped a hand into the inside pocket of his suit. 'She was planning on telling you soon.' He handed over the printout of a scan. 'We're having a little boy.'

Tears welled in Sally-Ann's eyes as she took in the grainy image. 'He's sucking his thumb.' She sniffed, touching the outline of the baby's face. 'I can't believe it.'

'That's why she wouldn't just disappear.' Donovan turned to Paddy who was resting a hand on Sally-Ann's shoulder. 'She knows I'd be out of my mind with worry.'

'I just thought she was under the weather,' Paddy replied as he came to terms with the news.

Donovan was pacing now, just as he did in the office when a big case came in. 'I can't help but think it's connected to the case. It's just a feeling, you know? That call wasn't a coincidence. She mentioned Amy by name.'

Paddy thought of the previous victims. Amy had nothing in common with any of them, although she'd been intricately involved in the case. 'It's only natural for you to feel protective. Don't worry. She'll turn up soon.'

But Donovan was biting his thumbnail, speaking his

thoughts aloud. 'Abbie, Mallory, and Yasmin. Why would Amy be next? What connects her to them?' His pacing came to a sudden halt. 'Why didn't I see this sooner?' He gasped, shaking his head.

'Boss?' Paddy was still trying to make sense of it all.

'The victims. Think about it.' Donovan spoke with a hint of wonderment in his voice. 'Abbie, Mallory, and Yasmin. Take the first letter from each name. What does it spell?'

The answer hit Paddy like a steam train.

'Amy.' Sally Ann spoke in a whisper. 'Oh my God. Has this been about Amy all along?'

CHAPTER EIGHTEEN

'We did it! We fucking did it!' Lucy's voice echoed around the timber-framed cottage.

They'd parked up and come inside as she'd desperately needed to pee. Now she was high on the rush of their crime, drying her hands on the back of her denim skirt, unable to stay still. Now she'd changed out of her black all-in-one, she seemed more like her usual self.

'This deserves celebrating,' she said, bouncing up to him. 'Where have you hid the coke?'

'Not yet.' Damo grabbed her wrist, stilling her movements. 'Not until we get her inside. We caught her off guard the first time, but now she's bound to put up a fight.'

'That's called the fun part.' Lucy smacked her fist playfully into Damo's ribs. 'Bring it on.'

He loved her when she was like this. Sexy and horny and full of life. He dragged her close before kissing her hard on the lips. Crime was an aphrodisiac like no other. Lucy was high on breaking the rules. He parted from Lucy as she toyed with his belt buckle.

'Not yet,' Damo murmured. 'Let's get her inside first, she's screaming bloody murder out there.'

Lucy's blue eyes were bright with excitement. 'Good. I'll soon shut her up. Can't believe I've bagged a copper. Soon it'll be all over the news.' She pushed aside the red-chequered curtains and peered out the tiny cottage window into the darkness and beyond. Here, in the middle of the forest, they were miles from life. 'You should have heard me on the phone.' Lucy stepped away from the window. 'Boohoo, poor me, I'm such a victim. That tosser lapped it up.' She stared at her boyfriend with a mixture of admiration and amazement. 'But you...going to her house was a stroke of genius. How did you know she'd be there?'

Damo's chest virtually swelled with pride. He'd never been called anything resembling a genius before. 'Cos I knew her pig boyfriend is as possessive of her as I am of you.' In truth, he hadn't expected to see Amy Winter walking down the street. He'd expected to force his way inside her home, at the very least. Seeing her standing there on the pavement, head bowed as she'd rooted in her bag, had just about made his fucking day.

Lucy walked her fingers up Damo's chest. 'Works both ways, hun. You're mine, and don't you forget it.'

'C'mon then.' He led her towards the door. 'Your present is getting cold.'

Lucy emitted another squeal of excitement before following him out. It was Lucy who'd insisted on pushing the boundaries by taking a copper. He'd been content with snatching drunken women off the street. What were the chances of someone like him getting together with Lucy in the first place? He'd never dared bring up his interests with the women he'd been with in the past. They probably would have called the filth. But not Lucy. She'd lapped it up from the start. She was always pushing the boundaries.

Taking the copper had started off as a dare. By now, they had so much on each other that they were both in it up to their necks. *Party hard, die young, and leave one sexy corpse*, was Lucy's motto. Being with her always made his heart pump a little faster in his chest. They were locked in a constant power struggle, and he loved every minute of it. For the first time in his life, he wasn't on the outskirts of things. But he would never have gone this far without her to egg him on.

He signalled to Lucy for silence as they approached the stolen BMW. It was a ringer, two different motors welded together with stolen licence plates to boot. His mate had loaned it to him for the month on the proviso he'd sell it for him afterwards. But there was no chance of that with Damo. It would go the same way as the van – up in flames. He watched Lucy lean over the boot of the car. Goosebumps pimpled her flesh as she peeled off her top and pressed her breasts against the shiny black metal.

'You're not serious,' Damo whispered, hitching up her denim skirt.

As she slipped down her thick black tights to the tops of her Uggs, it seemed that she was.

'Hey, baby.' She banged on the boot, awaiting a response. 'Wanna know what real fun sounds like?' Lucy glanced over her shoulder to Damo, giving him a wicked grin.

The more the woman in the boot screamed, the more Lucy got off on it. Damo wasn't going to turn her down this time. He unbuckled his belt, oblivious to the cold on his bare backside. Lucy licked her lips, and she was impossible to resist. Their coupling was quick and noisy, Lucy leaving their prisoner in no doubt as to what was going on above.

Minutes later, she was fixing her clothes, complaining of the English weather. 'If we lived somewhere warm, we could do it outside every day.'

'I think there are laws against that,' Damo said with a satisfied laugh.

'You've got a cop in the boot of your car and you're worried about getting caught for screwing outside?' Lucy gave the boot another bang of her fist for good measure, but there was no reply. 'She must have got bored of screaming. Do you think we put her off her little holiday?'

Lucy's eyes glittered mischievously, the sneer on her face hard. When she was like this, everything was about getting a reaction. But he had seen too much of the ugly side of the world. Nothing shocked him these days. Lucy's world was nothing like his. She found her privileged lifestyle claustrophobic, whereas he'd grown up with nothing. And now he'd given her the greatest gift of all. He pressed his ear to the cold metal of the boot of the car. Clouds gathered above, casting the sky in a monochrome hue. Had she passed out in there?

'You ready?' He looked at Lucy. She knew what was coming next.

'Shit. I left my knife inside,' she grumbled, fixing her skirt.

'You don't need it.' Damo blocked her path as she turned to go back in. 'I'm tired and hungry. Let's get this done.'

He guided Lucy back towards the boot. The cop was bound and beaten She wouldn't give them any trouble now.

He popped open the boot. The figure inside was unmoving, the bag masking her face.

'She's not dead, is she?' Lucy prodded her back.

There was nothing. Not a sound, or groan, or breath.

Damo ground his back molars. 'This is your fault. I told you to bring her in straight away. Instead, you had to go pissing about!'

'Oh yeah, that's right, it's all my fault.' Lucy turned on him, the wind playing with her long blonde hair. 'I didn't hear you complaining five minutes ago!'

Damo frowned. The mood between them had changed. She drove him mad when she was like this, a constant seesaw of emotions. 'I'm not arguing with you now. They could have choppers looking for her for all we know. Get her inside before someone sees us.'

Lucy was still grumbling as she grabbed Amy by the legs. Damo took his knife from the holster on his hip, sliced the cable ties from her ankles and swung her feet out of the boot. They would have to carry her inside and see what could be done.

'I'll take her shoulders from behind,' Damo instructed. 'You go in front and take each of her legs.'

Neither of them expected what came next.

CHAPTER NINETEEN

THIRTY MINUTES EARLIER

Amy predicted various scenarios while she lay in the back of the car. As the wind whistled past them, it felt like they were moving at speed. The road was motorway smooth until they came to some twisty bends, and the car bumped along the path. She'd tried to count the turns, but she quickly lost track. As she was jolted in her space, Amy tried to get a sense of her location, but it had been impossible to gauge. Music blared from the car radio as some heavy metal channel played. The journey had felt like it went on forever as they drove down the winding road.

She used the time to work out her escape. Panic was futile. She needed to utilise her strengths. She could turn her background to her advantage. As a child in a home with serial killers, you learned to make yourself small. You hid behind curtains, or squeezed into laundry baskets, or crawled beneath beds. You kept your eyes shut tight and clasped your hands over your ears until the bad stuff went away. There was no escaping this situation, but Amy could use what she knew to face them head-on.

Lying in the boot of the car, she tried to predict Donovan's movements. In her mind's eye, she saw him leaving the office.

Had he gone to Flora's or back to his flat? *No,* she'd thought, recalling their conversation. *He promised to come to mine.* He was too worked up about the pregnancy to leave her alone. He might talk to Flora, see the remains of the food Amy had ate. He'd see that she'd taken her bag, phone and coat. He'd double check with the office that she hadn't gone in while he was on his way out. When that came up blank, he'd contact Sally-Ann. But what next? Would he report her missing or presume she'd taken herself off somewhere and turned off her phone? He'd know for sure when she failed to turn up for work. Were there any clues to her abduction? Someone would have seen something. The police must have been called. Donovan would piece the clues together, and the team would track her down. *Breathe,* she told herself as her thoughts raced. *Keep calm...at all costs. Whatever they do to you...don't give them a reaction.* They were a man and a woman. They'd taken her in a silver van. This was connected to the previous attacks.

A muffled groan left her lips as a pothole jerked her hard. She pressed herself against the felt flooring of the car but her bindings refused to budge. Her heart faltered as the car slowed and eventually came to a halt. The radio was silenced. Car doors opened and closed. Judging by the tone of their voices, the woman was excitable and highly strung. She spoke like she was bringing home a puppy to her kids. The man, on the other hand, was steady and calm.

Amy's stomach clenched. What if this was some weird sex traffic setup? Given the sort of criminals who would be interested, a DI could be quite a prize. Especially one with her background. She had pissed off a lot of people over the years. Her emotions were hyper-sensitive as the worst-case scenarios played over in her mind. Her adrenaline was pulsing.

Keep calm, take everything in, find out what they want.

Her internal pep-talk went on. Sometimes surprise was the

best element. She braced herself for the car boot to open. But there was nothing. Time passed, and the temperature dropped. Had they abandoned the car? She shouted until her throat was raw. She kicked out with every ounce of strength. Then she lay in the darkness, forcing steady breaths and formulating a plan.

By the time the couple returned, she was almost relieved to hear signs of life. Her female abductor was making herself known as she shouted something about having some 'real fun.' Amy stiffened as the car bounced. Someone was sitting on the boot. The car vibrated in line with a series of moans, and it was obvious what was going on. Jack and Lillian resurfaced from the depths of long-repressed memories. It was as if her biological parents had returned to kill again. Sex had always been their pre-murder aperitif. The thought made Amy sick to her stomach. The moans reached a climax. As the boot finally opened, Amy played dead. She readied herself to run but made her body a dead weight as the couple tried to pull her from the boot. A serial-killer couple fuelled by violence and sex had not brought her here for a chat.

Amy was dragged out of the boot. The thin cotton bag over her head offered her little view of a cold and unforgiving outside world. Hope bloomed as the cable ties on her ankles were snipped. The moment she felt the ground beneath her feet, she threw back her head and butted her captor in the face before shouldering the other aside. Head forward and determined to keep her balance, Amy ran. Gravel skittered beneath her heels as she shouted for help, trying to draw the attention of someone, anyone who could hear. The air turned blue behind her as her captors came to grips with the fact that not only was their victim alive, she was heading away from them.

Panting hard, Amy ran blindly, her arms bound behind her back. The ground was hard beneath her feet, and the air was countryside crisp. The second she'd heard the male voice speak, she knew exactly who he was. There were no streetlights to guide her. Nothing but shadows in the darkness and the rustle of trees. It had to be the middle of the night. Nobody would find her out here. Her plans changing by the second, Amy ran for her life.

CHAPTER TWENTY

Overcome by a need to protect her unborn baby, Amy twisted her body so she would land on her side when she was tackled to the ground.

'You stupid whore!' a man barked in the darkness, grappling Amy's legs as he pinned her down.

Gravel tore into her side. She fought for escape. She was breathing heavily now, fighting for her life.

'Let me give her a good kicking!' the female accomplice screeched. 'That'll calm her down.'

The man's mood changed, and he broke into laughter, finally getting Amy under control. 'Babe, you can't go breaking your new toy when I've gone to such trouble to bring it to you.'

The cool outside air crept over Amy's skin. She'd had an inkling of the man's identity before, but now she was sure. His use of the word 'whore' chilled her to the marrow of her bones. It was the same thing Jack Grimes called his victims in the hours before he murdered them. How could the person grappling with her now be mixed up in all of this? Her astonishment was short-lived as her face was pushed against the ground.

'Get her inside then, I want to play,' the woman teased.

Knowing the identity of her male kidnapper changed everything. There was another way to win this game. If she choose her words wisely, it was possible to talk him around. The kicking the woman had wanted to administer could have killed her unborn baby. Like it or not, until the odds were in her favour, she had to comply.

The man grunted, gripping Amy's shoulders and pulling her up from the ground. As she was dragged backwards, she listened to the couple's interaction, trying to gauge the strength of their relationship. She couldn't place her voice. Who had he got himself tangled up with?

The woman emitted a dark laugh. 'She could have knocked out my fucking tooth.'

'I told you she wouldn't be like the others,' the man replied, a smile carrying on his voice.

'Still, she needs a slap for what she's just done.'

Amy prickled. *Untie me, bitch,* she thought, *and we'll see who's slapping who.* Her years of boxing practice were waiting to be tested. But now was not the time.

The man coughed up a ball of phlegm and spat on the ground. 'You know the rules. Good huntsmen look after their stock. Gives them a fighting chance. Otherwise, what's the point?'

'The point is she could have knocked my tooth out!' The woman screeched in a cry that triggered what sounded like a flock of birds to fly from their resting place.

So there are trees nearby, Amy thought. *Are we in another forest?*

'Shut your trap, you stupid cow!' Keys jangled as the man opened the door. 'Get her in the chair. Close the door. Then you can scream and shout all you like.'

It was interesting, listening to them bounce off each other. They had a spark similar to Amy's biological parents. One minute their voices were thick with lust, and the next, they were flying off the handle over the slightest thing.

'What do you want?' Amy said, finally asserting herself. 'What's your objective?'

'Ooh, *it* speaks.' The woman pulled Amy's arms behind her back as she forced her inside. 'Our objective is to hunt you down like the dog you are.'

'Follow the rules and you might just get away,' a man's voice rose behind Amy's ears.

The chair was hard against her frame, and the sudden sting of fresh cable ties to her ankles rendered her immobile. Logic suggested that it decreased her chances of release if she told him she knew who he was. But she knew how his insecure and often irrational mind worked. If she could manipulate him over time, there was a chance of a change of heart. If the couple before her were anything like Jack and Lillian, it wouldn't be that difficult to drive a wedge between them. Narcissists in love put their own needs first. Her male captor was angry at Amy, yes. He hated her, that was clear to see. But did he have it in him to look her in the eye and kill her and her unborn child?

Through a haze of pain, Amy tried to make sense of her situation. Surely they knew that by taking a police officer they were unleashing all sorts of hell upon themselves? But then she thought of all the times they'd met. How he'd glared at her with such intensity that it had turned her blood cold. Amy kept her silence. If the killer couple stuck to their MO, she would be left alone tonight. In the morning, the hunt would begin. But in the meantime, they could have other things planned.

'Let's get these off.' The woman's voice rose as she tugged on Amy's boots.

That was the first thing they had done with their previous victims – left them barefoot to slow them down. Amy flinched while a pair of soft hands caressed her foot.

'Ooh, you've got nice feet. Hasn't she got nice feet, hun?' she said, stroking Amy's polished toes.

Amy ground her back molars at the indignity of the situation. She wanted to kick her in the face and knock her teeth out for good, but where would that get her? A punch in the stomach? A knife to the face? She forced herself to stay calm. She had her baby to think about now.

'Mmm,' the woman murmured in a husky voice as she put on a show.

Amy's stomach heaved as she took her toe in her mouth and sucked. 'Tasty.'

'Stop playing around.' There was a hint of discomfort in the man's voice.

Amy's breath was shallow. She would not give the woman a reaction. Amy knew people like her. She was looking for an excuse to hurt her. She wanted Amy to lash out. If it wasn't for her baby, Amy would have given her more than she bargained for. But she had one ace up her sleeve – her kidnapper wasn't just an acquaintance, he was her biological brother, Damien Grimes. His female partner in crime had seriously underestimated the bond between them. Damien may despise her, but he was easily manipulated. His mother had run rings around him over the years. Family meant something to Damien – it was why he was so furious about Amy's perceived betrayal when she'd turned her back on them. But time alone together could heal the wounds of the past – as long as Amy could find the right words. Damien wasn't just her brother, he was her trauma buddy, too. Nobody, not even the woman before them, could understand what they'd been through. He hadn't just kidnapped Amy, there was her baby to consider, too. She would choose her moment carefully and furnish him with the truth. She could turn things around. Could he kill his unborn nephew in cold blood?

CHAPTER TWENTY-ONE

Donovan stood on yet another doorstep, checking and rechecking his phone as he waited for the occupant to answer. It was gone two a.m., and he was getting desperate. He'd been back to Flora's place, and there was still no sign of Amy. Her mobile phone was either out of battery or switched off.

It had taken him almost half an hour to get to Chelsea Bridge Wharf in Battersea, but he couldn't send up a flare without checking the address personally. Craig Winter was aware of Donovan's relationship with his sister, but he had no knowledge of Amy's pregnancy because she'd been in denial herself. Now, everything hung in the balance, making Donovan sick to his stomach. Was Amy hiding out here?

'Sorry to trouble you at this late hour.' Donovan gave a faint smile of apology as Craig opened the door.

The man was slim, athletic, and body confident, his skin tanned from a recent trip to Thailand. Paddy shuffled behind Donovan on the doorstep. It had taken all his powers of persuasion to stop Sally-Ann tagging along.

'What's wrong? It's Mum? Isn't it?' The blood drained from

Craig's face as he came up with his own conclusions. 'Somethings happened.'

'Flora's fine.' He paused as a dark, olive-skinned woman sloped down Craig's hall.

Bleary-eyed, she dressed in a man-sized tee shirt which skimmed the curves of her thighs.

She glanced at the gathering on the doorstep and back to Craig. 'What's going on? What time is it? I must have fallen asleep.' She picked at the false eyelash hanging loose from her eyelid and peeled it away.

She was one in a long line of casual girlfriends. Despite Craig being in his forties, he would never settle down. Amy was forever ribbing him for his womanising ways.

His frown deepened as he turned to his companion. 'Sorry, would you mind getting a cab home? It's...' He glanced at Donovan before resting a hand on her shoulder. 'It's work.' His voice softened. 'I'll call you.'

'No you won't,' she mumbled, before walking heavy footed back into the bedroom.

'It's Amy,' Donovan said. Craig gestured for them to come in. 'She's disappeared.'

But Craig didn't appear overly concerned. 'Is that it? I pissed off Alana because Amy's taken herself off somewhere?' He grabbed a pair of jogging bottoms from the back of the sofa and pulled them on. 'You two not getting along?' he added. 'She must be comfort eating because she's put on a few pounds.'

'There's more to it than that.' Paddy gave him a stern look. Craig may have been a couple of ranks above him, but his behaviour wasn't washing with Paddy. 'Amy doesn't just disappear. This isn't like her at all. She wouldn't leave your mum with no explanation and she'd *never* switch off her phone.'

They were standing in Craig's living room, which also doubled as an open-plan kitchen, like many London abodes.

Two empty wine bottles rested on a glass kitchen table, along with two half-eaten meals. The air was thick with the smell of sex, booze and the remains of a Thai curry which appeared to be home-made. Floor-length glass windows invited the night inside.

'Want me to call you an Uber?' Craig interrupted as Alana passed, fully clothed.

She responded with a shake of the head. 'I've got one waiting outside.' She paused, seemingly deciding against what she was going to say.

Craig joined her at the doorway and whispered into her ear. Whatever he said, it evoked a smile. Stretching on her toes, she planted a brief kiss on his lips before walking out the door.

Craig's smile was fleeting as she left. 'I take it you've rung around.' He pressed a button on a remote control, and the floor-length curtains closed.

Donovan responded with a nod. It hadn't taken long. Amy didn't have many friends outside of work. Her circle of trust was small. 'Sally-Ann rang her sister, Mandy, who hasn't heard from her. I've tried Amy's ex, Adam, but he's out of the country so she's not there. I rang Mama Danielle, but she's not heard from her either.' He paused as Craig gave him a quizzical look. 'She's someone Amy met through work.'

Mama Danielle was a London madam who Amy had met during a previous case. The pair had formed an unlikely friendship and Mama Danielle had been very concerned.

'And there's nobody else's door she could knock on?' Craig asked. 'What about Molly, from work?'

'God, no,' Paddy replied. 'She gets on with the girl, but there's no way she'd call on her at this hour, after working next to her for half the night.'

'Besides, Molly finished the same time as me,' Paddy added. 'Amy left a couple of hours before.'

But Craig was staring at Donovan. 'You didn't answer my question. Did you two have a row? When was the last time you spoke?'

There was a measurement of protectiveness in his voice that Donovan hadn't picked up on before. This was beginning to sound like an interrogation.

Donovan filled Craig in on the case he'd been working on and told him the meeting didn't bear fruit. 'Amy's committed to the case, and she didn't appreciate being told to stay at home. But now I'm wondering if that call was just a ploy.'

Craig snorted a disbelieving laugh. 'You told my sister to go home? Right in the thick of a case? Don't you know her at all? No wonder she was pissed off.'

Donovan exhaled in frustration. He was tired of justifying his actions and he didn't have time to waste. 'These people we're dealing with are dangerous. They asked for her by name.'

Silence fell and Craig appeared to give this some consideration.

'I don't know...' he said at last. 'She's probably in a hotel room, pissed off with you for excluding her from the operation.' He took his mobile phone from the side and scrolled through his contacts. 'I've always said you should never date work colleagues, especially when you're their boss. It's messy and awkward and never ends well.' He nodded to himself as if speaking from experience. He put his phone to his ear and waited for his call to Amy to connect. 'It's switched off,' he said, staring at the display.

'I know that.' There was a hint of irritation in Donovan's voice, but Craig spoke over him.

'If you two want to make a proper go of things, you should make it official. That's probably what she wants. Her ex really let her down. Maybe she needs some commitment...I dunno.'

His voice trailed off. 'I'm not the best person to give romantic advice.'

'This can't get out at work,' Donovan snapped. 'Not yet.' He was wasting his time here. Craig was missing the point.

'Why not?' Craig piped up. 'You two seem serious, don't you think it's about time?'

'Best we keep it to ourselves for now.' Paddy folded his arms. 'If she's reported missing then the boss won't be able to work the case. Conflict of interest and all that.'

'And what if she's spending the night in a hotel with the sole purpose of teaching her dear boss a lesson? You'll have egg on your face if you report her missing and they find her shacked up in the Hilton Hotel.'

'She wouldn't do that.' Donovan spoke with conviction. 'She knows I'd be out of my mind with worry.' Why wasn't anyone listening to him?

'Oh, for God's sake, man, stop smothering her,' Craig scoffed. He leaned against the back of his leather sofa. 'She's an independent woman.'

'She's five months pregnant!' Donovan shouted, his frustration coming to a head. 'Which is why she couldn't join in the operation. I'm losing my shit here. When are you going to take this seriously?'

Donovan's audience fell silent. Craig's mouth dropped open. He looked from Paddy to Donovan, clearly shocked to hear the news.

'Mum doesn't know about this, does she?'

'No,' Donovan said instantly. 'And there's no point in worrying her. Amy might turn up for work in a few hours. I'm heading into the office to update her as missing.'

'I hear what you're saying.' Craig was sombre now. Concerned. 'But if Mum's house wasn't broken into, how would Amy disappear into thin air? Think about it. If your suspects were gunning for my sister, how would they know where she lives?'

'It wouldn't take a genius to follow her home from work,' Paddy said. 'Although it doesn't make sense for them to set up a meet and then go there.'

'How about *I* report her missing,' Craig said. 'Just to play it safe. She only has herself to blame if she comes back to a fanfare.'

'OK,' Donovan replied, palpably relieved. 'Make the call. We'll meet you at the office and follow it up. There might be CCTV of her leaving the house. Don't mention the pregnancy,' Donovan warned. 'The team don't need to know yet.'

Amy's brother nodded, his face etched with worry as the situation sank in.

'Boss?' Paddy said softly as Donovan turned to leave. 'You don't think that she left to have a termination? She's just under the threshold. She could have herself booked into a clinic first thing.'

The thought had crossed Donovan's mind, but only briefly before it was dismissed. 'We discussed it when she found out, but Amy wouldn't contemplate it. We were all ready to tell your mother. We were making plans.' A shuddering breath left Donovan's lips as the weight of guilt bore down. 'This is my fault. I shouldn't have left her alone.'

'Don't be daft.' Paddy placed a firm hand on his shoulder. 'She's probably back at the office now, her phone in her pocket, her battery flat.'

'I hope so.' Donovan pulled his car keys from his pocket as he headed towards the door. He would never forgive himself if something happened to her.

CHAPTER TWENTY-TWO

Donovan had dealt with many high-stress situations during his career in the police. His previous cases were nothing compared to the tumult of emotions that Amy's disappearance brought. Only now did he truly appreciate the feeling of helplessness that overwhelmed you when a loved one disappeared without a trace. The sounds of traffic outside absorbed him for a few minutes as he tried to straighten his thoughts. On the grey, drab streets, hapless pedestrians were being splashed from puddles by passing lorries as they began their day.

This morning he was running on adrenaline, nauseous with worry but determined to project an image of calm professionalism.

He turned to his team, who hadn't hesitated in coming in, their gazes expectant as they waited for him to speak. Paddy was here to oversee them, and Craig was in the CID office making enquiries. In the last few hours, Amy had been reported missing and her home searched. Efforts to triangulate her phone had not produced any new leads, as a signal was last picked up in the region of her home.

Donovan hated to worry Flora, but his gut told him to

progress the investigation with speed. Feeling like a fraud, he'd searched Flora's home with two uniformed officers, hoping that Flora wouldn't let details of his romantic entanglement with Amy slip. She had sat on the sofa, her face gaunt with worry, and all the while Donovan was thinking no, no, no, Amy would never put her through this. And so he'd looked again at the undisturbed bed, the cracker crumbs on a plate in the kitchen, and tried to imagine where the woman he loved most in the world had gone.

'Thanks for coming in early.' He corrected himself as he realised he was pacing the office floor. 'You all know why you're here.' He took in his colleague's faces, each one shadowed with worry. 'Hopefully Winter will walk in at any minute and tear a strip off us for overreacting, but until then, we can't waste a minute of time.'

At work she was Winter, but in their quiet, private times she was Amy. It made it easier to separate the two as he directed his team today. A set of sharp footsteps echoed around the corner and the team seemed to hold their collective breaths. But it was just DC Steve Moss, whispering an apology as he joined them. There was nothing to apologise for. Light was yet to filter in through the blinds. It wasn't yet six a.m. Steve sat next to DC Molly Baxter and exchanged a few hushed whispers before turning his attention to Donovan. He was in shock. They all were. It was up to Donovan to hold them together.

He stood firm and addressed them. 'Our team has received more than its fair share of attention in the press. We have one of the best detection rates for our size, and we've interrupted a lot of criminal activity over the last year.' The office fell mortuary quiet as he issued a warning. 'This is a word of caution to any one of you. Don't take off without letting someone know where you are, otherwise you'll return to the same reception.'

Molly rose a hand. 'Is this off the record? I mean...given

she's our DI. Are we allowed to investigate her disappearance?' Her voice tense, she sat on the edge of her chair. Molly had been in awe of Amy when she'd first joined the team, but their relationship had grown into a strong mutual respect over the course of the year.

Donovan was ready with an answer. 'I've cleared it with the command team. We're best placed to investigate it. Nobody knows Winter better than us.'

In truth, it had taken Donovan some time to persuade his senior officers that they were best equipped to investigate. For once, Amy's icy exterior worked to her benefit. They weren't aware that the team was so tight-knit, and he had managed to keep his relationship with Amy under wraps. They wouldn't have had a look-in otherwise. There was a reason it was called a conflict of interest. When strong personal feelings were involved, anything could happen. Lines could be crossed. Procedure could be forgotten. People could be compromised, and jobs could be lost. Donovan would sacrifice anything to get Amy home safe.

'You know the drill,' he said, scanning the room. 'I've requested extra resources. If Winter doesn't show up for work this morning, it's likely they'll be approved. Officers from CID are checking CCTV, and Paddy's going to liaise with them to arrange house-to-house enquiries. We're researching her recent financial transactions, although I've spoken to her mother this morning, and she said Amy left her purse at home.' The more Donovan spoke about work, the more strength he drew from it.

He acknowledged DC Steve Moss as he waited to speak.

'Boss, do you think this has anything to do with last night's operation? They asked for Winter by name, didn't they?'

'I'm not ruling it out. Obviously, we'll take any calls that come into the office seriously. Every hour counts.' He didn't know how he got through the rest of briefing, but he was glad when it was over and he was able to make it to his office in one piece.

He looked across at Amy's empty chair. She should be here by now. Thanks to Flora, he'd quickly accessed her online banking. Amy's mum was far cannier than he gave her credit for. There were no transactions involving recent travel or hotel bookings. No payments to private clinics or spas. They had already rung around local hospitals to no avail. He'd been half hoping that she was safely in a hospital bed with some minor injury. Anything was better than the thoughts running riot through his head.

He threaded his fingers through his hair, a sick feeling returning to the pit of his gut. The woman who'd called last night was armed with intimate knowledge of their last victim, as well as asking for Amy specifically. Had the meetup been a diversion all along? He sighed as his thoughts kept hitting dead ends.

He snapped his head up as someone cleared their throat. It was Molly. She stood before him, nibbling on her bottom lip.

'Yes?' he said.

She clasped her hands together, looking like she wanted to run for the door. 'Boss, I...I've something to tell you.'

For one blissful second, Donovan expected Molly to tell him exactly where Amy was.

Molly's cheeks flushed pink as she struggled with her words. 'I...' She swallowed. 'I think I was the last person to speak to DI Winter. I called her last night. I told her about the op. Sorry. I shouldn't have got involved.'

As she told him about the call, it was clear that Molly had expected a telling off for getting involved. But Donovan had bigger concerns. If nothing else, details of the call gave him an insight into Amy's state of mind. Given what Amy knew, she would have been angry enough to return to work and have it out with him there.

Donovan was about to speak when Paddy strode in. He was pale, his face stony with concern. This was not good.

'Boss, we've had an update. It's definite. Winter's been snatched.'

FOUR DAYS LEFT

CHAPTER TWENTY-THREE

The sickly sweet smell of cannabis filtered through the material of the bag on Amy's head. She hated that smell because it reminded her of her biological parents. Back then, Lillian and Jack were too nose blind to notice the stench that clung to everything. But their teachers weren't, as they complained about the odour on Damien's and Mandy's school uniforms. But while a follow-up visit had been requested, it was never made. Somehow, the neglected Grimes children had fallen through the cracks. Not enough was done, until social services came to check up on Sally-Ann after she'd failed to turn up at school. Then four-year-old Amy had blown the whistle, and everything around them changed. That was the day Amy's big brother came to hate her more than anyone in the world. It was hard to comprehend how he despised his four-year-old little sister more than his murderous parents who were the epitome of evil in Amy's eyes.

Amy's humiliation hadn't last long. A phone call interrupted proceedings, and she listened with a keen ear as the woman who had been fondling her feet received a telling off from what sounded like her father on the phone. It seemed like an odd time to call. The man was either an early riser or had not yet been to bed. Amy could hear the pout in the woman's voice as she transformed from psychopathic sex kitten to spoilt brat. The call had been taken in the next room while Damien lit a fire in the hearth. As soon as the conversation ended, an argument had ensued.

'You'd better go round there, Luce, keep the old man sweet.' He had barely said the words before his girlfriend rounded on him, screaming a string of obscenities for using her name. An argument followed, but not enough to keep her there for long. She gave him a mouthful of choice words before slamming the door on her way out.

Amy sat in the sterile silence, with nothing but the crackle from burning timber and the aftermath of the woman's outburst still hanging in the air. A wave of nausea washed over her. She needed to eat, despite the sickness. She breathed through the covering on her head. It smelled of stale linen, and she wondered if it had been used before. She told herself to snap out of her moroseness. Moments like this were golden because it meant she could talk to her brother alone.

'You may as well take this off my head, Damien.' She spoke with the dull disinterest of someone who had seen it all before.

Silence was returned. But he was near. She could hear him breathing. Watching. Thinking. She stiffened, waiting for sudden recrimination. A sharp slap or a kick to the legs. A car engine revved outside, gravel clanking against metal as the vehicle skidded out of the drive. It was a relief to hear her drive away. It was just Amy and Damien in this lonely pocket of space.

The soft creak of a chair was followed by quiet footsteps as Damien approached. Amy's fists clenched as he fumbled with the neck of the bag and ripped it from her head. She blinked, growing accustomed to her surroundings. She was in a wooden log cabin. The lights were on, the shutters closed. Damien's face was unshaven, his unruly brown hair styled with gel. A hunting knife was strapped to his thigh. In his combat trousers and black top, he was dressed like a character out of an Xbox game.

'I need a drink,' Amy said firmly. She would not beg. Not yet. Their relationship had always been difficult. Amy was the youngest in the Grimes family, or 'pocket rocket' Poppy as she was known back then. Damien may have been her big brother, but Sally-Ann was the only sibling to show her an ounce of kindness. From what she could remember, Damien was the one who tore up her pictures or stuck out a foot to trip her up. But Amy could not blame him for everything. Being raised by serial killers would skew anyone's brain.

She looked up at her brother. He stood, bag in hand. His eyes narrowed, he watched her for a few seconds before leaving the room. A myriad of emotions threatened to engulf her. Damien had always been unpredictable. He could just as easily be reaching for a knife as a glass. She exhaled a breath of relief as the sound of a gushing tap filtered through.

She checked out her surroundings. The cottage was small and low-beamed, with old-fashioned furniture and deep, cosy rugs. A fire roared in the wide hearth, and the chill had left the air. In any other setting, the cottage could be viewed as homely, but this was a potential murder house. Her eyes darted to the doorway as Damien approached, glass of water in hand.

'Drink,' he grunted, poking a straw into her mouth.

Amy gulped, taking breaths through her nose as she finished it off. Damien's expression darkened and she could almost see the hateful thoughts passing through his mind. His eyes were filled with such malevolence that Amy was shaken by a flashback of her father's image. Damien even smelled like her father, as a mix of tobacco and booze lingered on his breath.

He rested the glass on the coffee table and brought her a Mars bar. His eyes never leaving hers, he unpeeled the wrapper. 'Eat it.'

It was a command Amy was happy to comply with. Chocolate may not help her nausea, but it would provide some much-needed energy. She bit down and chewed. She should be talking, not eating, but her body was trembling from her ordeal. Damien scrunched up the wrapper before sitting astride a wooden chair turned back to front. His dark eyes bored into hers. Amy licked her lips, tilting her head to one side. No doubt he expected her to reason with him or beg to be freed. But she was born a Grimes. As much as she'd reinvented herself, she could not deny the dark roots of her past. It was time to allow her inner child out to play.

'What is it?' she said sharply, her dark hair shadowing her face. 'If you've got something to say, then spit it out.'

'I've nothing to say to you.' Damien crossed his arms over the front of his chair, observing her as you would an animal in a zoo.

'Come off it,' Amy snapped. 'You've got all these thoughts swimming around in your head. Best you get them out before Luce comes back. What's it short for? Lucifer?' The words were out before Amy could stop them.

Damien jumped up from his chair, grabbed a handful of Amy's hair, and shook. 'Don't you fucking talk about her.'

Amy flinched as spittle showered her face. Her scalp prickled from the force of his knuckles against her skin. But he wouldn't kill her, not yet. It wouldn't hurt to push the envelope at this stage. She waited a few seconds until he calmed down. He was pacing now, chewing on his thumbnail as he gave her the side-eye. Already, she was getting to him. That, and the fact he probably needed a fix.

'I'm gonna do you a favour,' Amy said, grateful she hadn't been gagged. Deep down, her brother wanted to talk. She watched anger flare in his eyes and quickly continued. 'I've got some inside info on the investigation, but first you'll have to free my hands. I can't feel my fingers.'

Damien's mouth formed into a thin white line. He seemed lost without his sidekick to guide him. His eyes flicked to the door and back to Amy.

'I'm not going anywhere,' she said. 'I'd prefer a head start in the woods tomorrow rather than take my chances with you now.' She nodded towards the knife which was strapped to his hip. 'That's a nice piece of kit.'

'There's lots more where that came from.' A sneer rose on his lips as he ambled towards her. 'I'll free your wrists, but one wrong move and I'll slit your throat.'

Amy rolled her eyes at the dramatic turn of phrase. It didn't originate from Damien, who usually spoke in simple terms. It was an empty threat. He wouldn't go as far as killing her without his partner in crime. But as Damien's knife cut through the cable ties like butter, Amy was left under no illusion of the danger she was in. She winced, rubbing the soreness from her wrists. She only hoped her brother would keep their conversation to himself. Lucy was an unexploded bomb.

'Go on then,' Damien sat back down.

Amy's ankles were still bound, but he hadn't holstered the knife.

'What do you think you know?'

'I know about the case and what we have on you both. But I don't know why you took me, of all people. Jesus, Damien. I've got no beef with you. Kidnapping a police officer – it's a bit extreme, innit?' She measured her words, drawing on past experiences.

Damien gave her a one-shouldered shrug. 'If Lucy wants a cop then she gets a cop, and I can't think of anyone who deserves this more than you.'

As they fell into conversation, Amy could see who was pulling Damien's strings. She rubbed her wrists and the feeling in her fingers slowly returned. 'Have you thought this through? This isn't some computer game. If you get caught...you'll get sent down for life.'

'That's rich, coming from you.' Damien snorted. 'Given you were the one who put Mum in prison.'

Amy groaned. It always came back to this. 'I was four years old. A baby. Social services interviewed me in their car. I was playing with unicorn stickers while "The Wheels Of The Bus" played on the car CD player. I had no idea what I was saying. Hell, I barely spoke, just nodded in response.' She sighed, grateful to have Damien's ear. 'I remember one of them telling off the other for asking leading questions. I'd no idea what it meant back then, but I do now.' Her memory of that day was crystal clear. By providing Damien with enough details, she hoped to convince him of that, too.

Damien's expression relaxed. It was strange, watching his features contort. His brows burrowed deep in his forehead, but his eyes reflected something else. The haunted expression of a wounded animal that's been kicked one too many times. He looked away, apparently uncomfortable beneath the weight of Amy's stare.

'That's not what you said before.'

'When you turned up at my gaff and had a go at me? You had my back up the second you walked in the door.'

'Nah.' Damien shook his head. 'You're messing with me head. Trying to get me to back down.'

'I'm telling you how it was,' Amy retorted. 'Who found the evidence that set Mum free?' She was talking about the evidence she'd stumbled upon in Flora's loft. Calling Lillian 'Mum' did not come naturally, but she could make this work.

'You hate her.' Damien snarled, trying to compound the theories that had driven his hatred this far. 'I've seen the two of you together.'

'I'm a cop.' Amy matched his tone. 'I've got a nice number going on here. I'm hardly going to blow that, now am I?' A dark chuckle left her lips, and for a moment it scared her, because it was Lillian's signature laugh. 'You don't know me at all. I could have burned that evidence. My DCI told me to get shot of it.' She watched Damien's eyebrow rise. 'But I didn't. Even if it meant dobbing in my adoptive dad. I thought he framed her, and nobody wanted to know.' But it was Amy's conscience which had made her come forward with the evidence, not loyalty for her biological mum.

'Then why didn't you tell Mum that?'

'Because a serial killer mother doesn't exactly help my chances of promotion. Think about it, Damien. Look at the facts. If there's one thing my childhood taught me, it's that you've got to look out for number one.'

Damien fell silent as he took her words in. The fire crackled and spat as a breeze drove down the chimney.

'I'll tell you about the case and what we know,' Amy continued. 'But not your girlfriend. She's playing the victim, Damien. She blamed you for everything when she called it in. I don't see why you should take the brunt when the shit hits the fan.'

The sound of an approaching car signalled an end to their conversation. Amy's heart pounded frighteningly hard behind her ribcage. Had her colleagues found her? Her body tense, she prepared to fight her way out. Damien jumped up from the chair and peeked through the shutters. Amy's spirits fell as he visibly relaxed. The engine stalled. Lucy called out that she was back. Amy exhaled a long, quiet breath. At least part one of her plan had gone well, and Damien had dropped his guard long enough to hear her out. If he thought she held valuable information, then it bought her some time.

Damien holstered his knife as Lucy entered. She was just as Amy had imagined: a cosmetically enhanced beauty with sculpted cheekbones, fake eyelashes, plumped lips, and long blonde hair tied into a high ponytail. A tight-fitting denim skirt clung to her slim frame.

'I thought you were gone to your dad's?' Damien spoke with an expression of a man who had just been caught with his hand in the biscuit tin.

'No need.' Lucy flashed him a smile. 'I managed to get a phone signal a couple of miles down the road…worked my charm on him.' Her gaze turned to Amy. 'What are you playing at?' She shot an arm over her face to disguise her features. 'She can see me!'

Amy calmly watched their interaction. Would Damien mention her warning? His eyes flicked to Amy's, as if reading her mind. She held his gaze.

'Babe…' He turned back to his girlfriend. 'She already knew who I was. And if she knows it's me, then it won't be hard to trace you.' He leaned in and whispered, 'It's not as if she's ever leaving here…not alive anyway.' He snaked his hand around her waist, his actions evoking a chuckle as he whispered some more.

Amy's chest felt tight as she listened in on their plans. Damien's allegiance was clear, and her team may never find her. She had four short days to win her brother around.

CHAPTER TWENTY-FOUR

'Run that by me again.' Donovan wanted to be sure he'd heard Paddy correctly the first time around.

They were standing around his computer. He pulled up the software to reiterate what he'd explained moments ago. Only Donovan couldn't believe it. He couldn't imagine Amy ending up the same way as the victims who'd gone before her. As for his baby…he couldn't physically do his job if he sat down and thought about everything he had to lose. Molly fidgeted nervously next to him, and the rest of her colleagues crowded around. The mood was sombre. Donovan wanted to leave the room, to go up to the roof of the building and gulp in some fresh air. This wasn't happening. Not to Amy. But Paddy's Irish accent brought him back to ground as he relayed the harsh truth.

'We've got a hold of CCTV of Winter coming out of her house. Here. It's already on the system, but look…I'll show you.' Paddy was fraught with worry as he accessed his emails. It seemed to take forever for the file to open. 'It's not brilliant footage, but it's enough to see,' he warned. 'The camera is across the street, but you can make out their forms.' He clicked on his mouse and accessed the file. 'We've run a check on the van, what's left of it. Officers found it burnt out nearby. The plates are stolen.'

'Right.' Donovan's voice was gravelly as he acknowledged the update.

He tried to swallow, but his throat was bone-dry. Amy's image was a grainy black and white, clear enough to show her exiting her home. So she *had* left the house of her own free will. Donovan wanted to warn her to go back inside he watched her descend the steps. Then she was out on the street, not paying any attention to her surroundings as she fumbled with her bag. He leaned on his table as he watched two masked figures appear out of nowhere. Amy had been looking at her phone, too preoccupied to notice. One grabbed her in a bearhug while the other opened the back of the van. A bag was thrown over her head, her wrists bound to stop her lashing out. Anger rose as he watched the slimmer figure draw back their fist and rain down blows to Amy's head. But it was the glint of a handheld object being thrust into Amy's thigh that made Donovan want to rip the monitor from its station and throw it to the ground. His fists clenched as he watched Amy's body jerk before going limp.

'The bastards tasered her.' Paddy's words rebounded around the silent room.

Donovan rubbed a hand over his mouth. 'Looks that way,' he said, as calmly as he could muster.

His colleagues crowded around and he felt the strength of their emotions as a collective. The air crackled with the need to bring their boss home. Donovan had to put himself in Amy's shoes. What would she say? She'd tell him to put his emotions aside and use their collective experience to get her home. If there was one woman capable of taking control of a situation, it was her.

. . .

Paddy rewound the footage once more. They watched the slimmer abductor jump into the back with Amy, while the other attacker stopped to retrieve Amy's bag and phone from the ground.

Donovan pointed to the screen. 'Someone was ringing her. She was distracted by her phone when they pounced.'

'It could have been anyone calling...' Paddy began, peering at the screen.

'No. It couldn't,' Donovan said firmly. 'Winter has two phones. One for work and one for personal use. Her work phone is at home. Very few people know her personal number. Sally-Ann didn't ring her last night, did she?' He had already asked Amy's sister, but he needed to be sure.

'No.' Paddy shook his head. 'She last spoke to her a couple of days ago.'

'Then find out who else could have had Winter's personal phone number. Because I'm pretty sure she didn't spread it around.' He looked at his colleagues who appeared lost, a flock without a shepherd, of sorts. 'Back to work,' he said firmly. 'I know this has been a shock, but get over it. If we can't handle this case subjectively then it'll be passed on to someone else.'

Two office phones rang at the same time, cutting through a silence he could not bear to be a part of. All but one officer returned to their desks as instructed.

Molly stood before him, her face fixed in determination. 'We'll find her, boss. It won't be long.'

Donovan managed to nod before striding into his office and shutting his blinds. He had a myriad of strategy meetings and briefings set up for the day, he just needed sixty seconds to catch his breath.

From the moment he'd discovered that Amy was missing, this was what he had dreaded the most. There was no doubt in his mind – this was no random attack. Yasmin's kidnapper's had been gunning for Amy all along. But who was behind this operation – and why?

CHAPTER TWENTY-FIVE

Donovan stood on the pavement outside Amy's home. To think, that hours previously, she'd left the safety of her London abode to venture out into the night. Different scenarios played out in his mind, each one accompanied by a sting of guilt. He should have kept her in the loop. If he'd involved her in the operation, then she wouldn't have been on her own. He should have trusted her. He should have known. And now he had to face Flora, her mother, and tell her the truth. He had no idea how to break the news. Amy would hate for her mother to find out like this. Amy's pregnancy would come as a shock, but given the gravity of the situation, it would soon be breaking news. He couldn't risk Flora hearing of Amy's pregnancy from anyone else.

He sat in her living room, with Dotty snoozing on the sofa, just as he'd done many times before. He'd explained the seriousness of the situation without giving too much away. There was a fine line between being truthful and worrying the poor woman half to death. 'I know it's hard, but we need keep my relationship with Amy a secret for now.'

'But why?' Flora's ashen face relayed her concern. 'Surely if everyone knows that you're together, they'll try even harder to find her.'

'Flora, my team are one of the best in the Met. They'll sweat blood to bring Amy home. But if the powers that be find out that we're in a relationship, they'll take us all off the case. Right now, our best bet of finding her lies with the team.'

'So what is it you're not telling me?' Flora fixed him with a glare. 'I may be getting on in years, but I'm not stupid. You know more than you're letting on.'

Only now did he see similarities between Amy and her adoptive mother. Amy had looked at him in the same way many times before. 'Amy was kidnapped last night. We're following up multiple leads, but that's all I can say for now.'

'Oh my God.' Flora raised a hand to her mouth. 'Someone's taken her? What about the baby?'

Donovan stared at Flora. He wasn't aware that she knew. It seemed their secret wasn't so secret anymore.

'She must be...four, nearly five months gone?' Flora reached out and stroked Dotty while giving him a critical eye.

'Five.' Donovan sighed, a little in awe of the woman before him. 'She was going to break the news soon. I kept on at her to tell you, but she hadn't accepted it herself.' A sense of relief swept over him. Flora was taking it well. At least she'd had time to process the news. 'How did you know?'

'I found her pregnancy test in the bathroom bin weeks ago.' It was Flora's turn to appear sheepish. 'Don't look at me like that, I was emptying it. Then there's the all-day morning sickness, and the recycling got a lot lighter because she wasn't drinking so much. I told her she was putting on weight, just to give her some more time. I may have been secretly thrilled, but I knew Amy would have trouble coming to terms with it.'

Donovan smiled, and for a few seconds he'd been able to forget the predicament he was in. 'Then let me say it officially. Congratulations. You're going to be a grandmother.'

But Flora's smile was fleeting, and she replied in a soft voice, 'Only if you find her.' She reached across and squeezed Donovan's hand. 'Amy's strong. If anyone can pull through this, she can. But she can't do it alone. You will find her, won't you?'

'I swear on my life. I'll do whatever it takes to bring her home.'

Flora nodded in acknowledgement. 'Then go. We'll talk some more later. Your team need you.'

Donovan rose from the sofa, equipped with a newfound respect for the woman who had taken Amy in from the age of four. Flora had been married to Superintendent Robert Winter, a brilliant man who'd died suddenly from a heart attack. He imagined she had seen and heard all sorts of things when it came to her husband's work, but none as harrowing as this. Yet she hadn't fallen apart. She had grown stronger since Robert's demise. Then he saw a tremble in her hand when she reached out to stroke her dog. She would worry for her daughter in private, after he had left.

As Donovan returned to his office, Paddy's expression relayed that news had come in. Donovan steadied himself while he awaited an update. Had their waking nightmare come to an end?

CHAPTER TWENTY-SIX

Damien sat on the front porch, waiting for sunrise as he dragged deep on his spliff. The cold was biting through his tracksuit, the seat of the wooden rocker hard beneath his skin. But he liked the freshness of the air, and the smell of the forest around him, which was so different to inner-city smog. He hadn't slept a wink last night. Having Amy here was messing with his head. He knew it was a bad idea, but Lucy always got her own way. He was strong. He had to be, to survive his childhood. He'd never admit it to Amy, but the more time he spent with his mother, the more he realised she was just as bad as their dad. Yet he couldn't let go of the fact that Amy had betrayed them. Because living in that stinking house with bodies buried in the basement was better than being in care. Jack Grimes had let him drink, even bought him ciggies. He hadn't cared where Damien had gone or what time he'd come home. A couple of times a month, him and Lillian would have a big row, usually because one of them got a bit too close to the person they were shagging. There was only one rule: they weren't allowed to swing alone.

He remembered Poppy asking if they were going to the park because Lillian had said she had some swinging planned for the weekend. He and Mandy had laughed their heads off, and Amy's chin had wobbled before her little fists clenched. That's the way it was with her, she either cried or got real mad and would give them all a mouthful. It was how it had been with them all. As long as he'd kept out of Jack's way, he could usually avoid a beating, but when he was shoved in the care home, it was on the cards almost every day. *Beat or be beaten.* It had become a way of life. The worst thing was being torn from his family. There were times he thought he'd never see them again. Nobody wanted to foster a teenager, especially one with bruised knuckles and a chipped tooth.

Damien ran his tongue over his teeth at the memory. It was fixed now, but in a way, it was still there. When one of the staff had tried it on with him, Damien had given him what for. He'd known about sex and how it all worked, and there was no way he was letting some lanky nonce have a go on him. So he'd punched him where it hurt, and Damien had his face smashed in return. The skinny sod half packed a punch back then. But still, Damien had fought his corner, and the bloke had left him alone after that. That was life. *Beat or be beaten.* He was never going back to it.

He'd always despised the pigs, but Amy Winter brought out a whole new level of hatred in him. He hated how she talked with a posh accent. He hated her nice pad in the city and how she rode her bike to work every day like Jessica fucking Fletcher on speed. He knew what she thought of him, he could see it in her eyes. Sometimes it was all he could do to stop himself going around there and breaking her privileged neck.

'You should hear how she talks about you,' Lillian had confided in him one night. 'She said you give her the creeps – that you're her father incarnate.'

Being compared to Jack had disgusted him. He liked it rough, but he drew the line at underage girls. But there was a small part of him that nagged. Amy would never call Jack her father. She despised him too much for that. She didn't care for any of her biological family but she hated Jack the most. Had Lillian been messing with his head? Such thoughts were silenced when he'd seen Amy on that pathetic cop documentary on TV. She had loads of supporters on social media, too. Lefty twats, the lot of them. He'd tried to start a wave of hate against her but was quickly shot down. People couldn't get enough of DI Amy Winter, and he was sick to the teeth of it.

'I hear they're trying to make another documentary,' Lillian had said. 'Virtually throwing money at her, by all accounts. She's done quite well out of this.'

'You ain't done too badly yourself,' Damien had mumbled, but his mother had turned on him, slapping him sharply at the side of the head.

'You know nothing!' she'd warned. 'You call spending the best part of my life in prison doing well? The only time I wasn't beaten was when I was in solitary.' She'd lifted the leg of her trousers, displaying a twisted patch of skin. 'Boiling water. They held me down for that.' She'd pulled her sleeve up. 'They tried to cut my wrists to make it look like suicide.' She'd pulled up her jumper to reveal a jagged flesh wound. 'A shank did this. Bloody idiot was as high as a kite. They came off the worst of it.' She'd raised her hands to her head to part her hair.

'All right!' Damien had said, putting a stop to her sick display. He didn't want to see anymore.

'And you know who we have to blame for this?'

He knew the answer.

'I was going to get help, but thanks to Amy's big mouth, I was vilified.' On and on his mother went, in her tirade against the woman who had abandoned them all.

. . .

But now when he stared at Amy, he could see a spark of Poppy there. It jolted him to feel something other than hatred when he looked into her cool grey eyes. Maybe it had taken this for her guard to drop. He thought about the life she'd made for herself. Was it all one big act? The way she moved, the way she talked. Even her face seemed to change in line with the little sister he once knew. Gone was the poncey accent. In her dirty blouse and wrinkled trousers, she was just like the rest of the Grimeses now. He used to think she'd gone soft. But maybe she had a point. It was her who'd found the evidence. Her who'd dobbed her old police mate in. Lillian had her part to play in persuading her, but would he have done the same in her shoes? *I was only four years old.* Amy's words replayed in his mind. Every night, lying in his bed in the children's home, he'd focused all his hatred towards her. But now he just didn't know.

His mother was always bitching about Amy, and Lucy was wrapped up in her fantasy world. Had he ever stopped to think about what *he* wanted out of this?

'Who pissed on your cornflakes?' Lucy said as she was met with a scowl.

He hadn't even heard her come out. Dressed in her combat gear, she was ready to go, and he hadn't even laced his boots. Her fine blonde hair was tied high on her head, a slash of red lipstick stark against the paleness of her skin. Something clicked in his mind. Lillian always wore the same shade. Why hadn't he noticed that before? He realised she was waiting for an answer and he flicked his spliff onto the gravel.

'I'm just tired, that's all.' He stood, and Lucy gave his buttock a squeeze.

'Too tired for me?' She purred, running a tongue over her lips. Both hands were on his backside now, kneading roughly.

He felt himself get aroused and cast all thoughts of Lillian aside. 'If that's what you want,' he said, pulling her close. 'That's what you're gonna get.'

CHAPTER TWENTY-SEVEN

The rest of the night had passed slowly for Amy. She'd been bound and transferred into the dimly lit bedroom so Damien and Lucy could catch an hour's sleep. It was missing a bulb, but a fat porcelain lamp in the corner provided enough light to see. The low-beamed ceilings were clean, the wooden floor covered by a purple patterned rug. A bookshelf was against one wall, filled with well-thumbed paperbacks, which gave the room a holiday home feel. It was completely at odds with the situation that Amy had found herself in. Her wrist was cuffed to the double metal bed frame, all efforts to escape proving fruitless.

She'd tried to force sleep, because she needed her strength to face what lay ahead. Her captors had not drugged her, and she was grateful for it. Their weapons bought her compliance. It wasn't just the firearms that worried her. It was the venom in their voices and the hatred behind their eyes. For now, she had time on her side. If she could not escape the game, then she would play it. Four days. At least she knew the rules. They wouldn't hurt her while she was imprisoned – if she complied. The bruise on her jaw was proof of what happened if she as much as rolled her eyes. Each day that passed, her odds of escape lessened. Right now, she was at her fittest. Yasmin had been found badly injured, dehydrated and hungry. Amy was used to skipping meals, but what about tomorrow, and the day after that? If day four came, she would be running on nothing but adrenaline.

According to Yasmin's statement, the weapons of choice became more dangerous as time passed. She knew about their use of scrambler bikes and how they sometimes stalked on foot, moving in a pincer movement until their prey was caught. As Amy grew weaker, the weapons would become more life-threatening until her captors reached their end goal. But four days...Amy clung on to the hope that her team would find her in time. She would not die today, or tomorrow. But she may just escape.

She was shaken from sleep when Damien entered the room. Shafts of light splintered through the shutters which were closed and padlocked. Her body ached from being bundled into the van the day before. Damien ensured her compliance before dipping a spoon into a bowl of porridge. She stared deep into his eyes, drawing on painful memories in an effort to win him around.

'You used to make us this before you went to school,' she said, parting her lips to accept it.

But Damien scowled in response. 'I know what you're doing, trying to worm your way into my noggin. No gabbing, unless it's to talk about the case.'

'If I survive the day, I'll tell you,' Amy replied. 'It's in your interest to know.' She wolfed down the rest of the porridge, hoping it wasn't drugged.

Silence fell between them as Damien spooned the last of it from the bowl. The familiar taste evoked further memories. He'd sweetened it with honey instead of sugar, and used long-life milk instead of fresh. Anything fresh was a luxury in their household, and Damien used to shoplift for extra supplies when he could. She remembered Mandy explaining it to her, when she'd asked why he hid things in a special pocket inside his duffel coat. Amy recounted it in between spoonful's. Damien didn't need to speak, she could see the flicker of recognition in his eyes. Their bond was tenuous, but it was there. His hatred was evidence of the strength of his unresolved feelings towards her. She wanted to tell him that he didn't need to do this, that they needed to talk things through. But she'd be dropping the veil on the Grimes persona. Grimes' family members didn't talk about feelings. They looked out for themselves. She had a better chance of getting through by staying on Damien's wavelength. She only hoped she survived long enough to win him around. It was hard to think about her baby. All this time she'd spent resenting him... had she brought this upon herself?

She dutifully took a drink as Damien tipped a bottle of water to her lips. Suddenly she was four years old again, asking her big brother for a drink because her parents were out. The house she'd been born into was either a base for drug-fuelled parties or devoid of her parents for days. During the times Jack and Lillian were away, their children were left to fend for themselves. The cupboards were usually empty, apart from porridge or breakfast cereal. On the days her parents disappeared, Damien stayed home from school to look after her. It would earn him a beating when they returned. Jack Grimes wasn't worried about his school record, but he *was* worried about attracting attention. She had forgotten about the porridge until this morning. Was Damien remembering, too?

CHAPTER TWENTY-EIGHT

Paddy hadn't wanted to come home. It wasn't the need for forty winks that had brought him there, or the order from his DI to freshen up with a shower and a shave. It was the pull to see Sally-Ann. She was suffering, and he couldn't bear it. She'd come into his life when he'd been at his lowest point. Geraldine, his former wife, was a manic depressive who'd beat him more times than he cared to recall. Sally-Ann had been pure sunshine, generating a love so warm and nurturing that it had enabled him to move on. After divorcing Geraldine, he'd never imagined the day when he would want to wed again. But now he couldn't imagine life without Sally-Ann. Every day in her company felt like home. It was why an engagement ring was nestled in a box in the breast pocket of his jacket. But this was not the time, not while Amy was missing. He couldn't bear for Sally-Ann to suffer the worry of her sister's disappearance alone.

She was upon him as soon as his key entered the Yale lock. 'Have you found her?' she said, eyes wide and wondering as she opened the door from the other side.

Paddy hung up his coat and shook his head. 'Not yet, darlin'.

The boss sent me home for a break. How are you doing?' He lay his hands on her shoulders, which seemed to sag beneath his touch.

'I don't...I don't...' she began to say, crumbling into tears. 'I don't know what to do.'

His six-foot-four frame encompassed her in a bear hug as she cried. 'Shh, now. It'll be fine. She's made of strong stuff.'

When her sobs abated, he drew back, his shirt damp from her tears.

'Sorry.' She sniffed, giving him a watery smile. 'You're right. We'll find her.'

Their cat wandered down the hall, mewing as she curled around Sally-Ann's legs. She was a rescue and not the prettiest of felines. Like Sally-Ann, she had been through the mill.

'Let me fix you something to eat.' Sally-Ann scooped her cat up and walked into the kitchen.

'Are you talking to me or the cat?' Paddy grinned.

But Sally-Ann couldn't raise a smile. 'Haven't you any leads?'

'You know I can't tell you that.' Paddy watched her fill a bowl with kibble then turn to wash her hands.

He couldn't bear to see her this upset. 'We have our suspicions,' he relented. 'There are teams of specialist officers being drafted in to help. It's not just us.'

'Then you know something, because you can't work on thin air. Please. I might be able to help. Tell me.'

'I don't want to worry you.'

Sally-Ann folded her arms. 'I've never asked anything of you, Paddy. I've always been here when you needed me, always understood when you were late back from work. But if you don't tell me what's going on right now...' Her face was flushed with frustration as she raised a finger in the air.

'All right, all right!' Paddy guided her to the kitchen table. 'Sit down.'

Her chin wobbled as she followed his instruction. 'She's dead, isn't she? You're looking for a body.'

'Feck's sake, Sally-Ann, don't even think that. Not for a second. She's safe for the next few days.'

She listened intently as he explained about the silver van and the likelihood that her sister had been kidnapped by the same people.

'OK.' Sally-Ann breathed a sigh of relief. 'If that girl got away, then my Amy can, too.' She treated Amy more like a daughter than a sister. This was hitting her hard.

He brushed a stray hair off her face before cupping his hand over hers. Sally-Ann wasn't like the rest of her family. She dyed her dark hair blonde so she wouldn't look like her mother. She couldn't wait for it to turn grey so the roots wouldn't show as much. She didn't like to talk about her past, but she cared deeply about her siblings and would do anything to help.

'Have you spoken to Lillian yet?' He had to ask the question.

Amy wouldn't have wanted her biological mother to be involved, but this case had her MO all over it. Officers had already been in touch, and Lillian had denied all knowledge.

'I've spoken to Mandy.' Sally-Ann sniffed. 'I've not been able to get through to Damien. There's no love lost between him and Amy, so I don't think he'd care.'

But that wasn't what Paddy wanted to know. 'So you've not seen Damien about then?'

Sally-Ann shrugged. 'Mandy saw him yesterday…or was it the day before? I can't remember the last time we…' Her words evaporated as a thought struck. 'Wait a minute. You don't think he's involved, do you?'

'I'm not saying anything of the sort.' Paddy rubbed his bristled face. Time was ticking, and he needed a wash and a change of clothes.

Sally-Ann stood, unable to keep still. 'I feel like I'm walking on air, but not in a good way.' Her words were haunted with worry. She walked to the kitchen window, her words filled with pain. 'Have you ever felt like that?' She turned, searching Paddy's face for an answer. 'It's like I'm walking, but there's nothing there because the ground has fallen away.'

'Do something for me, will you?' Weary, Paddy glanced at Sally-Ann. 'Give Lillian a ring. Put her on speaker. I want to hear her voice.'

'I will if you tell me why you think my family is involved.'

'I don't...but this case, it has echoes of Jack and Lillian Grimes. She's always had it in for Amy. I want to hear what she has to say.'

Paddy could never bring himself to call Lillian Sally-Ann's mother, although she'd come to terms with her bloodlines. He despised the woman with a passion and kept his distance from Mandy and Damien, too. It had never been an issue, given how much they hated the police; the feeling had been mutual. Forever the peacekeeper, Sally-Ann never allowed it to become a bone of contention. Her caring nature meant she could never completely alienate herself from them.

He fiddled with his hands, desperate for a cigarette.

'If you think it will help.' Sally-Ann picked up her phone from where it was charging on the kitchen counter. It took seconds to connect the call. 'Have you heard the news?' she said, her face downcast.

'What news?' Lillian made a puckering noise as she smoked a cigarette.

Paddy shook his head. She was already playing games.

'Haven't you heard? Amy's been kidnapped.'

'Oh, that. Yes, the filth were here, knocking on my door.'

Lillian emitted a dark chuckle. 'But not out of any concern for me. They actually asked me where I was last night. Me, half blind from years of being inside!'

Paddy ground his back molars. She hadn't mentioned one word of concern for Amy. As usual, it was all about her.

'C'mon, Mum, you're hardly Snow White.' Sally-Ann spoke with a firmness reserved for her mother.

'I never said I was! Only that I'm sick of the pigs beating down my door every time something goes wrong.'

Sally-Ann leaned against the kitchen counter. 'Have you spoken to Damien today?'

Lillian barked a laugh. 'You don't think he's taken her, do you? The Hunters are all about sex. They're a pair of fucking wannabes. Even Damien wouldn't go as low as to screw his own sister.'

Sally-Ann's lips thinned. Each word from Lillian's mouth was an assault on the universe. 'How did you know about The Hunters?'

'It's all over social media. I keep my ear to the ground.'

'Do you know where Amy is? Have your followers said anything?' As crazy as it seemed, Lillian had a band of groupies online.

Lillian was in no rush to reply as she took another drag of her cigarette. 'What's it Amy said to me once? You live by the sword...some rubbish like that. She's pissed off a lot of people over the years. Perhaps it's time she got her just deserts.'

'You don't know the full story.' Sally-Ann's face darkened. She exchanged a glance with Paddy. He shook his head.

'I've got to go. I need to keep the line free,' Sally-Ann replied. 'Call me if you hear anything.' She hung up before her mother had a chance to reply.

'You were about to tell her Amy was pregnant, weren't you?'

Sally-Ann didn't deny it. 'Maybe if she knew, it might filter down. They might not be as hard on her.'

'If Amy wants her kidnappers to know she's expecting, then she'll tell them. Let her make that decision. We don't want this going public. Not yet.'

Sally-Ann sighed. 'She's enjoying this. What a bitch.'

'Are you surprised?' Paddy rose from the table. 'I'm going to get a shower and head back to the office. Why don't you go to bed?'

'How the hell could I sleep with that going round in my head?'

She had a point. It was the same reason Donovan would drive himself to exhaustion – he couldn't rest in a world without Amy, the woman who had battled her demons and won. He would not allow evil to take her down now.

CHAPTER TWENTY-NINE

Donovan shaved in the sink at work. He'd spent the last three hours with Superintendent Jones going through each minute detail of their investigation. Every minute in his office was torture because all Donovan wanted was to be out on the ground. His super had asked him if he was getting enough sleep, which was why he was shaving in the work toilets. Anything that helped him portray the illusion of having it together was worthwhile. The weight of responsibility was like lead on his shoulders. His super had requested a 'quick and decisive result' as the commissioner had 'grave concerns for DI Winter's welfare'. They were throwing everything at this case, but it was only a matter of time before the press got a hold of it. They were already covering 'The Hunters' with the cheaper tabloids making much of the impromptu Instagram strip tease. Sex sold newspapers. It was no wonder their readers were lapping up the torrid tale of the killer duo who labelled themselves 'The Hunters'.

. . .

Donovan stood before Amy's desk, hoping he was sending valuable resources in the right direction. The link to Amy's name was more than a coincidence. It hadn't been easy, coming to that decision. Perhaps if Amy's brother had been contactable, he might have thought differently. Damien may have spoken to Mandy, but that could have been a token visit to keep himself in the clear. CCTV was being checked for the appearance of a female companion, but that would take time. Amy had always said that Damien was a powder keg waiting to go off. He'd had a warped upbringing and harboured a grudge against his sister that spanned decades.

Perhaps they needed to look at Lillian, who could be living vicariously through her son. Either way, it was a lead worth chasing. Damien had sailed close to the wind before, with involvement in online Facebook groups which had harboured unsavoury sexual deviants in the past. Amy had investigated them all. The difficulty lay in directing the bulk of their resources towards catching Damien. The superintendent had warned Donovan not to be blinkered. Amy had worked on many high-profile cases during her career and was recently in the spotlight, starring in a fly-on-the-wall policing documentary. Any number of people could have been involved. But spreading the net wide in such a limited amount of time was a gamble. As far as Donovan was concerned, Damien was the main face in the frame. He had previous for sexual offences and had spent time in prison. His hatred for Amy was ill-concealed each time they met.

'Gov, have you got a minute?'

Donovan snapped out of his thoughts, embarrassed to be caught staring mournfully at Amy's desk. 'Come in.'

He opened his window blinds and peered out at his team before returning his attention to Paddy. He'd had a change of clothes but little sleep, judging by his haggard face. His navy trousers were freshly pressed, most likely by Sally-Ann, and his navy-blue tie displayed tiny yellow ducks. Amy loved his novelty ties. *Loves*, he caught his inner thoughts, the ones he couldn't yet bear to touch upon. *They may be sharpening their knives, but she's still alive.*

Paddy rested a mug of coffee on Donovan's desk. It was a James Bond mug, one of Amy's favourites. 'I thought you could do with this,' he said, grim-faced.

'Cheers.' Donovan raised the mug to his lips. Paddy wasn't the best at making it, but it tasted like nectar today.

Paddy fell into a thoughtful silence, change jingling in his pockets as he thrust his hands inside. 'For what it's worth, I think you're right. Winter's family is involved.'

'Family? Not just Damien?' Donovan rested the mug back on his desk.

Paddy nodded. 'From what I've learned about Damien, he takes instruction from his mother. She's the one pulling the strings.'

'True,' Donovan agreed. 'And there's no love lost between her and Amy. Lillian's good at holding a grudge.'

He was aware of Lillian's ability to hold on to things. She had kept the burial sites of some of their murder victims to herself for over thirty years. She'd only shared them to get herself off the hook.

'What about Sally-Ann? Has she tried talking to her?'

'Aye,' Paddy said flatly. 'But Lillian barely tolerates Sally-Ann. She sees her as a traitor for siding with Amy. Mandy is more accepting. She's always been on Damien's side. I've told Sally-Ann to work on her.'

'Good.' But Donovan was feeling guilty for drinking coffee while Amy was God knew where.

The divisional intelligence unit were working on tracking Damien down, but what about his accomplice? What sort of woman would be involved in such brutality? There was one person who knew. The woman the female suspect was most likely trying to emulate. He was going to have to speak to Lillian Grimes.

CHAPTER THIRTY

Every movement Amy made out of the bedroom was closely monitored. She guessed it was late afternoon by the time Lucy got out of bed. Had Donovan slept? How far were the team into the investigation? Had they made the link? Surely her brother would be in the frame. It came to her as she worked out the connection to each of the previous victims, that the first letter of each of their names spelled out Amy. It was the kind of twisted game that Lillian used to play.

'Move it.' A pointy finger jabbed Amy in the spine as her footsteps slowed. It sounded like Lucy, one half of the duo determined to make her life hell. Amy stumbled onto the cottage decking as she was pushed through what seemed to be the open front door. The air was icy but fresh and clean, a relief after breathing in the cannabis fumes that lingered in the cottage. She tried to imagine her surroundings, her thoughts one step ahead. The bag over her head was about control, as were the bindings on her wrists which were keeping her compliant. At least her ankle ties had been removed.

Lucy whispered huskily into Amy's ear, 'Here's the rules.

You get a ten-minute head start before we hunt you down like the dog you are. Think you can remember that?'

'Not without my boots,' Amy said firmly, before Lucy jerked her by the arm.

'You play by our rules,' she spat.

Amy was close enough to hear her breathing. To smell the sickly sweet scent of her perfume.

'Nope.' Amy replied, her feet rooted to the ground. She imagined Lucy glaring at Damien.

'Tell her!' Lucy's words were edged with impatience. 'Or do I have to get the taser?'

But they both knew that use of a taser would bring their games to a halt today.

Damien sighed. 'Just give her the bloody boots.'

'Aw, baby, why should *she* be treated any differently to the rest?' Lucy whined as her personality changed. Gone was the husky sex vamp as she spoke in a babyish voice.

Every second in her presence was winding Amy up. Their relationship had to be based on sex, because this was no meeting of minds. As much as Amy hated her biological mother, Lillian was good at taking control. But Lucy was nothing more than an entitled young woman who used sex to get her own way. This morning, it seemed that Damien was having none of it.

'Put her effing boots on,' he growled. 'Or we bring her in and call off the hunt.'

Was it wishful thinking, or was Damien softening towards Amy? She hoped it was the case. She said a silent prayer of thanks that she'd worn her boots on the night she'd disappeared. Already, the October air was raising goosebumps on her flesh. She wouldn't have got far in her heels today. She wanted to tell them to remove the bag. Given she'd seen both their faces, it was pointless to keep it on. But it was all part of the theatrics of the game. Amy made it her mission not to beg or plead, whatever they did to her. Her pulse picked up a beat as Lucy's bony hand guided each foot into her boots.

'Step forward,' Damien instructed in a no-nonsense voice.

Lucy had fallen silent, no doubt sulking for now. Gravel scrunched beneath Amy's feet as she was guided outside. This was all happening too quickly. She felt like she was being lined up for the firing squad. She focused her thoughts. Adrenaline flooded her body, making her limbs shake.

'You've got ten minutes,' Damien continued, speaking in a dead tone. 'You won't get far.' A dry chuckle left his lips.

But he wasn't fooling Amy. Change was in the air. He wasn't taking any enjoyment out of this. What would he do if she refused to budge? Punch her? Push her back inside? Finish her off there and then? Because there was no way Lucy was letting her go. Amy tried to regulate her breathing, but she was sweating, despite the chill, and had barely moved an inch. On they walked, the swish and creak of moving branches overhead. The wind picked up, rising goosebumps on her flesh.

'Are you ready, little rabbit?' Lucy caressed the side of her arms as she stood behind her.

The cool metal of what had to be a knife touched Amy's wrists. Lucy was pressed up against her now, her breath accelerating.

'Shame you're related. The three of us could have had some fun...' Then she was pushing the bag up from Amy's neck and nibbling on Amy's ear.

What the hell? Amy thought, remembering her vow not to give her a response. *I can do this,* she told herself. *I've seen worse.*

Damien murmured something so low that Amy could not make it out. Then the cable ties were cut with ease, and there was a sudden flash of daylight as the bag was pulled off Amy's head. She blinked to clear her vision and was pushed from behind.

'Run, rabbit, run!' Lucy's words were followed by a wild giggle that echoed around the forest.

There was no time to think. Amy's survival instincts kicked in, and she ran for her life. But the woodland was thick, with several overgrown paths. She sprinted through the trees, trying to get her bearings. But where the hell was she? The sun was high in the cloudy sky, and there was movement in the bushes as wildlife scrambled out of her way. There was no sound of traffic in the distance. The best thing she could do would be to find a hiding place and wait it out until Donovan tracked her down. At least she was physically fit. Even pregnant, she'd found the time to keep up her cardio routine. Her bump was small and neat, barely noticeable beneath her clothes. But she felt the weight of responsibility just the same. Her eyes scanned the forest, if there was a copse she could bury herself in, or a dense tree she could climb... But so far the path she ran was flat, with the occasional tree root sticking out. The trees weren't leafy enough to disguise her form. Above her, a flock of birds shot from swaying branches, giving a clear signal to her kidnappers. A series of whoops rang out as the motor of their bikes revved. It hadn't been ten minutes, it had barely been five. *Dammit,* Amy thought, scoping as much ground as she could. She ran off the path; they would have to follow her on foot. Brambles scratched her arms as she shielded her face. They were coming, she could hear them. The sound of the engine died. A branch snapped underfoot. It was another signal for Amy to run. But to where? Every path looked the same. She could see nothing but trees ahead. There were no clearings, no picnic benches or litter bins. No signs stating she was in a nature reserve. Where the hell was she?

Either she kept to the path and sent up flares from the birds above, or she moved slower through the overgrown woodlands in the hope of being able to hide. Today, she wasn't injured. Running was her best chance of escape. Minutes passed and she struggled to find a clearing. But the woodland was dense and disorientating. She was going in circles. A feeling of helplessness washed over her. They were near, and Amy was panting so hard she was sure they could hear her. It was no use. She had to find somewhere to hide.

She froze as an arrow shot into the tree before her.

'Hands up, or the next one is for you!' The sound of Lucy's gleeful voice rose from behind.

Damien stepped out in front of her, knife in hand. Amy raised her fists in defence. She could take on one of them, but two, both armed? She met his gaze as Lucy tore through the brambles to reach her. Damien delivered a tight shake of the head. An unspoken message passed between them. He was telling Amy to choose her battles. A slice of pain darted from beneath her stomach. It was her ligaments, stretching to accommodate her unborn child. She'd felt this pain before, and it was enough to weaken her legs.

'Turn Around,' Damien said. 'Game's up for today.'

Amy's head swivelled to see Lucy creeping up behind her, her arrow trained on Amy's head.

'That wasn't ten minutes.' Amy panted for breath..

'Yeah, and you weren't barefoot.' Lucy grinned. She turned to Damien. 'Can't I give her a warning shot in the arm?' She chuckled. 'Or her ankle, maybe? Nothing vital.'

'You know the rules, naughty girl.' Damien smiled, tugging Amy's wrists together as he bound them.

Amy could have fought. Most likely would have, had it been just her. Why had she trusted her brother? But yet her instincts told her it was the safest thing to do. She only hoped she was right.

CHAPTER THIRTY-ONE

'Look at all the pretty flames...' The words drifted from Lucy's lips in a moan. It was evening and she was lying on the floor, her head on Damien's lap as he stroked her long blonde hair.

He'd found her sprawled on the rug before the open fire after he'd finished securing his sister to the metal bed rail. In his absence, Lucy had found his stash in the bottom of the wicker basket used to store logs. Whatever she'd taken, she was enjoying the ride. Sighing, he watched as she stared at her hands, mumbling something about flowers coming out of her fingernails. In Lucy's world, it was all flames and flowers, dark and light, hate and love. Damien wasn't one for deep thinking, but he recognised the pattern just the same. He used to think that rich people had it made. Turned out, plenty of them were just as messed up in the head. He sat on the rug, wondering where this was all heading. Those were the thoughts that scared him the most.

For so long, his hatred for Amy had eaten into his life. Sometimes his thoughts were so noisy they felt like a swarm of hornets bouncing inside the walls of his head. Some days it got so bad that dying from a drug overdose would have brought sweet relief. He'd come close to it several times and had woken up choking on his own vomit more than once. That's when Lillian had come to him and told him to stop being stupid. She spoke about feeling alive again and how drugs weren't the best way. *Why kill yourself when you can get so much more pleasure by bringing others to their knees?* That's when she'd talked about sex and giving himself up to his needs.

'You're just like your father.' She'd spoken in a sultry voice as she'd relived her youth. 'He was always at odds with the world.' It was weird how sometimes the comparison to his dad was a compliment, and other times an insult. Lillian and Jack's relationship was twisted beyond belief. It was hard to imagine how they'd be together now, had he not died.

During the long dark nights when rain spiked against the window of his flat, Damien and Lillian would talk for hours over the phone. These were conversations that no mother should have with her son. She'd told him that he was different. That you were either the hunted or the hunter in life. That weakness was not an option – not if he wanted to keep calling himself her boy. She'd told him to find a partner. Someone with the same desires who would stand by his side. She'd said women were less suspecting of a couple, and when you brought home a plaything it was much more fun with three…true, Damien had balked a couple of times when Lillian had gone into detail, but it *had* given him food for thought. For once, his thoughts were focused as he'd made plans. Then he'd found Lucy, who was also looking for an escape. Lillian was right. It was easy to become hooked on power and control.

Lucy finally fell silent, her eyes two slits as a thin string of drool left her lips. Damien wiped it away with his sleeve. Her face was scrubbed of make up, with nothing but the scent of soap on her skin. He preferred her this way. He chewed on spearmint chewing gum as he mulled over his plans for the rest of the evening. Soon he would light the fire, and when Lucy came back to herself, he would persuade her to eat. But first, he needed to check on Amy, make sure she was behaving herself.

Damien's limbs were stiff as he rose. He was heading towards middle age, and today he felt every second of those years. He placed Lucy's head on a cushion and rested her on her side, just as he'd done many times before. He tried to imagine a future for them both but couldn't see past the present. He'd thought it would feel good to get his own back on Amy, but now when he looked into her defiant grey eyes, all he could see was his little sister staring back at him. Defiant, yes, but she needed him, too, and a little piece of him wasn't ready to sever their bond. When he'd spoken to Lucy about killing her, his words had felt hollow.

A knot formed in the pit of his stomach. Whatever he thought about it, Amy was too dangerous to keep around. It was too late to fix things, and he didn't trust her not to rat him out. At the end of the day, she was a copper. She'd made her choice. Lucy would have her way. Soon, Amy Winter would be buried in a shallow grave. He hadn't expected to feel shitty about ending her, but it was too late to stop the hunt now.

CHAPTER THIRTY-TWO

The police station car park was half empty, with many of the uniformed officers out on patrol. Local intelligence was always worth following up, and it was just as important to prevent any further kidnappings as it was to track Amy down.

Donovan glared at the marble sky, feeling angry with the world. The thoughts of going begging to Lillian filled his mouth with bile. His throat was scratchy from talking, his limbs heavy from lack of sleep. He was functioning on adrenaline, coffee, and flapjacks which Molly was keeping in constant supply. Her mother had baked them for the team, no doubt picking up on Molly's anxieties at home. It was comforting to know that he wasn't alone, even if he was lying to his team.

He dry washed his hands, needing a crutch but not giving in. A cigarette or a shot of whiskey would really take the edge off things. But the last thing he wanted was to visit Lillian Grimes with the smell of either on his lips. The woman had a nose like a bloodhound and uncanny insights into the human psyche which had furthered her crime sprees for years.

His car key dug into the palm of his hand as he thought of her smug smile and the way her gaze raked his body every time they met. It was impossible to spend time in her company without having the sudden urge to scrub his skin clean. He thought about Amy and her aloof nature which masked a vulnerability shown to very few. Never had a mother and daughter been at such polar opposites. The heavy security door clicked behind him as DC Daneil Negussie Aberra stepped outside. The young African man was a highly valued member of the team, given his experience working for the professional standards department. Denny was conscientious but worked without fanfare, but he was a silent watcher who took everything in.

'Everything all right?' Donovan said as Denny greeted him.

'Yes, boss,' Denny replied with his usual smile of encouragement. 'I was just wondering if you needed company.'

'To see Lillian Grimes?' Donovan arched an eyebrow. 'Thank you, but no. To be honest, I think my visit will be a waste of time. She enjoys stringing us along.'

Denny seemed to consider this. He tilted his head to one side. 'You've had results in the past, haven't you?'

'Yes, but that was down to Winter. All of it. Even then, Lillian only complied for her own gain.'

'But you think she's involved in DI Winter's kidnapping?'

Donovan's frustrations rose as he thought of his unborn baby and how stupid he'd been to fall for the phone call that night. 'I think I shouldn't have let Amy out of my bloody sight. Suspects don't just fall in your lap like that. I should have known the call was a wind-up.' His stomach clenched at the thought. 'She could be out there right now, running barefoot in the woods with those monsters chasing her down. Why didn't she wait for me to get home? I could have explained things then...' The words fell from Donovan's lips. He realised he had said too much.

Tiredness had worn down his defences. They both knew

that Amy shared little of her home life with the team. Yet here he was, giving Denny chapter and verse of how he was meant to join her that night. This was a man who studied people's emotions and reactions in his former job in the Professional Standards Department. He was meticulous in every way, from his polished black shoes to the creases in the legs of his suit trousers. He was bound to pick up on this.

Donovan cleared his throat. 'Sorry. What was I saying? I lost my thread.'

But Denny delivered a measured smile. The man was a pillar of calmness. 'It's good that you have such a rich understanding of Amy and share in her home life. Perhaps we can work together to play it to its best advantage. What about getting close to Lillian's daughter, Mandy? Is there any way she could be persuaded to squeeze the truth from her mother?'

'We've tried. She doesn't want to get involved. Besides...' Donovan sighed. 'Lillian would never confide in her. She knows Sally-Ann would blab.'

'Anyone else? What about boyfriends? Is Lillian seeing someone?'

Donovan shook his head. 'She's had some bunk-ups since being released from prison but nobody she cares about.' Caring relationships were a rarity in Lillian's adult life. He paused, remembering something Amy had told him once. 'Lillian had a little brother. His name was Kevin. She looked after him right up until social services took him into care.'

'Then find Kevin. Perhaps someone from the past may make her see the little humanity she had before she turned violent.' Denny paused. He shifted his stance. 'May I speak to you frankly?'

Rain spit from the sky, but Donovan barely noticed it. A creeping sensation told him that Denny was building up to challenge him. 'Of course,' he said, hoping he wouldn't regret saying so much. If Denny reported his relationship with Amy, Donovan would naturally be thrown off the investigation. They were hanging on to it by their fingernails as it was.

Denny was watching him intently, reading every reaction as it leaked from his tired face. He began to walk away from the building, and Donovan fell into a slow step beside him. In such a busy police station, conversations were easily overheard.

'When I first joined the team, I was made to feel welcome, but my colleagues were cautious of me. But as I explained, just because I worked for PSD, it doesn't mean I'm out to get everyone.'

'It takes time to embed yourself in any team.' Donovan blinked against the sprinkle of rain.

'I respect my colleagues,' Denny said. 'As I respect you. But I admit, I can't help but notice things.'

'Like what?' Donovan knew what was coming, but he had enough on his plate right now.

'Like the fact that DI Winter is pregnant, and you are the father.'

Donovan blinked. He had only himself to blame for letting it slip about their relationship, but Amy's pregnancy? For once, he was lost for words.

'I'm no mind reader,' Denny continued. 'I'm just surprised nobody else has picked it up. The sickness, the side-effects. Your attentiveness, and over-protection.' He raised a finger. 'Not a criticism, just an observation.'

'I'm not confirming or denying,' Donovan replied. 'But why are you bringing it up now?' He ran a hand over his rain-damp hair.

'My father had a saying. "Rain does not fall on one roof alone." If there's an aspect of the investigation you need help with then I'm here for you. We all are.'

Denny had always carried an air of wisdom, and today Donovan was grateful for it.

'You're not bringing up your findings with the command team?'

Denny looked surprised. 'Why would I? You're not breaking any laws.'

'Then why mention it?'

'Because if I can see that you're...' He paused, searching for the right words. 'Challenged by the situation, then others will notice it, too. Winter needs you to run this case, but we have to pull together as a team. You need to confide in them. If not about your relationship, then her pregnancy, at the very least.'

'I had hoped it wouldn't come to this.' Donovan sighed. 'I thought she'd be home by now.'

'I'll leave it with you.' Denny turned his gaze to the station as the rain grew heavy. 'Your team are behind you. But they need to be kept in the loop. Good luck with Grimeses.'

Denny's words replayed in Donovan's mind as he drove out of the station. He had obviously come to find him out of earshot of their team. But sharing news of his and Amy's relationship could shoot him in the foot.

CHAPTER THIRTY-THREE

Amy awoke to yet another argument. She calculated the day in her mind. It was Wednesday, 5th October, and more important than ever for her to keep track. She had four days left. Her head was fuzzy from tiredness. The couple who took her had only two settings: ferocious fighting or noisy sex. There was no in-between. No moments of peace or contentment that most normal couples enjoyed. The similarities to her biological parents were frightening. Both Jack and Lillian were killers, but when they were caught, Lillian had turned on her husband, blaming him for everything. It was a tragedy that his heart attack had killed him before the families of the victims reaped the justice they so richly deserved.

Would Damien do time for Lucy, should she act the victim? That would be dependent on two things – them getting caught, which they invariably would, and having no witnesses present to contradict Lucy's account. Or at least, witnesses who weren't too scared to speak up. Lucy was unpredictable and violent, most likely suffering from a whole host of personality disorders which she self-medicated with alcohol and drugs. Such treatments would serve to exacerbate her conditions, and so the cycle continued, and more people got hurt.

Amy was grateful that so far, she had not been drugged. Nor had she been seriously injured – yet. Compliance was necessary for her baby's survival until she found a way out. A part of her had come to terms with never seeing her little one's face. Of never staring at them in wonderment or cradling their warm body in her arms. The rational part of her brain told her that survival of one was unlikely – but two would be a miracle. In the small hours of the night, Amy had wrestled with her conscience, wishing she'd got to know Damien better so she could second-guess his next decision. It must have been a novelty for him to meet a woman like Lucy, hungry in every sense of the word. For people like Damien, with little or no education or prospects, Lucy's admiration must have felt like a high.

She was a well-spoken young woman, and Amy guessed her to be someone who squandered her private education with promiscuity and drugs. Damien was a novelty, cheap and disposable. Her well-to-do parents would no doubt get her off the hook, leaving Damien to cop the lot. Amy had no sympathy for her biological brother, but she *could* drive a wedge between them. Amy and Damien had a bond, like it or not. From what she knew about him, family was everything. It was why he was so angry with her for bailing. It was also why he'd visited Lillian without fail and why he helped Mandy out when he could.

Amy stared at the wooden ceiling as she mulled it over, her stomach growling with the need for food.

She was experienced in interviewing suspects, and Damien could be manipulated – if she had enough time. She formulated a plan. If she got Damien alone for long enough, she could inject a tiny seed of doubt. All these years she had denied being a Grimes, and now she was about to embrace it. The thoughts of walking down memory lane with Damien made her feel physically sick.

She scooted up on the bed, her muscles taut as Damien swaggered in. In one hand was a carrier bag. In the other was a gun. Yasmin had mentioned a firearm but wouldn't elaborate any further. Officers presumed she'd been talking about a flare gun. But this added another element of danger, not just to Amy but to anyone who approached. Where on earth had he sourced that from? He wasn't taking any chances as he threw the plastic bag on the bed. It contained food, and a packet of toilet wipes, to use with the bucket placed nearby. Another element of humiliation. But using a bucket as a toilet didn't faze Amy. all her attention was focused on the gun.

'Eat.' Damien delivered a deadening stare before turning for the door.

'I knew you were pissed with me, Damien,' Amy called after him. 'But why this?'

He stopped in the open doorway. Amy tried to look behind him, but there was no sign or sound of Lucy, just the soft crackle of a fire in the hearth.

'I told you that you'd get what was coming to you.' His words were spoken with venom. 'You deserve this and more.'

'I'm your sister.'

'Oh, *now* you're my sister? What about all those times you denied being any part of this family? In your posh house with your well-paid job in the filth.'

His nostrils flared in anger, but Amy responded in a soothing tone.

'I know,' she said calmly. 'And I don't blame you for being angry. But can you honestly say that if you were adopted instead of me you wouldn't have appreciated it? I won the lottery with Flora and Robert...but you're right. It's time I faced up to who I am.' She kept her gaze straight ahead, solid and unwavering. Her life depended on her ability to convince him.

But Damien scoffed in her face. 'Funny what people say when a gun is pointed at their head.'

Amy smiled. 'It sure has a way of focusing your thoughts.' She would not be afraid. There was no point in freaking out.

Damien's eyebrows rose. He seemed taken aback by her acceptance of the situation. It was a far cry from the previous victims who would have screamed and begged for their lives. But Amy was equipped with the bones of a schedule. Her brother wouldn't kill her. Not today.

'Luce won't let you live,' Damien said coldly. 'You know that, don't you?'

'I thought this was a fair fight.'

'If you think you can talk your way out of this then you're wrong.' Damien folded his arms.

He used his words sparingly. He didn't have a wide vocabulary, and Amy knew it brought him shame. Just what did Lucy see in him?

'So, what's the state of play for tomorrow?' She decided to change tack.

Damien narrowed his eyes. 'You're enjoying this a bit too much.'

Amy forced a wry smile. 'What's it Lillian always says? We're cut from the same cloth.'

'All right then,' Damien replied. 'Tomorrow will be the same as today, except we up the ante. Next time, I won't hold Lucy back.'

'OK,' Amy said. 'What are we talking? Crossbow? Knives, guns?'

Damien took two swift strides towards her. 'Why are you asking me all these questions? What difference does it make? You're fucked.'

Amy didn't flinch as she returned his gaze. 'Because I get it, Damien. I get why you felt like you had to do something. I don't blame you for coming after me. But it's all based on lies. I know Lillian's been pouring poison in your ear.'

'You know nothing!' Damien growled, flecks of spittle gathering in the corners of his mouth.

'Maggoty Mandy,' Amy shot back. 'That's what she calls her. 'As for the rest of us... Simpering Sally-Ann, Arsehole Amy, and Maggoty Mandy. Check her phone if you don't believe me. She's given us all names.'

The information had come from Sally-Ann. Lillian had told her when she was drunk, even showed her the contacts list on her phone. It wasn't long after her release from prison, when Sally-Ann was trying to mend bridges by bringing her some food around. But she'd received the sharp end of Lillian's tongue as she'd told her to 'fuck off' along with the rest of the 'useless shower' she had raised. It was doubtful Lillian even remembered the outburst, but Amy had filed it away for later.

She waited for the question. Damien's jaw was firm, his mouth a thin white line. He took a step back, his eyes never leaving Amy's.

'Well, go on then, what does she call me?'

Amy swallowed. Her body tensed as he waved the gun in the air. It was like an extension of his hand; he barely seemed to realise it was there. She didn't want to aggravate Damien, but she needed to make him doubt the woman pulling his strings. If he turned against Lillian, then Lucy would follow as he realised he was being played. Bit by bit, Amy would chip away. Because Damien was listening, at least while they were alone.

'Dopey Damien,' she said at last, waiting for reprisal.

But instead, her brother barked a laugh. 'Holy shit!' His voice was loud and off kilter. 'Is that the best she could come up with?' He hadn't denied that it was possible. Hadn't paused to defend Lillian in the least. Rubbing his mouth, he didn't appear to give Amy another thought. He shoved his gun in the waistband of his trousers and turned.

The log cabin reverberated from the force of the slamming door as he left. Amy exhaled a sudden breath. She was playing a dangerous game. He could have blown her brains out for that. She only hoped it was worth the risk.

CHAPTER THIRTY-FOUR

If someone had told Donovan that one day he would be having lunch at The Ivy with one of Britain's most notorious serial killers, he would have presumed it was a sick joke. Nowhere in the realms of his imagination could he have stretched to that. Yet here he was, perusing the menu while Lillian Grimes, aka, one half of the Beasts Of Brentwood, sat across from him. Not only was she a serial killer, she would be the biological grandmother to his baby when it was born. Any of these statements were enough to blow his mind. He bumped his knee against the table as he crossed his legs, trying to focus his thoughts. The woman before him was an expert at picking up weaknesses, and up until recently, she wouldn't have had much luck with him. But the foundations of his world had been shaken, and he was struggling to stay upright.

Lillian sat, wearing giant sunglasses and a colourful headscarf befitting of any A-list celeb. She was slim yet shapely, and while she had some resemblance to Amy, her features were cold, her eyes glittering flints. Donovan wasn't one for designer clothes, but he could tell her cream blouse and black leather trousers must have cost her a bob or two. If her LouLouboutin shoes were knockoffs then they were impressively like the real thing. He'd seen the flash of red soles as she'd strode to the table ahead of him, her bottom wiggling from side to side. But her gait wasn't quite steady – it was the walk of a woman who'd been wearing flats for the last few decades of her life.

'They're prescription,' she said, catching Donovan's gaze at her oversized sunglasses. 'My eyesight is shot.'

If Lillian was looking for sympathy, she wasn't getting it from Donovan. 'It must be quite a novelty to have her every whim catered for. You've come a long way since prison.'

The Ivy had been her idea. Lillian gave nothing for free, including time in her company. Donovan's jaw tensed when he noticed her new haircut – a shoulder-length bob with layers and mahogany highlights – the same as Amy's new cut. Copying the hairstyle was her way of winding Amy up.

'You could say that life has changed for the better,' Lillian's lips curled in a smile. 'I got quite the advance for my autobiography, which went to auction for my TV deal.'

Yet you still expect me to pick up the bill, Donovan thought, resting his menu on the table. He didn't feel up to food. His stomach was in knots. But it was the only way to gain an audience with the woman who had declared herself a victim of both domestic abuse and a corrupt justice system. He couldn't believe that people were falling for her story, much less lining up to buy it in droves. Lillian was creaming profits off the murders, and sharing a meal with her made him feel sick. At least the restaurant was relatively quiet, with room between tables and discreet staff. If they recognised Lillian, they didn't show it.

Guilt rose inside him. Amy was God knows where, and here he was, sitting in The Ivy. But he had to eat to keep up his strength. His stomach growled as his nostrils were assailed by the smell of freshly cooked food. He couldn't remember the last time he'd eaten. While Lillian ordered steak, Donovan went for The Ivy cheeseburger and hoped he could keep it down. He had to distance himself from Amy if he had any hope of progressing the case.

'Lillian,' Donovan said, as soon as the waiter had delivered their starters. Kingfish sashimi for Lillian, and butternut squash soup for him. 'This isn't a social event. I need your help in finding Amy.'

'And I've told you, I don't know where she is,' Lillian replied without missing a beat. 'Oh, don't frown, darling, it spoils your handsome face...' She swallowed a mouthful of food. 'You're lucky I didn't order the caviar. Horrible stuff. You should have seen my agent's face when I spat it out the last time we were here. Imagine paying a hundred pounds for something that tastes like dirt?' She chuckled to herself.

The sound of her laughter grated on Donovan's nerves. 'You must know something.' He reluctantly spooned his soup. As the creamy broth slid down his throat, it was medicine for his soul.

Lillian chewed methodically. 'Nice. A little too much salt.'

Donovan snorted. *As if she could judge fine food, given the canteen muck she'd been living off for most of her life.*

Lillian swallowed, reading his thoughts. 'Mocking me isn't going to get you what you want.'

'Sorry.' But the word stuck in Donovan's throat. 'But we're running out of time. She's not got long left.' A tiny flare of hope lit inside him. This time, Lillian hadn't denied knowing Amy's location.

'Have you stopped to consider why I'm reluctant to help? You lot stitched me up. I've spent most of my natural life in prison, thanks to you. You think I'm in a hurry to send one of my own down?'

Donovan rested his spoon. 'You're talking about Damien. He has something to do with this?'

'Oh, please...' Lillian toyed with her food. 'I know you're after him. He's gone to ground, hasn't he? Doesn't mean he's guilty of a crime.'

'Then tell me where Amy is. That's all I'm interested in.'

Lillian rested her fork, having cleared her plate. 'Until you set me up with fake evidence, like before. Amy only has herself to blame.'

'How do you figure that out?' Donovan quietened as the waiter took their plates away.

'She should have been loyal to her family. How do you think the rest of them feel, watching her live the high life while their old mum wallowed behind bars for crimes she didn't commit?'

'Come off it, Lillian.' Donovan shook his head. 'There are no cameras or reporters here. You're not on TV now.'

Lillian bit back a grin. Minutes later, the waiter approached with her steak, and she flashed him a flirtatious smile. Donovan watched Lillian stare at his bottom while he walked away.

'What I wouldn't give for half an hour alone with him,' Lillian said beneath her breath.

Donovan fought a shudder as she turned her gaze upon him. 'Or you, for that matter. After all, you've had the daughter...' She licked her lips salaciously. 'Why not the mum?'

'Cut it out,' Donovan said in a harsh whisper as her foot brushed his leg beneath the table.

'You're no fun.' Lillian pouted. 'I thought you wanted to find Amy? You're not trying very hard.' Picking up her knife, she sliced into her meat with an expert hand. Blood pooled on her plate, and she closed her eyes, savouring the first chunk.

'What do you mean by that?' But deep down, Donovan knew, and the very suggestion made him queasy.

'Oh, c'mon now, we're both adults. You scratch my back and I'll scratch yours...' Her gaze lingered as she chewed, her lips shiny from grease.

'So you're saying you know where she is?'

'I'm saying it wouldn't be that hard to find out. Spend the night at mine, and I'll see what I can do. You'd better be good mind, none of this half-hearted stuff.'

Donovan leaned over the table, keeping his voice low. 'You want me to have sex with you in exchange for saving your daughter's life? You're one sick...'

'Now, now, not in front of all these fine people, DCI Donovan.' She leaned heavily on the pronunciation of his name, loud enough for nearby diners to hear.

Some recognised her, judging from their expressions. They glanced at her not with hatred but curiosity. The PR team had done a good job of protesting her innocence. If only they knew of the ultimatum she had just given him.

Donovan pushed his plate to one side. It was embarrassing to be seen out socially with this woman, particularly now she had let slip his name. He closed his eyes, took a breath, and gathered his thoughts. There was no point in getting emotional. As much as he wanted to shake her by the shoulders, he would have to stay calm.

'Now, Lillian,' he said, watching her sip her champagne. 'You've asked to meet me here, and I've bent over backwards to keep you happy. You can call Damien and warn him to do a runner, I don't care, as long as I get Amy back alive.' He imagined Amy, tied up, bleeding and broken. Waiting for him to arrive.

'Oh, she's my daughter now, is she? Funny, that.' She sliced through her steak. 'You're the nearest thing I have to a son-in-law, yet you've never acknowledged me until now.'

'Lillian...' he said again with a weary sigh. 'If it wasn't for Amy, you'd still be in prison.' He was referring to the time Amy had reluctantly assisted with her appeal. 'All I'm asking is that you return the favour...'

'And I will,' she winked, 'if you play ball.' Lillian took a chip from his plate. She licked the tip before sucking it into her mouth.

Donovan bumped against the table as she wriggled her toes against his crotch. He swallowed back a swear word, pushing back his seat. Lillian pouted as he slipped his wallet from his pocket. He couldn't do this anymore.

'You're not leaving, are you? We haven't had dessert.' Another sly smile. She was getting off on this.

'Last chance.' Donovan slid his mobile from his pocket and laid it on the table. His voice was a low rumble. He didn't need to attract attention. Any one of them could be a journalist, and he couldn't publicly link Lillian to the case. 'Ring Damien. Find out where she is. Then tell him to get out.'

Smiling, Lillian chewed the last of her steak. 'You know the deal. Don't you love my daughter? She doesn't have to know...' She winked, speaking with a whisper. 'It'll be our little secret. You may even enjoy it. I'm *very* good in bed.'

There was no point in asking Lillian if she loved Amy. The only person she loved was herself.

'What if I agree? Tell me where she is, and I'll do it.' There was no way he would sleep with this woman. She made his skin crawl. But he *could* deliver an empty promise in exchange for an address.

'Do you think I came down in the last shower?' Lillian's eyes twinkled. 'You've got my number. Call me when you're ready. I keep my word. I've come good in the past.'

She had. That was the trouble with this situation. But Donovan couldn't contemplate her indecent proposal. He turned to her with a parting shot. 'Why can't you do the decent thing for once in your life?'

Lillian simply smiled. 'Because there's nothing in it for me.'

CHAPTER THIRTY-FIVE

Damien sat on the front porch, waiting for Lucy as he inhaled his spliff. She didn't get up until lunch time, still recovering from her blowout the day before. He'd fed Amy her porridge, just how he used to years before. The cold was biting through his tracksuit, the seat of the wooden rocker hard beneath his skin. But he liked the fresh air, and the smell of the forest which was so different to the inner-city smog. He hadn't slept well last night. Amy was messing with his head. He'd always worried that this was a bad idea, but Lucy kept pecking at his noggin until she'd had her way.

The more time he spent with his mother, the more he realised that she was just as bad as their dad. He'd had a right go at her about his nickname, and she didn't even care.

'It's just a bit of fun,' she'd said, laughing down the phone before telling him to lighten up.

It seemed Amy had been telling the truth. Yet he couldn't forgive his sister for blabbing to the social services, who in turn had called the cops. Not many would believe him, but living in that stinking house with bodies buried in the basement was better than the children's home where he'd been sent to next. His dad had even bought him ciggies and let him drink leftover booze. Back then, nobody had cared where Damien had gone or what time he'd come home. There was only one rule in the Grimes' household: Jack or Lillian swung together or not at all.

He stared out at the trees, lost in the past. Poppy was standing in their kitchen, in her stained dungarees, holding her cloth doll close to her chest. Her pigtails were lopsided, her face unwashed. Her hand-me-down shoes clopped on the floor as she walked because they were a size too big for her feet.

Now when he looked at Amy, he could see a spark of Poppy there. It jolted him to feel something other than hatred when she stared at him with those defiant grey eyes. He thought about the life she'd made for herself. Was it really one big act? The way she moved, the way she talked. Even her face seemed to change in line with the little sister he once knew. Gone was the poncey accent. In her wrinkled clothes and messy hair, she was a Grimes again. Would he have done the same in her shoes? *I was only four years old.* Amy's words replayed in his mind. He took another drag of his spliff. What did it matter? Why was he driving himself crazy like this? Soon it would be over and they could carry on picking girls up off the street, just as they'd done before. The pigs had nothing on him. But would Lucy be satisfied with that? She was obsessed with being a social media influencer and the thought of it made him restless. There was nothing Damien wanted less in the world than fame.

'Who pissed on your cornflakes, darling?' Lucy said, as she was met with a scowl. He hadn't even heard her come out. Dressed in her camouflage gear, she was ready to go. He hadn't even laced his boots. Her blonde hair was tied high on her head, a slash of red lipstick stark against the paleness of her skin. Something clicked in his mind. Lillian always wore the same shade. Why hadn't he noticed that before? He realised she was waiting for an answer and he flicked his spliff onto the gravel. 'I'm just tired, that's all.' He stood, and Lucy gave his buttock a squeeze. 'Too tired for me?' She purred, running a tongue over her lips. Both hands were kneading his backside now. He felt himself get aroused and he cast all thoughts of Lillian aside.

THREE DAYS LEFT

CHAPTER THIRTY-SIX

Amy's eyes snapped open. She'd been dreaming that she was back there, in the Grimes' family home. She was four years old again, barefoot and hanging around the corridors. But the nightmare she woke up to was no better than where she had emerged. She blinked in confusion as someone slammed the bedroom door.

'Wake up, sleeping beauty,' a female voice cackled. 'It's gone two o'clock, time for the hunt.' It was Lucy, in full combat mode, and she was armed.

Amy wanted to tell her where to go, but Lucy was handy with her fists. She couldn't afford to piss her off. The woman was a manipulator through and through. To think that she'd called Donovan, sounding scared and out of her depth. Amy knew another woman like that – Lillian Grimes. A dagger was strapped to Lucy's thigh, and a gun holstered to her hip. She watched Amy with interest, her skinny hips swaggering from side to side as she ambled across the room.

Amy scooted up in bed, scrutinising her with the mind of an investigator. True crime attracted a lot of attention. Perhaps

Lucy was seeking fame. Lillian had played the victim, and now she was raking in money from film and book deals. A thought struck. Was that how Damien had funded this? She remembered Mandy saying that her mother had 'sorted her out' financially. Sally-Ann didn't need her money, and the fact she was living with a police officer meant she was never in line for a pay out. But Damien would have been – especially if Lillian could persuade him to inflict violence upon the one person she hated the most. And now Lucy was upon her, pulling her hair as she forced her to comply.

'All right!' Amy shouted as Lucy yanked her upright.

Lucy pulled out a handcuff key from an extendable key chain hooked to her belt. She was enjoying her role.

The skin on Amy's wrist was raw, and all she'd had today was a bowl of porridge, but a wave of nausea washed over her just the same. 'Water,' she croaked. 'I need a drink.' She scoured the bedclothes. Yasmin had mentioned being given a tracksuit in its plastic wrapper before each hunt. But there was no change of clothing for her. What would be the point, when she could identify them both? There was no playing fair either. Neither planned for her to live.

'What time is it?' Amy blinked. With no watch or phone, she was completely disorientated as the days merged into one.

'Aw, why, are you sleepy?' The woman pouted. 'Are we keeping you up? Cos, if you prefer to stay in bed, I'm sure we can find something to do...' She stroked Amy's cheekbone with the tip of her finger.

'No,' Amy replied firmly. 'I'll go.'

'I figured you'd say that.' She chuckled. 'I bet you run fast, too.' She glanced over her shoulder.

Damien was standing in the doorway, scowling. He wasn't enjoying the show.

'What's wrong, babe?' Lucy said, briefly looking his way.

'Nothing,' Damien said flatly. 'Get a move on. The quicker we start, the quicker we get back.'

His uneasy expression lifted Amy's spirits. Maybe the heat was on and her colleagues were making press appeals. Perhaps Damien wanted to hurry up because he was scared they would get caught. Donovan must be pulling out all the stops to get to her. She had to run with hope. Run with the belief that any second now, she could be picked up. But she wasn't ready to go just yet. The minutes before they let her go were the safest she'd ever be from them. She needed to hold things up.

'Water. I need water.' She ensured she croaked as she made the request. She'd been to jobs in the past when they'd attended minutes too late. Every second counted when it came to buying time. 'And I need to pee,' she said as a bottle of water was thrust into her free hand.

'What's wrong, little rabbit?' Lucy stared with contempt. 'Anyone would think you don't want to escape.'

'I want a fair crack at it,' Amy said softly. 'It's two against one. You're armed and have wheels. I won't get far if my kidneys are screaming for the loo.'

'Fine,' Lucy said. 'Drop your knickers. You can use the bucket while we watch.'

'She can go in the toilet,' Damien overruled her. 'And take that stinking bucket with ya. The place reeks of piss.'

Amy was grateful for his intervention. Perhaps he was fed up of playing Lucy's games. Amy rubbed her wrist after Lucy released the handcuff. She didn't dare make any sudden movements, because both of them were armed. She had more chance of winning this game with her mind than her fists.

'Go with her,' Damien instructed Lucy, speaking in a voice that wasn't to be messed with.

Amy walked to the bathroom, being prodded in the back with what felt like the barrel of Lucy's pistol.

'Don't look so pleased with yourself, pig,' Lucy spoke in an angry whisper as they entered the hall. 'Cos your time is coming. Damien may not want to screw you, but I will, and soon. You'll be crying out for the day I'll put a bullet in your brain.'

Amy didn't give her the satisfaction of a response. Covering her stomach with her sweatshirt, she pulled down her tracksuit bottoms and sat on the cold toilet seat. She still wasn't sure if she could trust Damien not to share news of her pregnancy, which was why she hadn't told him yet. Lucy had a sadistic streak, and the easier Damien went on Amy, the stronger Lucy's resentment became.

By the time Amy got outside, she had wasted as much time as she could. She scanned the gloomy autumn skies for helicopters, willing them to appear. But there was nothing except the chill of the wind and the swish of the trees as their yellow-brown leaves floated to the ground.

'You have ten minutes,' Lucy said, joining Damien at the front door. 'We won't shoot you, at least, not today. But I'm an excellent archer, so keep that in mind. I hope you live to day four. I *really* want to put that bullet in your skull.' She paused as Damien set the stopwatch on his phone. 'Anything to say, babe?'

But Damien shook his head, his brows knitted in a frown. Lucy's smile faltered. The pair of them were like two dogs gearing up for another fight.

'Babe?' Lucy tried again.

The corners of his eyes crinkled as he responded with a smile. Amy was wrong. It was impossible to read the couple before her, and that made them dangerous.

'Ten minutes.' Damien turned his attention to Amy as he

brandished his knife. 'And you better hope Lucy gets you, cos if not, I'm gonna cut you up.'

His words brought a squeak of delight from Lucy who dragged Amy out to the front. Two scrambler motorbikes were loaded up with crossbows on the back.

As Damien counted down the timer, Amy was on her own.

CHAPTER THIRTY-SEVEN

'Any news?' Sally-Ann was in the hallway the second Paddy entered his front door.

The day had slipped through his fingers. It was gone one a.m., and he couldn't function much longer without sleep.

'Why haven't you been answering my calls?' Sally-Ann's face creased with worry for her sister. Amy's disappearance was affecting them all.

Donovan shrugged off his coat. 'I've been working. Would you prefer me to chase up leads or spend my day answering the phone to you?' He met her eyes and instantly regretted his outburst. 'Sorry.'

Sally-Ann rested her hand on his back. 'It's OK,' she said softly before following him into the kitchen. 'We're both wound up. I know you're doing your best.'

But Paddy's best wasn't good enough. Every time he came home, he felt like a failure who had let everybody down.

Sally-Ann switched on the kettle. 'Tea?'

But Paddy shook his head. 'Not before bed, love. We both need a good night's sleep.' He poured himself a glass of water and took a sip.

Sally-Ann searched his face for answers, clearly not ready for sleep just yet. 'Have you had any leads?'

Paddy nodded wearily. 'The team have spent all day on them, but it feels like we're chasing our tails. What about you?' It pained him to hear the defeat in his voice as it rebounded around the room. He wished he had something more positive to say. But there was no point in sugar-coating things for Sally-Ann. She could see right through him.

'I've been working on Mandy all day.'

'And?'

Sally-Ann shrugged. 'It's impossible to know with that one. She doesn't wish any harm to Amy, but neither does she want to get involved.'

Paddy shook his head. 'That's the Grimes' family spirit for you.'

'Paddy, you have to understand. Mandy may come across as hard-faced, but she's never got over her childhood. She's scared that if she gets involved, Damien will come after her.'

'We won't let that happen.'

But Sally-Ann looked at him dubiously. 'With all respect, it already has. If someone like Amy can get kidnapped, then what hope does the likes of Mandy or her kids have? Lillian's warned her to keep her nose out of Damien's business. I doubt she knows very much.'

'So what now?' Paddy leaned against the kitchen counter, feeling ready to drop off to sleep right there.

'I'm hoping Mandy will speak to Lillian and plead Amy's case. Mother dearest won't listen to me. She accused me of picking sides a long time ago.'

'That's rich coming from the woman who tried to kill you.'

'She's done her time.'

Paddy was amazed by Sally-Ann's loyalty. He knew that a

small part of her wanted to buy into the story that Lillian had been a victim of domestic abuse.

'Sure will you look at the pair of us.' He rested his glass on the counter. 'We're getting nowhere arguing between ourselves.' Paddy's eyelids may have grown heavy, but his emotions remained strong. The feeling of helplessness was overwhelming. It didn't matter how many leads his team were following, it always felt like he wasn't doing enough. He stared at Sally-Ann's face. She was desperate for a crumb of hope. Perhaps if he shared just a little of his working day, it would give her some much-needed rest. 'Molly spoke to one of the victims today, Yasmin.' He raised a smile. 'She's a bright spark, that Molly. She's going to go far.'

'I thought you said Yasmin wasn't talking.'

'She wasn't.' Paddy sat to take off his shoes. 'But Molly persuaded her just the same. Yasmin remembered something significant. It may come in handy when we're ready to prosecute.'

Molly had told him she'd approached Yasmin in hospital, sympathising with the young woman, because she'd been through something similar herself. He recalled how Molly had relayed the story in the office, her chin wobbling as her emotions shone through. She went on to say how she'd been walking home from school when she was sixteen, and a car pulled up. She talked of being bundled into the back and kept overnight before managing to escape the next day.

'It was horrendous,' Molly had said. 'And I never reported it because I couldn't bear to talk about it again.'

'God, poor Molly.' Sally-Ann rested a hand on her chest. 'I had no idea.'

'That's what I said,' Paddy replied. 'I told her she didn't have to work on the case if it got too much.'

'What did she say?' Sally-Ann replied, invested in the story.

She'd only met Molly a couple of times but cared for her just the same.

Paddy raised a half-smile. 'She told me I wasn't to worry because she'd made the whole thing up. She said she wasn't proud about lying to a victim, but she'd do whatever it took to get the lead.'

'Wow.' Sally-Ann seemed a little in awe. 'I suppose it helped Yasmin, having someone she could relate to.'

'It helped her enough to remember that the woman who took her had studs on the back of her neck.' Paddy wriggled his toes, grateful to be free of his hard leather shoes.

'Studs? What kind of studs?'

'It's called dermal piercing.' Paddy plucked his phone from his trouser pocket, brought up a browser, and typed it in. His bones creaked as he stood to show Sally-Ann the images flooding his phone screen. 'According to Yasmin, there were three vertical studs from her neck to below her hairline. 'She said it must have been recent because she told the man off for grabbing the back of her neck because it was sore.'

'I've never heard of a piercing there.' Sally-Ann rubbed the back of her neck.

'Aye. They're not that common, which is good for us. We're making enquiries with piercing and tattoo studios in the area.' He didn't tell Sally-Ann that they were also delving into CCTV in the surrounding area of Damien's flat. If they could identify Damien's girlfriend on CCTV, and she happened to have the piercing, it could prove to be a good result. Little by little, the pieces were coming together. But would they be on time?

'C'mon.' Paddy guided Sally-Ann out of the kitchen. 'I need to get my head down. I have a feeling I'll need it for the day ahead.'

CHAPTER THIRTY-EIGHT

Donovan kneaded his forehead. He hated being home. At least in the office he had a sense of doing. But he couldn't function without sleep, and God knew, he'd needed a bath. His limbs had been weary from being on his feet all day. It was a function, a necessity. A charging of the batteries to keep him going for another day. But he had pushed past the tiredness of forty-eight hours without sleep and come out the other side. But now he lay in bed, having awoken at five a.m. *Four hours sleep is better than nothing*, he thought, staring at the ceiling. He reached over for his phone. No texts. No messages. He should try to go back to sleep.

Instead, he flicked up to his personal emails. There was the usual rubbish, sales and subscriptions to newsletters he hadn't remembered signing up for. *Junk.* He thought. *I should check my junk mail.* Now he really was grasping at straws. Who or why would anyone email his personal account at this hour of the night? There was nothing of value there. He switched to social media, checking the hashtag #TheHunters. He squinted at the reel which had gained thousands of views. The Hunters had uploaded another recording. His heart skipped a beat as he fumbled with the night light. He read the text: *Amy says hello. Or should that be goodbye? Catch us if you can...The Hunters.*

Donovan inhaled a sharp intake of breath as Amy's image filled the screen. Her left eye was bruised and swollen, her hair matted and in disarray. She spoke into the camera, but she was not crying. Instead, she gave it a steely gaze. Her arm was in a makeshift sling. A dirty sheet was placed as a backdrop behind her. She looked overhead before returning her gaze to the camera.

'My name is Amy Winter. I have lost two hunts, I have three left to go.' Her eyes moved from left to right as she read what was apparently placed in front of her. 'These are the most dangerous killers in history. I am not...' She squinted, making it obvious she was reading the words. 'Good enough for them. I am a...loser... a pathetic piece of trash.' She rolled her eyes, and a muffled argument ensued.

'Shh!' a male voice rasped as the couple squabbled between them. The woman released an anguished cry before the video came to an abrupt end.

What the hell was that all about? Donovan rushed around the room, pulling on a fresh shirt before sliding his grey suit off the hanger. There were no demands, no ransom. Just a declaration of how they were the most 'dangerous killers in history'. Was that what they wanted – fame? Was the woman following in Lillian's shoes – acting the victim one minute then a dangerous killer the next? The footage would be picked apart. Played and replayed for clues. Each sound would be analysed as they drew out each muffled word. He played it again, resting his phone on the floor as he tied his shoe laces. She was alive, and that was all that mattered, but the days were counting down.

CHAPTER THIRTY-NINE

As Donovan drove to the woodlands, he asked himself for the hundredth time what he was doing here. He'd never felt as frustrated as he did this morning. His body was jittery at his inability to relax. No matter where he went or what he did, he felt guilty for wasting time. Talking to Lillian, spending time in the office, reassuring Flora that he'd bring her daughter back. None of these things gave him an ounce of satisfaction because it didn't seem to change a thing. Amy was a brilliant detective. He needed her on the case. Only now did he realise just how lost he was without her, both work wise and emotionally. Then he asked himself what Amy would do, and he found himself driving to Epping Forest first thing, where he arranged to meet Malcolm, their head CSI. He wasn't sold on the value of Malcolm's suggestion, but Amy always had a lot of faith in him. Nicknamed the Nigel Havers of Notting Hill, Malcolm was a well-spoken ex-high court judge. He was known for his nonconventional ways which got results, but Donovan wasn't relishing the prospect of meeting him in the woods. It was covering old ground. POLSA had the unenviable job of searching the vast forest land. The killer couple were unlikely to return, so why had Malcolm suggested they meet there?

Donovan pulled up to the clearing in the woods and he had to blink twice to make out Malcolm's form. What he'd expected to see was a tall, skinny man with perfectly groomed hair wearing his usual suit and bow tie. Instead, Malcolm had the appearance of someone who had broken free from prison. He stood, hands on his narrow hips, slightly flustered and out of breath, his hair dishevelled and a scratch above his eye.

'Malcolm?' Donovan stared, bewildered. 'Everything all right?'

'I'm good...' Malcolm said between breaths. Thanks... Just getting in a trial run before you got here.'

'Trial run?' Donovan stared at him quizzically. 'You asked to meet. You didn't say anything about going for a run.'

'Ah. Yes. It was a last-minute flash of inspiration. I like to put myself in people's shoes. I identify more with the investigation that way.'

'Do you *need* to identify with the investigation?' Donovan raised his hand to shade his eyes as a ribbon of sunlight cut between the trees.

'Don't you?' Malcolm tilted his head, as if Donovan was the one acting odd. 'Are you telling me it's not the last thing on your mind each night when you go to sleep?'

'Well, yes...if I manage to sleep.'

Malcolm's brow creased. 'Amy means the world to me. She's an exemplary officer and a beautiful person, both in and out.' He was flushed now, in a rare show of emotion. 'Sorry...' He finger combed his hair. 'I've been utterly beside myself since she went missing.'

Donovan felt humbled by his show of emotions. He'd been so stressed that he hadn't thought of how Malcolm felt. Malcolm had known Amy for longer than him. From what Amy had said, there was a deep well of mutual admiration and respect.

'Don't apologise,' Donovan said, reminding himself that to Malcolm, he was nothing more than Amy's DCI. 'We've all been hit hard by what's happened. What do you have planned?'

'I want you to hunt me down, just as the victims have been hunted. It would help if you put yourself in the minds of the killers. Try to understand what they're getting out of this. Maybe this way we can narrow down the sort of place they're likely to be with Amy now. They can't have taken her far. It's surely worth a shot.' He glanced down at his feet. 'I wanted to do it barefoot, but my wife talked me out of it. My plimsoles will be the next best thing.'

Donovan nodded, a smile almost reaching his face. Nobody could fault Malcolm's commitment to the job. But Donovan continued to be surprised as Malcolm led him around the corner.

'I don't suppose you can drive a motorbike, can you? This is going to be horribly delayed if you can't.'

Donovan stared at the motorbike which, given recent reports and tyre treads found, was believed to be a similar match to one of the vehicles used.

'It's been a few years but...' He looked at Malcolm uncertainly. 'I take it this reconstruction hasn't been authorised.'

'Heavens no,' Malcolm scoffed. 'Can you imagine the red tape?' He shook his head and exhaled a sigh of disappointment. 'If you'd rather wait for health and safety evaluations then perhaps you should go. I'll call upon someone else. I don't want to waste any more of your time.'

Donovan held out his hand. 'Keys.'

He was met with a smile. 'Smashing.' Malcolm paused to check his watch. 'Give me ten minutes then come looking. Take the time to accustom yourself to the bike.' He looked Donovan over. 'You won't fall off, now will you?'

'I may be rusty, but I'm not an idiot,' Donovan said, inhaling a lungful of crisp forest air.

'Good. Try to imagine you're hunting me down.'

'In for a penny,' Donovan mumbled as he threw his leg over the quad.

Malcolm was hugging a tree, his eyes cast upwards as he breathed in the scent of bark. Finally releasing his hold, he shook his head. 'Even if I could climb, I'd never scramble up one of these in time.'

Donovan exhaled in relief. At least he hadn't completely lost the plot. In theory, a re-enaction wasn't a bad idea. But in order for Donovan to think straight, he had to detach himself from his relationship with Amy.

Malcolm gave him a tight nod before taking off like a hare into the woods. *Amy will laugh about this one day,* Donovan thought to himself, immediately forgetting his earlier vow. He turned the key in the ignition, revving the throttle. He'd forgotten how good it felt to drive something powerful outdoors. In his youth, he'd started off riding BMX bikes along the dirt trails. He'd progressed to motorbikes in his spare time, when he wasn't working in his parents' café. But here in the heart of the forest, his youth was a million miles away. He checked his watch and inhaled a deep breath of crisp morning air. It was time.

TWO DAYS LEFT

CHAPTER FORTY

Today is Thursday, Amy reminded herself. *Twentieth of October.* She needed to focus, because if she lost track of time, it would be hard to grasp it again. There was no iPhone, no calendars, no TV shows to orientate her. Amy found comfort in her regimented routine. Without it, she was adrift. She didn't need to be cuffed to her bed after Damien and Lucy brought her back from the hunt number two. The Ring camera that Damien fixed to the corner of the ceiling gave him every opportunity to watch her on his phone. Amy groaned as she shifted, hoping no serious damage was done. Her arm wasn't broken, but she'd told them that it was. The more incapacitated they thought she was, the more they would underestimate her. But it still hurt like the devil from where Lucy's arrow had sliced through her flesh, almost pinning her to a tree. Had Amy not moved in time, that could have been her head.

Damien had not carried out his promise to 'cut her up', and Lucy did not hide her disappointment as he called it a day. Amy winced as she touched her eye. Lucy had hit her with a lucky punch. It was no teeth-rattler, but enough to produce a bruise. Had Amy not been cuffed, she would have shown her what a real punch was. She was grateful that they'd made another video, despite the humiliation involved. Anything that assisted her team seemed like a good idea to her. But Lucy's demands had got on Amy's nerves as she spoke about stripping Amy of her clothes.

'You won't get any traction,' Damien had argued. 'Ain't no point in making this video if it's taken offline straight away.'

'But babe, I just want to play...' Lucy had said, making a grab for Amy's breast.

That's when Amy had decided enough was enough and headbutted her to the face. Lucy's response had been instant, and Amy was left seeing stars. Damien had barked a laugh for the first time that day.

'It's not funny!' Lucy had screamed, rubbing her forehead.

It was a shame, as Amy had been aiming to break her pretty little nose.

Now the couple were back to arguing loudly, outside Amy's bedroom door.

'At least let me play with her,' Lucy pleaded. She spoke about bondage gear and her array of sex toys.

'Are you sick in the head? I've told ya, she's my sister. I'm not into that.'

'But, Damo...' Lucy purred. 'I just want to have some fun.'

'It's not about sex, is it?' Damien said. 'You get off on the danger. Haven't you seen the appeals? The reward for info? Isn't this enough for you?'

She'd been so intent on listening in, Amy almost forgot to breathe.

'Oh, my big gangster man...' Lucy continued. 'You'll always be enough for me.'

Amy exhaled a breath of relief as the couple walked away. Her thoughts returned to Donovan. Was he sleeping? Pacing? Planning? She couldn't bear to think about Flora. It pained her to imagine her anxiety. She had already lost her husband not so long ago. She hoped Donovan had spared her from the truth. At her age, she didn't need any more grief.

Another thought washed over Amy. What if she died? How would Flora cope with losing a daughter and a grandchild? She closed her eyes. *Pace yourself.* It was Robert Winter's voice, the only man she had been proud to call her father. She took comfort from his presence in the back of her mind. She wasn't going to die. She would see Flora again. Donovan would be fine. She rested her hand on her stomach, sending her positive affirmations to her unborn child.

Damien walked into the room, his tracksuit bottoms hanging low on his hips, his concave chest pasty white. He threw her a cereal bar and watched as she ate. It was food she would never had received if Lucy had her way. Amy couldn't figure him out. Why was he feeding her if his intention was to see her dead? She wanted to say something snarky about Lucy, but it would only tip him off to the fact she could hear them in the next room. The last thing she wanted was for them to be guarded with their words. She watched as he sloped around the room. Today *he* seemed like the one behind the cage. Then she saw the glint of paranoia in his eyes as he chewed on his fingernail. She'd seen it before, but this time he wasn't turning on her. Amy sensed that he was thinking about Lucy. He wanted to talk, but Amy couldn't ask if he was OK. He knew when he was being played. She sat in silence, waiting for him to speak. People like Damien couldn't bottle their emotions. He had to find release. And right now, she was all he had.

CHAPTER FORTY-ONE

'Christ,' Paddy said, wondering if his ears had been playing tricks on him. 'I must be hallucinating.' He was sitting at Amy's office desk, nursing a steaming cup of coffee as DCI Donovan he brought him up to speed.

They had just come from briefing, but these updates were confidential. The lines of professionalism had become blurred due to their intricate personal relationships, and Paddy was grateful that Donovan was confiding in him.

Rain tapped against the windowpane. A storm was brewing outside.

'Are you seriously telling me that you were riding around Epping Forest chasing an ex-high court judge who was on foot?' Paddy felt guilty for laughing, but the mental image brought tears to his eyes. 'Feck's sake, close the blinds, they'll think I've lost the plot.'

Donovan did as instructed as Paddy tried to control himself. Shock, tiredness, anxiety, and now amusement...a mixture of feelings were bubbling up inside him, and he could not keep them contained.

'What did you do when you found him?' Paddy pressed a tissue to his face and blotted his tears.

'That's the thing.' Donovan failed to share in his mirth. 'I didn't. No matter how hard I tried, the forest was too dense. There were too many places to hide, and a bike can only take you so far.'

'What do you make of that?' Paddy gave him a curious eye.

'They've got to be using trackers. They must be stitching them into their clothes. I can't see how else they do it, even armed. I've asked for Yasmin's clothes to be re-examined.'

'But Yasmin escaped. If that was what they wanted, they wouldn't have tracked her that day.'

'Of course…you're probably right.' Donovan rose from his chair as a police siren blared from the car park.

The man had been haring around all day, and Paddy felt like telling him to sit. They were all working as hard as they could, but sometimes quiet moments of reflection could produce the biggest results.

'What about Lillian's indecent proposal?' Paddy rested his mug on the table. 'Was she messing with you?'

That was another surreal piece of information that Donovan had shared. Wherever Amy was, she would never have expected this. He took in Donovan's worried face. If Paddy's mother were still alive, she'd be elbowing him in the ribs, saying the man looked 'fierce shook'. A couple of shots of Jamieson would be prescribed, along with a 'little lie down' for an hour or two. But it would take more than his mother's medicinal whiskey to help Donovan today.

'She was deadly serious.' Donovan's voice interrupted Paddy's thoughts. 'She left a message on my phone, going into details about some hotel where we'd do the deed.' His face soured at the thought. 'Then she said she'd keep her word and swore not to tell a soul.'

'Sounds like the old lush means business.' Paddy stood and joined Donovan at the window. They stared onto the darkening streets below. Pedestrians ran for shelter as the skies opened above them. He hoped that wherever Amy was, that she was warm and dry. 'Sure she's kept her word in the past,' he continued, his thoughts filtering back to the insatiable Lillian.

'She has.' Donovan's brow creased as a thought struck. 'Wait a minute. You don't think I should sleep with her, do you?'

'Are we speaking as colleagues or family?'

Donovan rubbed the knot in his brow. 'Family.'

'I don't know...' Paddy sighed. 'If it were Sally-Ann, I'd do anything to get her back.'

'Including sleeping with Lillian Grimes?'

'Mate, I'd shag the auld fella that mops our floors if Sally-Ann's life was hanging in the balance.'

'What's this about you sleeping with the caretaker?' Sally-Ann's voice rose as she crept in behind them. She gave them a sheepish look. 'Molly let me in. I got fed up of being fobbed off by you both.'

'You shouldn't be here,' Paddy grumbled, but he was happy to see her just the same.

Sally gave him a knowing look. 'And *you* shouldn't turn your back on your office door when you're having sensitive conversations. Now what's this about you sleeping with your caretaker?' She folded her arms, waiting for an answer. Her hair had been washed, and she was wearing a clean pair of jeans and a pink woolly sweatshirt. She was keeping it together for Amy's sake.

'Your mother's given Donovan an indecent proposal,' Paddy explained, much to Donovan's dismay. 'If he sleeps with her, she'll make it her business to find out where Amy is.'

Sally-Ann's eyes widened as she stared at them both. 'No way. You're kidding me.'

'I wish he was.' Donovan shook his head. 'She'll stand by and let Amy die if I don't go through with it.' He turned away from the window, looking Sally-Ann squarely in the eye. 'What should I do?'

It was a novelty for Paddy to watch Donovan ask for advice from his other half. When it came to investigations, he was usually self-assured but this had knocked him for six.

'It's a power trip,' Sally Ann said with authority. 'Another way for Mum to get one over on Amy. She hates her and everything she represents.' Her gaze wandered to Amy's desk, to her Post-its and neatly stacked paperwork. She straightened the pen that Paddy had moved and put it in line with the rest.

'Why?' Donovan asked. 'Why does she despise her so much?'

'You know why.' Sally-Ann blinked away the tears forming in her eyes. 'But there's a small part of Lillian, a tiny part, that doesn't want Amy to die.'

In the outer office, phones rang, printers were in constant motion, and officers raced through their tasks. But here, in the stillness of the room, time seemed to stop. Sally-Ann didn't often talk about Lillian's feelings, but it was obvious she'd tried hard to understand what made the woman tick.

'It's hard to believe,' she continued. 'But every now and again, Mum nurtured us. It wasn't often, mind. I don't think her demons would allow it. But her motherly instinct occasionally surfaced. Maybe by issuing you with an ultimatum she can let Amy live while still believing she's the one in control. Lillian is very complex. But if there's something in it for her then she'll usually keep her word.'

'Aye,' Paddy acknowledged. 'But like everything she promises, it comes with a cost.'

'I need more time to figure her out.' Donovan's biceps

tensed as he tightly folded his arms. 'Find a way of appealing to that small percent of her that's good.'

Paddy snorted at their optimism. Lillian Grimes was one hundred percent evil as far as he was concerned. Sally-Ann had always claimed that if Lillian was brought up differently she may not have turned to murder, but he wasn't so sure.

Sally-Ann appeared thoughtful. 'Appeal to the part of her that still exists from before she met Jack. She had a shitty childhood, but from what she's said about her past, she had a few happy memories, too. She hates the police because she said they didn't help her when she needed them the most.'

'She was a victim of abuse herself?' Paddy asked. There were plenty of articles written about the woman, and so far, he'd avoided them all.

'It's not unknown for victims to become abusers.' Donovan rubbed his chin. 'We need to dig into her past, speak to her friends or family. Maybe there's someone out there who can persuade her to do the right thing.'

'Her friends abused her,' Sally-Ann replied. 'She was groomed as a teenager and sold for sex. Her parents are dead, and according to Lillian, they're no loss.'

'No brothers or sisters? Cousins? Anything?' Donovan was grasping at straws.

Sally-Ann frowned, deep in thought. The topic of Lillian was only discussed during one of the many dramas she brought to their door. The woman was no spring chicken. Wasn't it about time she had a quiet life?

'She had a brother!' Sally-Ann clicked her fingers as she suddenly remembered. 'She cared about him, too. One of the only people I've ever heard her talk about with any affection.'

'I don't suppose he's kept in touch?' Donovan asked.

Quiet moments, Paddy thought to himself. *You never know*

what they'll bring. Had he not persuaded Donovan to sit down, he wouldn't have been here for this discussion.

'I think his name was Kevin,' Sally-Ann continued. 'He was taken into care when he was little. Child neglect. It's hardly any surprise.'

'Do we know where he is now?' Donovan replied. 'Anything?'

Sally-Ann thought for a moment. 'Mandy might know.'

'Sounds like a lot of work, with time we don't have.' Paddy was always grateful for a lead, but could they spare the resources to follow it up? He hated pandering to Lillian, who left nothing but a trail of devastation in her wake. The only decent contribution she'd made to the world was giving birth to Amy and Sally-Ann. But both of them would be dead if it were left to Lillian had her way.

'I think it's worth a shot.' Donovan seemed a little brighter. 'If we can set up a meeting, Kevin might persuade Lillian to do the right thing.' He slipped his phone from his pocket. 'But first, I need to buy some more time.' He tried to draw up his contacts list but seemed all fingers and thumbs. 'Lillian?' He spoke into the phone, pausing as he listened to the voice on the other end. 'It's me. Donovan. I'll do it. But I need more time. Get me an extra day and you've got a deal.' He hung up, exhaling the breath he had been holding. 'This better work,' he replied, looking at them both. 'Because I can't contemplate the alternative.'

CHAPTER FORTY-TWO

Damien was glad to get a break from Lucy. Living with her twenty-four-seven was really beginning to grate. He didn't know what love was. He wasn't even sure it existed outside TV rom-coms and books. But he did feel something towards her, outside of sex. Up until recently, she had been his world. Her father pay-rolled her for doing nothing. Every business he helped her launch fell flat on its face because she lost interest weeks later when things became hard. She was visiting her father now, placating him because her latest venture was losing money hand over foot. The truth was, she was siphoning money from it to pay for drugs and designer clothes.

She'd argued a lot with Damien since they'd grabbed Amy off the street. She had other ideas, and in the beginning, he had, too. But this was different to taking the other girls. They had been nothing more than objects, but Amy's presence was impossible to ignore. He couldn't face the idea of Lucy having sex with his sister. They'd been through some wild times, but the idea of involving Amy in the mix made his stomach churn.

The sooner all this was done with, the better as far as he

was concerned. His fake passport was nestled in its hiding place along with euros and the address of a place to stay. Lillian had ensured him that her friends in Spain would be more than happy to put him up. But would they accept Lucy into the fold? Did he want them to? Her need for internet fame was getting on his wick. He'd said no to TikTok videos and dressing up for some stupid dance. He couldn't see the value in her Instagram videos either. He'd heard the quiver in her voice, the sharp cry of fear at the end of each video just before she'd turned it off. It was all for show. She was a lot more bloodthirsty than him. So why did she make it look like he was always the one in control? He felt like he was on a runaway train. Her father wouldn't fund her for much longer. Was she gearing up to make money from him, just as Amy had said? His late-night chats with his sister unsettled him, but he needed to know.

He cast his gaze across the kitchen to the ink gun that Lucy was dying to use. If Amy lived to day four, Lucy would give her a brand-new tattoo. But Damien didn't want such a permanent marking on his sister's skin. He took the tattoo gun from the shelf and hid it beneath some towels at the back of a dresser drawer. As for the rest of the stuff Lucy wanted to get up to... having Amy involved in their sex games left a bad taste in his mouth. Why couldn't Lucy understand that it was all wrong? Was it another shock tactic to sell more stories to the press? Was she trying to outdo Lillian Grimes?

The ring of his phone interrupted his troubled thoughts. It was Lillian. She always had an uncanny way of knowing when he was getting wound up.

'Yeah?' he said, lighting a spliff as he cradled his phone in his shoulder.

'I have news,' Lillian simply said. 'But you didn't hear it from me.'

'What sort of news?' He grimaced.

'The kind you need to know. Are you alone?'

'Yeah. Why?'

'Because I'd like to speak to my son without Little Miss Moneybags listening in.'

'What do you want?' Damien said, preferring to get to the point. He opened the window a crack. Not that the owners would ever know he'd smoked here. They planned to burn the place to the ground when they left.

'Where are you?' Lillian dodged his question. 'I called to the flat twice this week.'

'What does it matter?' Damien scratched his head. 'Ain't it a bit late for you to start acting like a mum now?'

'It matters because you shouldn't go back there. The filth are looking for you.'

'Yeah, well, they ain't gonna find me here.' Damien dragged on his spliff, locking the smoke in his lungs before letting it go.

'Where's Amy?'

'How the hell do I know?' Damien instantly replied. He couldn't afford to get his mum tied up in this. She'd spent enough of her life behind bars.

'Fine. Play it your way.' She paused. 'Look, I'm glad you took my advice to have some fun. Life's short and all that. But I don't want you to end up inside like me. I can talk my way out of most things, but you...you're a man. They'll throw away the key.' Her words became indistinct as she began to mumble. Damien pressed the phone to his ear as he tried to make them out 'I don't trust her. She's setting you up for a fall.'

'You don't need to worry about her. Soon she'll be out of your hair for good.'

'Christ!' Lillian screamed down the phone. 'Are you not listening to me? I don't mean Amy, I'm talking about that piece of fluff you've hooked up with. I mean...I can see the attraction. She's sex on a stick. But stay the fuck off social media. She's making it look like it's all your fault.'

'What are you on about?' Damien's frown deepened. He'd purposely stayed away from all the online stuff. Now Lillian was messing with his head. Then again...she could have a point. In the first video, Lucy had made him hold the knife. In the second one, she'd ended the video with a strange squeal. It was as if he'd hurt her, but he was nowhere near. He hadn't wanted to make the bloody thing in the first place. He'd told her as much after she'd stopped filming, but maybe the damage had been done. He took another drag of his spliff. They kept each victim for four days, but Lucy only made two videos, just enough to prove her point. Damien shifted, uncomfortable with the thoughts in his head.

'What am I always telling you?' Lillian hissed. 'Trust nobody. You know how much I hate your scheming bitch of a sister, but right now, she's worth more to you alive than dead.'

'Mum,' Damien said firmly. 'I ain't getting into this with you.'

'The silly cow is pregnant,' Lillian blurted. 'That's what I've been trying to tell you. DCI Donovan is the father. If you kill his kid, he'll nail you to the wall. Get yourself out of there. You've still got some money left...haven't you?'

'Yeah...I...' Damien's thoughts were staggered as he came to terms with the news. 'Who told you she's pregnant? Has someone put you up to this?'

'Ask Mandy if you don't believe me. You're not a hunter anymore, Damien, they're coming after you. Think long and hard about your next move.'

Damien stood in silence. If this was some kind of setup, he'd admit to nothing. Amy, Lucy, Lillian, he didn't know who to trust. A part of him wanted to run. To get in the car with the bag he'd packed and leave it all behind. But he couldn't leave Amy alone with Lucy. If she came back and found him gone, there would be hell to pay. He was no baby killer, but if he left like this, he'd have innocent blood on his hands.

CHAPTER FORTY-THREE

Donovan took a seat near the hotel bar, barely able to believe his luck. He never imagined that Sally-Ann would track Lillian's brother down with such ease. She had wanted to come to the meeting, but Donovan didn't want to muddy the waters with a family reunion of sorts. Now he was sitting in the Hilton London Hyde Park Hotel as Kevin was staying there on business from the night before. The bar area was richly furnished, and Donovan sat in the deep upholstered chair, an Americano on the coffee table before him. He hadn't known what to expect. The Grimes' family tree had produced a mixed bunch of apples, and with the exception of Amy and Sally-Ann, some were rotten to the core. Donovan still struggled to comprehend Amy's true origins, particularly during times like these.

The middle-aged man before him was suited and well-spoken – a world away from Lillian Grimes. Thankfully, Kevin had remained in touch with extended members of the Grimes family on and off for years. Lillian's cousins lived in London and had provided refuge to Sally-Ann when she'd run away from home as a teen. But while Kevin spoke to distant relations, he was too scared to touch upon whatever evil encompassed his sister. Now he was sitting across from Donovan, somewhat intrigued by his request to meet up.

'Thanks for agreeing to see me at such short notice.' Donovan placed his cup back in its saucer after taking a sip. He'd had too many coffees already, and the caffeine in his bloodstream was making his heartbeat accelerate.

'I feel like I had little choice in the matter.' Kevin crossed his long slender legs. 'It's difficult to ignore a DCI.' His suit was navy, but a pair of bright-red socks poked out from the tops of his black leather shoes.

'I appreciate this is a sensitive matter,' a stern-voiced Donovan replied. 'And I wouldn't have got in touch if I had any other choice.' The image of Lillian sucking on a French fry bloomed in his mind. His stomach rolled.

'It's more than sensitive,' Kevin pressed. 'If this gets out, it will damage my career.'

'Amy felt the same way at first.' Donovan recalled how she'd coped when the truth of her biological mother had hit the press. 'She's an amazing woman. She wouldn't let it bring her down.' He had already furnished Kevin with details about Amy in his email when he'd asked to meet up. It felt alien to be so helpless, at the mercy of others. He crossed his legs, forcing such feelings down.

'My wife is a fan of police documentaries,' Kevin replied. 'She followed you both on TV.'

'You knew she was your niece, though, didn't you?' Donovan was keen to make the connection. Anything to enlist the man's help.

'I knew,' he said, 'but we're hardly a conventional family. Amy seemed to be doing well enough without any interference from me.'

'You made contact with Lillian once, didn't you?' Donovan

had done his homework, and Sally-Ann's extended family had been helpful when they'd discovered what was going on.

Kevin delivered a non-committal shrug. 'I wrote to Lillian in prison. I was curious, that's all. But as soon as I posted the letter, I realised it was a bad idea. It was a blessing that I never heard back.' He cast a glance over Donovan. 'I was young and foolish back then, finding my way in the world.'

'And now?'

Kevin gave him a considered look. 'And now it's better to let sleeping dogs lie. In my world, people not only judge you by your actions but by your acquaintances and family, too. I can't afford for this to get out.'

'Amy is fighting for her life. Please. She's five months pregnant. If we don't find her soon those monsters will kill them both. What if it was your wife? What would you do?'

And how Donovan wished that Amy *was* his wife and the world was aware of their relationship. 'Girlfriend' came nowhere close to describing his commitment towards her. He would sleep with Lillian if he had to, but the woman made him shrink in his skin. He wasn't sure he could bring himself to go through with the physical act. Every minute that passed brought Amy closer to the end. Lillian wasn't the only one who kept her promises. He was in no doubt that Damien would, too.

Donovan explained the situation. He was taking a chance, sharing so much of the investigation with a stranger. But he had checked him out on PNC and he wasn't known to police. Kevin was the head of a well-known charity which helped countless victims of domestic abuse. It came with the backing of high-profile celebrities, which was why he needed to be squeaky clean. There were no guarantees that Lillian would entertain the brother she'd lost as a child, but if Donovan threw enough darts at the board, one of them may just stick.

As Kevin finished his coffee, his expression relayed that he was about to burst his balloon. 'I'm afraid I can't help you. I'm sorry about Amy, but Lillian's a heartless psychopath. She won't listen to me.' He pushed back his sleeve and checked his watch before getting to his feet.

Donovan rose, crestfallen. 'Is that it? You're leaving? You're not even going to try?'

'I can continue as I am, saving countless lives, or I can risk everything I've built over the last ten years to help just one.' Kevin wasn't exaggerating. Without charities such as his, victims of domestic abuse may not have been able to find the strength to get away. Four women died a week at the hands of abusive partners, but without help, that figure would rise.

'Kevin. Wait.' Donovan could feel him slipping away. 'Lillian cared for you once. I'm sure you can get through to her. Nobody else needs to know.' He was grasping at straws. His team were making good ground, and all the arrows pointed to Damien and the girlfriend they were working hard to identify. But something in his gut told him he was on the right track, if only he could persuade Kevin to listen.

'I can't help you,' the man said firmly. 'And I'm going to be late for my train.' His steps quickened as he made his way out.

Donovan followed, raising his voice over the sounds of the traffic on the busy London streets. 'At least sleep on it. You have my number if you change my mind.'

Kevin turned to face him. 'I hope you find her in time.' Then he was running towards the Tube station before Donovan could utter another word.

CHAPTER FORTY-FOUR

'Why didn't you tell me?'

Amy blinked, surfacing from the fog of sleep. She was weak from hunger, her pregnant body demanding more than she could provide. 'What?' she murmured, making out Damien's form as he stood over her.

His face was hard with suspicion, his t-shirt grubby and sweat-stained. He handed her an energy drink. A blast of warm air floated through the open doorway, and the crackle of a roaring fire rose from the hearth.

'I said, why didn't you tell me?' Damien demanded.

A chill of realisation overcame Amy as she saw him staring at her modest bump.

'Because I can see it now,' he continued. 'I just don't get why you kept it to yourself.'

Amy swigged from the bottle, reminding herself to act like a Grimes. 'Because that pretty girlfriend of yours would be training her crossbow on my stomach the second she found out.' Her head was spinning, her legs weak. She knew by Damien's tone that Lucy wasn't about. He was different when she wasn't around. And now, as he stood, his expression a maelstrom of emotions, he didn't dismiss her concerns.

'You should have told me.' He folded his arms, watching her every move.

'When?' Amy snapped, slowly regaining her strength. 'When you were jabbing the taser into my thigh or after you threw me into the back of the van?' She wiped her nose with the back of her wrist. 'Get me some grub, will you? I'm fucking starving.' She shot her big brother a belligerent look. This was the sister he remembered, but did he care enough about her to stop?

'Yeah, well, you've done this to yourself.' He shrugged, non-committal. 'You only have yourself to blame.'

'Funny that,' Amy said, in no mood for his excuses. 'Those are the exact same words Dad used to say to Mum after he belted her one. Is that what you want, Damien? To end up like them? Because from what I can see, that's where you're heading. And for what? Is it worth growing old in prison just to get rid of me?' She edged to the side of the bed, pushing the duvet away. 'Because you won't just be known as a rapist. They'll label you a baby killer, among other things. And you know what they do to people like that inside.'

Damien rubbed the back of his neck. Amy had touched a nerve.

'Why don't you just go?' She continued. 'You've had your fun. You've taught me a lesson. I've been beaten and humiliated for everyone to see. You win.'

'I can't.' There was an edge to his voice as he stared, lost in thought.

'Why not?' Amy planted her feet on the floor as she sat on the side of the bed, conscious that Damien's hand was hovering over the sheathed knife strapped to his thigh.

'Fuck's sake, don't you get it? I can't leave you alone with *her!*' His gaze flicked to the shuttered window, as if expecting the sound of Lucy's car to rumble up onto the drive.

The room fell silent. All Amy could hear was the beating of her heart. The rush of blood pulsed in her hears. If Damien went now, he was going alone. He had created a monster. Perhaps if it were up to him, Amy stood a chance of survival, but if Lucy came back and found him gone, it would be the end of Amy.

'Then let me go,' Amy said quietly. 'Please. I swear down, I won't hang you out to dry. I'll say I lost my memory...however you feel about me, it's not the baby's fault.' Her hand rested on her stomach. All these months, she'd been too scared to acknowledge her pregnancy, but in this moment, she wanted her baby more than anything in the world. She hadn't realised that she was crying until her vision blurred. 'He's kicking.' Amy's voice quavered as her unborn baby moved. 'Please, Damien, let him live.'

Damien stood, statue like, his brows furrowed as he appeared to give it some thought.

Amy thought about Yasmin and her need to see her daughter again. Was that why Damien had let her go? All this time, Amy had thought Yasmin's escape had been part of the plan. But Amy could have found the girl whether she was alive or dead. For the last few days, Amy had battled to stay strong. Being emotional equated to weakness in her eyes, but what if she was playing Damien all wrong?

'*You* let Yasmin go, didn't you?' she said. 'Not Lucy. I know you have a heart, as much as you try to bury it. Please. Do the right thing.'

A sharp beep of a car horn signalled that Lucy was back. As her car pulled up on the drive, Damien yanked Amy's hand and cuffed her to the bed.

'There's bacon in the fridge,' he said, in a low voice. 'I'll make sandwiches. You'll need all your strength for the hunt.'

CHAPTER FORTY-FIVE

As Donovan drove towards King's Chase, he hoped his visit would bear fruit. It was an impressive three-storey building, its long, tree-lined driveway dappled by yellowing leaves. Donovan should have been enamoured by the beautiful surroundings. The lawns were immaculately trimmed, with impressive ornamental equine water features dotted each side of the expansive front drive. The road to the left led to a stable block which housed many of the UK's finest racehorses. Donovan wasn't averse to a flutter or two. He would have loved to have had a tour of the grounds. As a child, he'd briefly fantasised about becoming a jockey, but the nearest he'd come to it was patting donkeys on Southend's beach. But now he was a different person to the cheeky kid who'd worked part-time in Nancy's Café, his parents' greasy spoon. He held a responsible job. People depended on him. Each moment was consumed with thoughts of bringing Amy home.

Amy's brother, DI Craig Winter, had been of immense help. He wasn't officially investigating due to a conflict of interest, but he'd freed up some valuable time for Donovan by allocating officers from CID to help.

Donovan eased his grip on the steering wheel of the unmarked Ford. Every muscle in his body ached from being tensed, but he was conscious of Molly's presence and needed to keep a professional front. Her enquiries around dermal piercing had provided good results. Several people had studs placed into the back of their neck recently, but only one matched the distinctive formation of piercings reported by Yasmin. Officers had also obtained CCTV from outside Damien's flat. It wasn't a perfect image, but enough to make out the features of the leggy blonde accompanying him. The same blonde woman who was captured heading into Eternal Tattoos and Piercing in Shoreditch the week before. She had a name, a double-barrelled one at that. Lucy Baron-Hart was the daughter of George Baron-Hart, a racehorse trainer and self-made millionaire. But much to her father's disappointment, Lucy did not follow in his footsteps. A socialite party girl, she had a string of failed businesses behind her and was a 'fame hungry wannabe' according to socialite gossip online. She had dated a couple of footballers as well as a dancer from a well-known band, but her relationships never lasted. Molly also discovered that Lucy was one of the first to comment on all Instagram posts with the hashtag 'The Hunters' with concerns for the women involved.

As he parked up on the gravel driveway, Donovan was hopeful he was at the right place. They couldn't yet assume Lucy's guilt, but she was officially a person of interest who was proving hard to track down. Molly had been warned to step carefully today. The detective was young and impetuous, but she was wholly devoted to Amy's case.

Donovan wiped his feet on the indoor mat as they were shown inside by the housekeeper. He breathed in the clean, sharp smell of leather and saddle soap which lingered in the air. The hall was spacious and old-fashioned, with countless paintings of racehorses hanging on its mahogany-panelled walls. A central curved staircase led to a grand landing illuminated by chandeliers. Molly's mouth had fallen open as she took in the opulence.

Donovan cleared his throat as George, Lucy's father, marched into the hall. A slim, stern-looking man, he had the presence of someone who was used to getting his own way. He was dressed in a sweatshirt, jeans, and brown leather Chelsea riding boots. Donovan guessed him to be in his late-fifties, and his weathered face spoke of time spent outdoors.

'You'll have to be quick. I'm rather busy today.' His voice carried down the echoey hall as he led them into a library, with books on racing and equine health lining the shelves.

'Believe it or not, Mr Baron-Hart, so am I,' Donovan said curtly. There was no time for politeness here. 'We'd like to speak to your daughter, Lucy. Is she about?'

'Oh, I see. My housekeeper was under the impression that it was me you wanted. I've already told officers, I don't know where Lucy is. She's not answering her phone and she hasn't darkened my door.'

'There must have been a miscommunication,' Molly added, despite having made the call herself. 'We would very much like to speak to Lucy. Can you tell us where she is?' Speaking to Lucy's father was better than nothing and a means of getting inside the door. According to their enquiries, Lucy's mother had taken off on Lucy's third birthday and never returned.

'I take it she's in some kind of trouble then.' Mr Baron-Hart heaved a sigh. 'If only she was more like her brothers. *They've never brought the police to my door.*'

From what Donovan had read online, Mr Baron-Hart's disappointment was not something he kept to himself.

'What has she done? Been speeding again? Or has she been fighting? I don't know where she gets her violent streak from.'

Molly arched an eyebrow. Lucy didn't have a police record

according to PNC checks. Her father was obviously kept busy keeping his daughter's nose clean.

'Excuse me.' Molly slipped her mobile from her pocket. 'Do you mind if I take this call outside?'

Donovan responded with a nod, but he hadn't heard the phone ring.

He returned his attention to Mr Baron-Hart as Molly left the room. 'It's in Lucy's interest if she comes to the station and helps us with our enquiries. Can you tell me when the last time you spoke to your daughter?'

'I don't know...' Mr Baron-Hart blew out his cheeks. 'She comes and goes, sometimes we don't see her for weeks, but when her money dries up, she suddenly remembers her old dad again. Just like her mother, that one. I expect one day she'll take off when she finds someone foolish enough to pay her way.'

Donovan's fists tightened, his fingernails biting into the palms of his hands. Every second was precious, and Lucy's father was being vague. Mr Baron-Hart was staring at him now.

'You may as well spit it out, man, because I haven't got all day. What has she done that brings a DCI and his sidekick to my door?'

'Let's just say that the sooner she speaks to us the better it will be for her.'

'Right, well, if that's all...' Mr Baron-Hart seemed unconcerned as he checked his watch.

Donovan could have asked him about Lucy's piercings, but he did not want to give too much away. If Lucy was on the premises, the less she knew about the evidence they'd gained, the better.

Molly clicked her seatbelt into place as Donovan joined her in the car.

'What was all that about a call?' He started the engine, looking from left to right before pulling out of the drive.

'We weren't getting anywhere with Lucy's dad, so I took myself off for a wander. Got chatting to a nice groom.'

Donovan admired her ingenuity. 'Oh yes? And what did he have to say for himself?'

'She. Her name's Tiffany, and very nice she was too.' A satisfied smile rested on Molly's face. 'And, boss, you'll never guess what – Lucy came to see her dad earlier today. He's been lying through his teeth.'

'And you believe her?'

Molly nodded quickly. 'It's all off the record, mind. Tiffany doesn't want to lose her job. She's even seen the neck piercings. She said Lucy does stuff like this all the time to piss her father off.'

'Anything else?'

'Apart from her asking me out on a date?' Molly smiled. 'She said Lucy's the talk of the stables. Her dad threatened to cut her off because she's dating a bloke with a prison record. I couldn't get a name, but I can guess who that is.'

'Good work.' Donovan flicked on the car indicator before turning onto the main road. It served to confirm what they already knew. Lucy Baron-Hart was one half of The Hunters. Now all they needed to do was to track her down.

CHAPTER FORTY-SIX

Paddy hated the way that people stared at Amy's desk when they entered her office. He couldn't bear people treating it like some kind of shrine. It was why he'd rested his chipped mug of tea on her coaster and taken up residence there today. He'd moved the neatly stacked journals and Post-it notes to the right of her computer and stacked printouts and folders to the left until it looked like anyone else's desk.

Paddy's natural inclination was to be pessimistic but they couldn't lose hope – not yet. The press had run with the story since Amy's appearance online. Just getting into work without having a camera shoved in your face was a challenge these days. And then there were the documentary producers who were desperate to get inside their doors for another fly-on-the-wall account. Letters of support for Amy's plight had come flooding in. The hate mail was being closely monitored, many were filled with vicious words which stated Amy got what she deserved. The media team were working around the clock dealing with it all, and extra officers were being drafted in to deal with all the work. Overtime was limitless, and the budget was generous for now. But what happened after the fourth day? Paddy had a sneaking suspicion that things would be scaled down. Never had the team given so much to a case. Sally-Ann hadn't slept properly in days, and they tried to protect Amy's mother, Flora, as much as they could. But today, she demanded answers, and Paddy would not let her down.

His footsteps were heavy as he made his way to the vulnerable victim interview room. He wished he'd been able to see more of Flora, but he couldn't afford the time. Sally-Ann had invited her to sleep at their place, but Flora had been adamant that she was staying where she was. She was a strong, spirited woman, much more than Paddy gave her credit for. For years, she had lived in the shadow of her husband, Superintendent Robert Winter, a man whose legacy lived on.

Flora rose as Paddy entered the warm but clinical room.

'Flora, how are you doing?' He already knew the answer.

Grey roots leached the colour from her auburn hair, and her face was devoid of her usual bloom of blusher and lipstick. She was not a big woman, but today she seemed even smaller than before.

Paddy looked around the room before she could reply. 'Are you on your own? Where's Floyd?'

Floyd, the FLO, had been allocated to assist, but there was no sign of the family liaison officer now.

'I insisted he take a break,' Flora replied matter of factly. 'You're working him too hard. He has six-month-old twins at home, you know.'

Paddy didn't know, but it was typical of Flora to care, even now, with everything going on.

'Can I make you a cuppa? Tea? Coffee?' The witness interview suite came equipped with a kettle, milk, and biscuits. It was also fitted with cameras, but Paddy would not need them today. DI Donovan was due back at any second. Paddy aimed to make this quick.

Flora gave him a half-hearted smile. 'Floyd made me one already. Now sit down, you and I need to have a chat.'

But Paddy didn't know what Flora wanted to hear. They had already told her as much as they could. 'I can't stay long,' he warned. There was a clock ticking down in his head that he could not escape.

Lillian's chin jutted upwards as she got to the point. 'I want you to arrange a meeting with Lillian Grimes.'

Paddy sat beside her, contemplating her request. 'We've already spoken to her. Sally-Ann...'

'But *I* haven't,' Flora interrupted. 'I know she's got something to do with this.'

'Maybe she has and maybe she hasn't,' Paddy said softly. 'But no good can come of you getting involved.'

'But I've got to do something,' Flora said sharply. 'That dreadful woman has always hated me, from the day the adoption papers were signed. I'll do anything, give her anything she wants, if it means getting my Amy back.' Her chin began to tremble and her voice rose a notch. 'She can have the house. Robert's pension...my savings.'

Her words fell away, and Paddy leaned forward and patted her hand.

'Now, now, what would Amy say if she were here? She wouldn't want any of this. And she certainly wouldn't want you bowing down to the likes of Lillian Grimes.'

'There's nothing I won't do to get my daughter back. Because she's mine...not hers. And she has no right to take her away.'

'Lillian wouldn't have the strength to whisk Amy off the streets,' Paddy countered. 'But she might know something, and I promise you, we're working on it.'

The door clicked open, and both of them looked up. It was

Donovan. Had he been watching them on camera from the monitoring room?

Paddy searched his face for signs of hope, but all he could see was his own frustration reflected at him.

'Don't you worry about Lillian.' Donovan approached Flora. 'If anyone's going to get the truth out of her it will be me. I've arranged a meeting. She's open to negotiation, so let's not lose hope yet.'

Flora nodded, unable to find the words to reply.

'Let's get you home, eh? Molly will give you a lift, and I'll update you as soon as I can.'

Paddy's thoughts descended into gloom. It seemed Donovan's visit to Mr Baron-Hart hadn't produced results. He had no doubt they would catch the kidnappers. They were erratic, disorganised, and unintelligent. Leads were coming in thick and fast, and officers were gaining ground. But time was their enemy. Finding Amy was like looking for a particular pebble on Brighton beach.

'You're a good man,' Flora said, taking Donovan's arm.

He exchanged a glance with Paddy – a mixture of hope and dread. It appeared that Lillian's indecent proposal was being given some thought. Just how far would Donovan go to bring Amy home?

CHAPTER FORTY-SEVEN

Rain spat against Amy's face as she ran, disorientated, through the woodlands. She was sure she'd seen this tree before. October winds bit into her skin, chilling her to the bone as the sun lowered in the sky. The hunt times were inconsistent, fitting in around Lucy and Damien's naps. Sunlight was beginning to fade, which meant it was gone four o clock. Engines roared in the distance. So much for a head start. But it was when the bike engines were silenced that she was most at risk. They were coming, and she was lost in a sea of trees. How were they finding her so quickly in such a dense forest? A creeping suspicion told her that they weren't playing fair.

Tears streaked from the corners of her eyes as she dodged tree roots and muddy paths. Panting, she blinked to clear her vision. She wasn't crying or upset, she was too focused on escaping for emotions to get in the way. She could hear her father's voice in the back of her mind, willing her on. Her real father, Robert Winter, not the sperm donor who had shacked up with Lillian Grimes. Robert would instruct her to keep her mind clear and ask what she'd learned from the hunt so far.

Experience told her that if she hid, Damien and Lucy would still find her, even if both were coming from different directions. Yet there were no walkie-talkies in use that she had seen, and she hadn't seen either of them communicate to each other by phone during the hunt. So how had they approached her in a pincer movement and known exactly where she was?

She thought of Yasmin's account and of how her captors had provided her with a special tracksuit to wear. But Amy's clothes were dark, they didn't make her stand out. The only thing they'd given her were her boots.

She pressed a hand against her side, her chest heaving as she gulped in lungful's of air. Why had they offered that one act of kindness? Unless...had they double-crossed her all along? Made Amy think it was her idea to wear her boots so she wouldn't be suspicious of what they had hidden inside? Because if they were going to use a tracker, it had to be planted there.

As much as it pained her to remove them, that's what she had to do. She leaned against a tree and tugged off each one. No wonder they'd made her leave her boots outside the door each night. She couldn't see anything at first glance, but it could be burrowed inside the heel. She could be making things a whole lot more difficult, but there wasn't time for a more thorough check. She had to go with her gut.

Dampness seeped into her stockinged feet. Gathering up all her strength, she threw her left boot behind her. Then she reached back and threw the other in the opposite direction. Pain shot through her at the sudden exertion, but there was also a sense of freedom. If there *were* trackers in her footwear, at least now she was free.

She darted through the forest, her jaw tightening as the sharp scratch of twigs and debris penetrated her feet. It made sense to go right, in the opposite direction of the sounds. They were closing in, but if she was correct about the trackers, Damien and Lucy would only get so far.

'Come find me now, you bastards,' Amy whispered beneath her breath as she took off down the isolated path.

CHAPTER FORTY-EIGHT

'One hour,' Donovan told himself. 'Just one hour of my life. Then I move forward, and whatever happens, I'll have done my best.' Because if Amy and his baby died, his disgust at sleeping with Lillian would be nothing compared to a lifetime of recrimination.

Seeing Flora offer up her home, her savings, and her husband's pension to get Amy back had put him to shame. She was willing to give up everything, when all Lillian wanted was an hour of his time. But he was lying about the impact this would have on him. How would Amy feel about it? Or worse still, what if Lillian was lying about knowing where she was?

He pressed his digital key card against the door. He'd come to the Premier Inn hotel early because he needed time to collect his thoughts. He was wearing his work suit and would shower at home after it was over. He would scrub his skin raw, but no amount of soap would wash the shame away. He had to keep the end goal in sight. Finding Amy was at the heart of everything.

He slid off his jacket and rested it on the back of a chair. The room was comfortably warm, with a large double bed. It made him nauseous to look at it. He couldn't believe he was doing this.

He jolted as the door clicked open. Lillian was here already, a salacious smile on her red-glossed lips. Her black hair was loose around her face, a diamanté-encrusted necklace around her neck. Donovan grimaced as she parted her coat. He was half expecting her to have nothing on underneath. He exhaled in relief as she smoothed over her low-cut black dress, following his gaze.

'Like what you see?' She winked, resting a small holdall on the bed.

'I'm not sure I can do this.' Donovan drove a hand through his hair as he tried to stay emotionally detached.

'Oh, honey, don't you worry,' Lillian purred as she approached. 'I've brought toys. We're both going to have so much fun.' She chuckled, running a long red-varnished nail down his chest. 'Relax. How many men get to have guilt-free sex?'

The smell of Poison perfume rose between them, making him want to gag.

'You know you want to,' she whispered, her hand lowering to his groin. 'Or at least a part of you will.'

Donovan jerked back as Lillian squeezed.

'So shy!' She arched an eyebrow, amused. 'But nothing I haven't encountered before.'

This wasn't just about being unfaithful. This was about sleeping with a sexual predator and serial killer. Lillian was getting off on the power. The more reluctant he appeared, the more it turned her on. He straightened his posture. He would not give her the satisfaction of being a victim.

'Let's get this over with,' he said firmly. 'I haven't got all day.' He raked her body with a gaze, just as she had with him. But now he portrayed a look of disgust. 'What are you, sixty-five? Seventy? Probably best you don't overdo it. You don't want to break a hip.' Donovan wasn't ageist, but he was hitting Lillian where it hurt. Suggesting she was well past her prime would bruise her ego.

'I assure you,' Lillian quickly recovered from the veiled insult, 'I am *very* flexible and perfectly capable of teaching you a thing or two.'

Donovan couldn't stop himself from stepping back as Lillian began to undo his tie.

'Oh, for God's sake!' She threw her hands in the air. 'Are we getting on with this or what?'

But he couldn't physically make himself undress. Each time Lillian moved forward, Donovan stepped back. All he could think about were the women and children she had hurt in the past.

Lillian lunged at his belt buckle, releasing it with expert speed. 'C'mon, big man. Let's see what you're hiding in there.'

'Get your dirty hands off me!' Donovan shouted, Lillian's fingers feeling like insistent maggots burrowing against his skin. He pushed her onto the bed and began to fix his clothes. He couldn't go through with it. He had let Amy down.

Lillian sat up on the bed, her dark eyes glittering in fury. 'You don't say no to me!' She jabbed the air with her finger. 'Because this time tomorrow, your precious Amy and that *thing* growing inside her will be dead!'

Donovan's eyes widened in surprise. So she knew about the pregnancy, and yet she was still playing games. 'I can't do it. Physically. I can't bring myself to...' His words were lost in torment as Lillian clambered off the bed.

'Oh, for fucks sake!' Lillian screeched, her fists bunched. 'I can't believe you dragged me all the way here for nothing! If you think I'm going to tell you...'

There was a soft knock on the door. Donovan half expected to see Paddy on the other side, ready to 'take one for the team'.

'Kevin.' Donovan exhaled in relief as he opened the door to him. 'I didn't expect you to show.'

Judging from his expression, he hadn't expected to either. 'Sally-Ann talked me into it. I was held up on the Tubes...' He looked over Donovan's shoulder. 'I'm not too late, am I?'

'No harm done,' Donovan said gratefully, finding the situation quite surreal.

'Who's this?' Lillian's voice rose behind him. 'Are you sending in the troops? Managed to rustle up a replacement?'

'Not quite.' Donovan opened the door wide and allowed Kevin inside.

He was dressed down today, in a navy woollen coat, scarf, and blue jeans.

'Who are you?' Lillian glanced from Kevin to Donovan, her expression tight with annoyance. 'If you think you're going to arrest me...'

'He's not a police officer,' Donovan talked over her. 'He's your brother, Kevin. If I can't talk some sense into you then perhaps he can.' He took a seat in the farthest corner of the room. Lillian staggered back and plopped into a chair.

Her voice descended into a whisper. 'No. It can't be.'

'Hello, sis.' Kevin tentatively walked into the room. 'Remember me? I wrote to you in prison.'

Lillian was shaking her head. She kicked off her high heels, unsteady as she forced herself to stand. 'Kevin? Is it...is it really you?' Her eyes narrowed. She turned to Donovan. 'Is this some kind of sick game?'

'I sent you a poem,' Kevin interrupted. 'We wear the mask that grins and lies...'

'It hides our cheeks and shades our eyes,' Lillian picked up the rest of it, handling each word with care.

Donovan watched with a sense of amazement. For once in her life, Lillian appeared vulnerable. He had never seen her like this, not even when she'd been in hospital after being stabbed. She always carried an air of wickedness, but right now, in the confines of the hotel room, her defiance fell away.

'Is it really you?' The corners of Lillian's mouth fell into a sad smile.

Donovan had always believed that Lillian was a psychopath who didn't feel love, remorse, or empathy. But emotion was blooming inside her as her eyes welled with tears.

'Yes, it's me.' Kevin stood awkwardly in the centre of the room. He cast his gaze on Lillian's bag resting on the bed, then glanced at Donovan, as if imagining what could have taken place. He cleared his throat. 'Lillian...the reason I'm here...'

But Lillian raised a hand, slapping away a tear as if it had no right to be on her face. 'I know why you're here and I'll give you whatever you want, but please...give me a moment to savour this.' She stood, drinking in his form. But this was the look of someone returning to a long-lost friend. 'If you only knew the amount of times I've thought about you.' Her skinny hand rested on her chest. 'I agonised over replying after you made contact. But I couldn't bear to taint you with what I did.'

Donovan dropped his gaze to the floor. She hadn't minded contacting Amy. It seemed Kevin was placed on a pedestal beyond any of them. Her admittance of wrongdoing also came as a surprise. Lillian stepped towards him, holding out a shaking hand. Kevin took it without hesitation.

'You look...' She shook her head as more tears rose. 'Amazing.' She sniffed. 'Tell me, how has life treated you?'

She was talking to him as if she were his mother rather than a serial killer sister who'd created so much carnage. Forensic psychologists could have had a field day with this. Lillian was displaying emotions Donovan didn't know she was capable of.

'I'm good, thanks,' Kevin said as Lillian released her grip. 'I used to be a barrister but now I lead a charity which defends victims of domestic abuse. People who need it the most.'

'My little brother, a barrister. I always knew you'd make something of yourself. I don't suppose you remember me from before.' A chuckle rose up her throat. 'Probably for the best.'

'I remember more than you know.' Kevin looked at her, unblinking. 'They say that victims of trauma can remember right back to when they were babies. I remember being hungry and waking you up by tapping your face. I remember the bedtime stories you told me. I remember Mum getting black eyes and broken ribs.' His words trailed away.

'She was a right dishcloth.' Lillian's voice hardened. 'She should have protected us.'

Donovan rolled his eyes at the sentiment. That was rich, coming from a predator.

'You always felt more like my mum than she did. But...' Kevin opened his mouth to speak but closed it again.

Pain was etched on his face, and Lillian looked away, clearly unable to witness it.

'What happened to you, Lillian?' he said, at last.

'Well now.' Lillian gave him a sheepish grin. 'That's a story for another day. You came here for a reason, and I won't stand in your way. It can't have been easy, but it means more than you can imagine.'

'I know,' Kevin said. 'But if we could make some good come of this...I'd like to get to know my niece.' He looked at Lillian earnestly. 'Where is she?'

Lillian turned her attention to Donovan as she slipped on her heels. 'I'll make the call.'

'You mean that?' Donovan's heart fluttered in his chest. Was this finally coming to an end?

Lillian ignored the question as she took her brother's hand

for one last time. You'll come visit me, won't you? I want to hear all about your life.'

'Try and stop me.' Kevin smiled. 'Once we get this nasty business out of the way. I have your number. I'll be in touch.'

Lillian stood, awkwardly, a stupid grin on her face. She stared at her brother expectantly as he said his goodbyes. It was too soon for hugs for Kevin as he extended his hand.

'Thank you,' Donovan said to Kevin as they walked shoulder to shoulder down the hotel corridor.

'I'm still shaking.' Kevin raised his hand to demonstrate.

'I'd no idea you were nervous. You seemed so calm.'

'I'm used to putting on pretences. It doesn't do to show your nerves.'

'I'll let you know how I get on,' Donovan said when they reached the elevators. 'If this goes to plan, you'll save Amy's life.'

'And I appreciate your gratitude.' Kevin pressed the button to call the lift. 'But that's as far as it goes for me. No offence, but I don't want anything to do with Lillian, or her extended family.'

'But you said...' The words died on Donovan's lips as the lift doors parted and an elderly couple stepped out.

Kevin glanced over his shoulder, waiting until they had passed. 'I said whatever it took to help you out. That woman's a monster. I felt sick in her company. I want nothing to do with her. So if she asks for my number – don't give it to her.'

'Of course.' Donovan understood. 'And thanks.'

They stepped into the lift, taking the four floors down in silence. Donovan usually prided himself on being a good judge of character, but he'd believed Kevin when he'd declared an interest in seeing Lillian again. Lillian had not been born a psychopath, life had made her that way. But he could not blame her brother for wanting nothing to do with her. There was no excuse for what she'd done.

His thoughts returned to Amy, and he felt hope for the first time in days. If Lillian was true to her word, she would be on the phone to Damien right now, telling him to make a run for it and let Amy go. He fingered the hotel room key card. The room was booked for twenty-four hours. It was unlikely Lillian would stay the night, but she was a sponger, so you never knew. Regardless, he would not be handing his key in yet. Donovan had thrown another dart at the board. He had a recording device to collect.

CHAPTER FORTY-NINE

Damien sat, staring into the fire, a million miles away from peace. Sometimes he just wanted everything to slow down long enough to take a fucking breath. His feet ached from traipsing through the forest, all the while his gut churning as he decided whether to run or stay. Amy thought she was so clever, throwing away her boots. In the minutes that followed after the discovery of the tracker, Lucy had been a nightmare. She wasn't as worried about getting caught as she was about finishing his sister. Now the silly cow was half comatose in her room after taking the last of their stash.

She was getting bored of him, he could hear it in the way she spoke. Last night, he'd seen her checking out Tinder and almost caved her skull in there and then. But then he'd caught the glint in her eye, and it had thrown him off. She'd wanted him to hurt her, but this felt different to before. Bruises and broken bones could go in her favour if she was caught later on.

Damien's gaze flicked to the Ring app on his phone. Amy hadn't moved in over an hour. She was in a bad way. Lucy had kicked her a few times in the spine when they'd finally found her, passed out after falling down a ravine. Lucy had acted like a wild animal, froth gathering in the corners of her mouth. She'd just unholstered her knife, screaming she would skin her alive, when Damien had pulled her away. He'd been livid, too, but he couldn't afford for it to end that way.

'She's a witness!' Lucy had argued. 'We need to finish her, now!'

But why had Lucy made those stupid Instagram videos if she was worried about being caught? Unless she was set to play the victim and blame the whole thing on him. She couldn't do that while Amy was alive. She'd seen what Lucy was really like. The same worrying thoughts cycled in a loop through his mind: the little frightened gasps Lucy made while filming, and how her hand had shaken when she'd held the camera. Sure, her words suggested that she was enjoying herself, but those sounds of fear could be picked apart. Was he looking too much into it?

Damien's brows furrowed as the flames crackled and spat. They had too much on Yasmin for her to blab; the videos of them in bed bought her silence for now. Amy was a different matter. She couldn't be blackmailed or threatened. She was a Grimes, after all.

He ignored his phone as it buzzed with yet another call from his mother. He didn't have the energy to speak to her today. Why was the silly cow having a change of heart now? It was her money that had bought the equipment that tracked Amy down. A thermal-imaging drone was just one of the tools in his armoury. The taser, the gun, even the rental for the cottages, Lillian had pay-rolled the lot. He hadn't given her the finer details, but she'd made him promise to share the videos when it was all over.

He shook his head. She was so screwed up. Judging by her texts, she'd lost her taste for the hunt. She wasn't the only one. He couldn't rid himself of the feeling that Lucy was ready to betray him – all for a slice of fame. The talk show appearances, the book deals, the impending movie deals – it was everything she wanted – as long as she could make it work. *One more day*, he told himself. Then it would all be over. But where did that leave him?

CHAPTER FIFTY

'Sit down before you fall down,' Sally-Ann instructed.

Paddy knew better than to disagree. She had channelled her stress into cooking, and the smells coming from their modest kitchen were mouth-watering. Donovan rested his mobile phone on the table. It was attached to a portable charger – he'd barely been off it all day. Eating at irregular hours seemed to be the new normal as they sat down for a slap-up meal at two a.m. It wasn't indigestion that would keep Paddy awake tonight, it was the digital clock next to his bed. He told himself that no news was good news – that Damien was dragging things out to give himself time to get away. But nothing in life was certain where the Grimeses were involved.

'You shouldn't have gone to so much trouble.' Donovan pulled up his chair.

'It's just pie and mash,' she said simply, even though it had been made from scratch.

Then there were the side dishes of red cabbage, dauphinoise potatoes, sautéed carrots, and cauliflower cheese. She had also baked an apple and a rhubarb pie as well as various pastries which would no doubt end up in the freezer because they'd never get through it all. But she wasn't doing this for Donovan. It was to capture their attention long enough to interrogate them both.

'Winifred's staying over with Flora tonight.' Sally-Ann passed the gravy boat. 'She won't leave the house in case Amy comes in through the door.'

'I'm glad she's not on her own.' Paddy's stomach growled in anticipation as he spooned mash onto his plate. He'd been living off a flapjack and a snatched bag of crisps all day. From what he'd seen of Donovan, he'd been the same.

'I don't have anything new to tell you,' Donovan said, anticipating Sally-Ann's line of questioning.

'You *don't* have anything new, or you *can't* tell me anything new?' She poured gravy on her plate, never taking his eyes from his.

'I don't,' he said shortly, shovelling pie into his mouth.

With Sally-Ann on one end of the table and Donovan at the other, Paddy felt like he was watching a verbal tennis match. Donovan bought himself a few seconds of silence as he chewed slowly and rhythmically, his gaze on his phone.

'I'm sure she'll call soon, love. This is smashing grub.' Paddy patted Sally-Ann's hand. 'And that was great work, how you persuaded Kevin to speak to her. I'm sure we'll hear back soon.' He was aware he was repeating himself, but platitudes were all he could offer right now.

'Lillian's not answering her phone,' Sally-Ann said mournfully. 'I've left a dozen messages, begging her to call me back.' She glanced up at Donovan, her food untouched. 'And there was no other recording in the hotel? Nothing you're keeping from me?' She rested her fork on the table. 'Because I'd rather know the truth than be kept in this...this...limbo.'

'I put my neck on the line telling you about that,' Donovan replied. 'So why would I try to cover it up now?'

'Now then, darlin',' Paddy comforted Sally-Ann. 'You know what we know.'

Donovan couldn't get the recording analysed because he'd done it off his own back. The fact a DCI from the Met had almost slept with a serial killer for information could never get out. The papers would have a field day with it. Sally-Ann was highly fortunate that she'd been included in the circle of trust.

'Play it again.' Her blue eyes were wide and pleading. 'Please.'

Donovan sighed, pressing play on the recording now stored on his phone. Paddy chewed quietly. Soon, Lillian's insistent tones were invading their space as she made the call to Damien.

'Hello? Why aren't you answering your bloody phone? You know I hate leaving messages. Ring me back.' The recording was followed by a couple more attempts to call. 'This is important, you twat. Call me back.'

Donovan forwarded the recording by fifteen minutes. They didn't need to listen to Lillian pacing the room again.

'Try to eat something,' Paddy said to Sally-Ann. 'You need to keep up your strength.'

Sally-Ann reluctantly spooned some mash potatoes into her mouth as the next section of the recording played.

'Damien. This is important. The filth are on to you. But don't worry, we can sort this, as long as you tell me where you are. Just leave Amy and go. She's more trouble than she's worth. That wanker Donovan, will string you up by the balls if you harm his kid. I only hope I'm not too late...' She exhaled a long sigh. 'I've done everything I can this end. Just ring me, all right?'

Paddy could hear the desperation in her voice. But who was it for, her brother, Kevin, or Damien, because it certainly wasn't for Amy...was it? Paddy wasn't sure. Lillian had more layers than an onion. There was no second-guessing her next move.

'What I want to know is...' Donovan began, after taking a sip of water. 'Is how Lillian knows about the pregnancy.' He gave Sally-Ann a stern eye. 'Because I didn't tell her, and I can count the people who know about it on one hand.'

Paddy watched the exchange with interest as Sally-Ann took a breath to reply. He wasn't going to allow Donovan to tell her off when she had done so much to help. Had she not got involved, Donovan would have been forced to have sex with Lillian Grimes.

But Sally-Ann smiled. 'Sometimes I shock myself with the clever things I do, and other times I can't think straight. I thought that if Lillian knew about the baby, she might get through to Damien.'

'You know it's going to be headlines tomorrow, don't you? I can see it now...' Donovan's hand rose in the air as he framed the words. 'My secret sorrow by Lillian Grimes. Sad grandmother shares news of Amy Winter's pregnancy.'

'Probably,' Sally-Ann replied. 'But at least I know I'll have done everything I could. There's only one day left, Donovan. Why haven't you found her? My brother's not all that clever. He must have left a trail.'

Donovan wiped his mouth with a napkin, and Paddy prepared to intervene. But instead of arguing with Sally-Ann, Donovan educated her on the intricacies of their investigation so far. She listened, fascinated, as he provided her with details of the different teams working on the case. He talked about the Divisional Intelligence Unit and how the Public Protection team worked. He explained what a CHIS was and how they'd been leaning on them for information. Then he went into depth about the scenes of crime team and what they had on the killer couple so far. He patiently answered every question Sally-Ann threw at him. The conversation was more thorough than any briefing Paddy had attended, and he was grateful to Donovan for letting her in.

'Thanks for the meal, I needed it.' He turned to Paddy as he stood at the front door. 'Get your head down. I'm heading back into the office.'

It was three in the morning, but nobody argued with him. Donovan had been napping in his office, in case anything came in.

Paddy locked the front door. 'Leave the dishes,' he said to Sally-Ann. 'I'll help you clear up in the morning. Try to get a couple of hours' sleep.' But the truth was, he didn't want the night to end. He wasn't ready to face the morning and what the day would produce.

ONE DAY LEFT

CHAPTER FIFTY-ONE

Splinters of light broke through the boarded cottage window. Amy ticked off her mental calendar. It was Friday, the twenty first of October. The last day of the hunt. She could tell that Damien was itching to move on. Last night, he and Lucy had an explosive argument over her father leaving countless frantic messages on her phone. Lucy had screamed about Lillian's endless attempts to get in touch. Things were smashed, furniture was knocked over, but no sex session followed. It seemed Lucy and Damien were falling apart. Did this mean that the police were on their trail? Amy had listened keenly to their shouting match as Damien smashed Lucy's phone. The silence that followed was eerie, and Amy's mind was on the array of weapons in the house. What if one had killed the other? She'd sat, her knees to her chest as she imagined Lucy entering the room. She wouldn't kill her quickly. She would take things slow, fulfilling all her promises before ending her. Amy had been overcome with relief to hear Lucy scream Damien's name in quick succession as they eventually made up.

. . .

There had been plenty of time for Amy to think over the last few days. She was grateful to be left alone while Damien while Lucy got stoned. The women who proceeded her had not been so fortunate. At least Damien had refused to go along with Lucy's suggestion to 'break her in' or give her a tattoo. Amy tried not to dwell on dark thoughts as she shifted to her side, one limp hand cuffed to the metal bed frame, the other resting on her growing stomach. Yesterday had been rough. She was so sure she would get away, because if Yasmin had done it, then so could she. But she wasn't in Epping Forest. She was in the depths of rough terrain with no visible roads. The forest had to be privately owned, because people hadn't walked the pathways in years.

After throwing away her shoes, hope had softened her focus, and she'd allowed emotion to creep in. Had she been paying more attention, she may not have slipped in mud and tumbled down the ravine. Stars had exploded in her vision as her head hit a rock, then she was released into a void. In those heart-stopping moments as darkness closed in, she believed it was the end of the line. She'd felt sorrow, not for herself but the baby she would never have.

Lying in wet leaves, Amy had briefly come to as pain closed in from every angle. Curling up in the foetal position, she'd tried to protect her bump as Lucy kicked and spat. The woman had sounded like a crazed animal, howling and screaming with rage as she'd grabbed a fistful of Amy's hair. Then Damien had stepped in, and the next time Amy came to, she was back lying in the cottage bed.

Amy groaned as she shifted her weight. It felt like a herd of cattle had galloped over her back. What sort of person would beat up an unresponsive human being? Lucy was losing her grip on reality. Amy touched her split lip, then ran her fingers over the dried blood on her injured arm. Her trousers were caked with mud, and the stink of body odour rose from her blouse when she moved. Her ankle was swollen, her legs weak, her feet scratched and bruised. How was she going to walk, let alone run for her life?

For the first time, she came to terms with the fact that her team may not find her in time. She imagined each one of them in turn. Molly would be pushing the boundaries, frustrated by red tape slowing her down. Denny would be calm and methodical, picking up things others had missed. Steve would be acting like a DI, going to meetings, coming up with strategies and retaining his focus throughout. Paddy would be worried sick, reassuring Sally-Ann that everything would be OK, but not believing a word. Flora would have the support of her friends but would be constantly asking Craig for updates. Lillian would be lapping it up. As for Donovan...it pained Amy to think about how he was coping with it all. If she was to get through the day, she needed to keep a clear head.

So she lay in bed, feeling relief and sadness in equal measures each time her baby moved. He was a fighter, just like her, but she was under no illusion of the danger they were in. She pressed her face into the pillow, trying to imagine a future for them both.

The noises rising from Damien's room told Amy the couple were awake. She knew what came next. A breakfast of lumpy porridge to sustain her before the final hunt.

CHAPTER FIFTY-TWO

Damien lifted the spoonful of porridge in the air. 'Open up,' he said, a curl of steam rising from the breakfast he'd made.

He was no Jamie Oliver, but he could rustle up some tasty grub. Porridge for breakfast, bacon sandwiches for lunch, and chips, beans, eggs, and gammon for tea. Not that Lucy ate much any it, preferring something poncey rubbish like smashed avocado on toast. Mushed-up green crap, more like.

'I need a doctor,' Amy said, in between mouthfuls of porridge. 'There's no point in letting me go if I'm dead before I reach help.'

Damien looked at his sister in amazement. She was back to her feisty self. 'Well, I hate to disappoint ya, but we ain't letting you go.'

'I know she's got no intention of letting me live.' Amy said, and he watched her gaze flick to the door.

On the other side, Lucy was happily singing 'Don't Stop Believing' at the top of her lungs.

'But you will, if you've any sense.' Amy's eyes bored into him, and for a split-second, Damien saw his mother there.

Christ, he thought. *What the hell am I doing?* If he let Lucy murder Amy, the rest of his family would turn against him. Even Lillian, who'd planted the idea to begin with. If she thought it was a bad idea, then alarm bells should be ringing in his head.

'All right, now listen,' he whispered in a low voice, resting the porridge to one side. 'What's it gonna take for the both of us to get out of this alive? Cos I ain't doing no jail time for you.'

'Then let me go and run,' Amy whispered. 'Get as far away as you can. I'll buy you time. I swear on my baby's life.' She rested a shaking hand on her stomach.

Maybe it was desperation, but Damien wanted to believe her. He had exorcised his demons as far as Amy was concerned. She was beaten, inside and out. His grudge had fizzled out.

'There's an empty cottage, not far from here. You've never found it because it's at the back of this place and you've always run straight ahead.'

Amy shook her head. 'It's too open. There's a clearing behind here. She'll see me.'

'Not if I distract her. You'll have about five minutes to double back. Then follow the trail straight ahead. Hide out there, and when we're clear of this place, I'll let someone know where you are.'

'Don't mess with me, Damien. No more surprises.' Amy may have had the stuffing knocked out of her, but she wasn't down just yet. Despite the bruises on her face and the injuries she'd suffered, there was still fire behind her eyes.

'Look at these if you don't believe me.' Damien grabbed his phone from his pocket and drew up some of Lillian's texts. *Pigs are baying for your blood. Leave Amy be and get the hell out of there.* Lillian had sent the text yesterday. He'd spoken to her since. He should have taken her advice straight away, but he didn't trust Lucy not to rat him out. He needed to work out what he was going to do with her first.

Amy nodded, reading the text. A silent understanding passed between them as Lucy's tune came to an end in the other room. He picked up the bowl of porridge, but Amy shook her head.

'Right then.' Damien stood to leave. Nervous energy surged through his body at the thought of what lay ahead. One way or another, the shit was about to hit the fan.

CHAPTER FIFTY-THREE

Donovan glanced up from his monitor as a figure entered his office. It was Superintendent Jones, and he did not look best pleased as he carried a folded-up newspaper in his hand. Donovan knew what he was going to say. As predicted, the headlines had already hit the papers. Donovan had predicted Lillian's exclusive story almost word for word as she told the world that the renowned DI Amy Winter was pregnant with Donovan's baby.

'Yea Gods, man! Why didn't you warn me!' Jones' face was thunderous as he slammed the paper on Donovan's desk.

'Sorry, boss,' Donovan replied. 'But I didn't want to be kicked off the case.'

'Well, you are, as of this moment.' He just noticed Paddy who had taken up residence at Amy's desk. 'Did you know about this?'

Donovan spoke up before Paddy could reply. 'Nobody knew. Lillian must have heard it from Damien. We didn't want it to come out like this.'

The superintendent shook his head. He was a large man who had put on weight in recent months, and judging by the pink flush rising up his throat, his blood pressure was going through the roof. 'When I told you to look after Winter, I didn't mean like that! How long have you two been seeing each other?'

'With all due respect, sir, that's none of your business.'

'It is if it affects this bloody case! How unprofessional does this make us appear, not one but two Met police officers splashed all over the papers, and that awful Grimes woman making money from it. I thought you were better than this, Donovan.' His words descended into grumbles as he mumbled something about people 'shacking up with each other' behind his back.

'How is DCI Jones these days?' Paddy interrupted, an amiable smile resting on his face. I hear she's taking early retirement.' DCI Jones was his wife.

Superintendent Jones shot Paddy a look which suggested he keep his comments to himself. He returned his attention to Donovan. 'You're off the case. In fact, go home. We'll discuss this tomorrow. In the meantime, you shouldn't be here.'

Donovan knew there was no point in arguing, not with the mood Jones was in. His superintendent was right. There was no point in him being here. Besides, he had plans which would not be authorised in time by his peers. He picked up his belongings and, after giving Paddy a nod, walked out the door. Time was running out. He knew what he had to do.

CHAPTER FIFTY-FOUR

Damien's head was pounding. He couldn't wait for this hunt to end. Even Lucy seemed distracted today. She'd already packed her belongings. Everything was ready to go. All her thoughts were focused on finishing Amy Winter off. He'd always known that he and Lucy were there for a good time, not a long time. She wouldn't risk being cut out of her inheritance for him. While he may not always agree with Lillian, her words rang true. A pretty rich girl like Lucy was not destined for prison. But one way or another, he'd be making a return visit to the clink soon. In prison he was respected, at the top of his game. He knew every trick in the book. How to get drugs, how to sell them without getting caught. His business had been lucrative, and protection was always there. But this was different. If Lucy put him on the hook for this, he'd be put away for life, and nobody would have his back.

The tinny sound of his scrambler reverberated through the woodlands as he led Lucy away. He'd managed to distract her for a few minutes while Amy doubled back. He only hoped she made it to the empty cottage in time. He pointed straight ahead, signalling to Lucy to send her astray. Her bike roared past him as she overtook him on the overgrown trail. But his mind was on his backup plan as he negotiated the path ahead. He'd been breaking the law for years. He may not have a fancy education, but he knew how things worked in his world. His passport was ready, his bag packed. He could begin again. Lillian had friends in Spain who were happy to give him a job. Prison was a last resort but no worse than the life he'd lived up until now.

'There she is!' Lucy's excited screams pierced his ear. She swerved her bike, doing a U-turn. 'I see her!'

Damien's jaw tightened as he saw the app open on his phone which was attached to the handlebar of the bike. He hadn't counted on Lucy using a tracker today. His grip tightened on the throttle. He tried to keep up with Lucy who was now racing ahead. A small part of him hated to put an end to the craziness of it all. Last night's argument was mental, and he had the bruises to prove it. Lucy had lost the plot, smashing up the cottage and throwing vases and glasses at his head. It could have been worse. She could have been holding his gun.

Lillian had been on his back, ringing every five minutes before Lucy had got a hold of his phone and told her to fuck off.

'I'm your woman now,' she'd spat as she'd turned on Damien. 'You don't need her anymore.'

But that wasn't the way things worked. Lucy had him until she grew tired of him, but Lillian was always there.

His eyes were streaming from the wind as they brought their bikes to a halt. He blinked to make out the form of the woman standing in the old cottage doorway.

'Let me do it!' Lucy screamed, in a tone that was growing to irritate him.

'Clip her legs,' he ordered. 'Don't kill her.' He was beginning to regret trusting her with a gun.

'Why not?' She sulked. 'You said…'

'The game's over,' Damien shouted, the wind taking his words. 'She's preggers, and I ain't no baby killer.'

'She's pregnant?' Her eyes widened gleefully as she turned to face him. 'A belly shot it is then.'

'No!' Damien growled. 'Shoot her in the leg!'

He rubbed his eyes which were blurry from grit. They were streaming now.

'Oh, wait a minute, that's...' Lucy's words faded as she looked through her viewfinder.

'That's what?' Damien sniffed, his heart a drumbeat in his chest.

'Nothing!' Lucy licked her lips, curling her finger around the trigger. 'I thought I was too far out.' Her lips rose in a smile. 'But I can see her just fine now.'

Damien was about to utter a warning, but Lucy pulled the trigger, and there was a deafening crack as the sound of gunfire filled the air.

Damien's vision cleared, and the figure went down, an explosion of red blasting from their temple. 'You stupid bitch!' He roared in anger and disbelief. 'You shot her in the head!'

'Oops.' A tinkle of laughter left Lucy's lips as she jumped back up on the quad.

A sick feeling washed over him, and he was overcome by anger and disbelief. There was no surviving such a head shot. He hadn't planned on killing Amy. He was going to let her go. But now she was lying dead, half her head blown away. His breath was heavy as he came to terms with it. Amy Winter was dead.

CHAPTER FIFTY-FIVE

TWENTY MINUTES PREVIOUSLY

Every muscle in Amy's body screamed for relief. She forced her steps forward, her injuries on fire as the wind swept the hair off her face. Her movements were primal now. Not for her, but the life inside her. Damien had proved true to his word, distracting Lucy long enough for her to double back towards the cottage and into the woodlands beyond. She forced one foot before the other over the clearing, where she was a sitting duck for anyone taking a shot.

She ran through the pain, one hand supporting her growing stomach as she made it past the clearing and into the trees. She searched for a solid structure. Maybe she could find a weapon of some kind. She paused for breath. What if Lucy and Damien were there, waiting for her? *Keep moving forward,* she told herself. But was she running to her death? There was no police helicopters or sirens. She was on her own. *No.* She caught her thoughts as a lump formed in her throat. She wouldn't do this. The only way to play the game was subjectively. She was a Winter, not a Grimes, despite the stories she'd fed her brother.

She wouldn't look at her feet. Right now, it felt like she was walking over hot coals. She found the softest route, dodging twigs and rocks. In the distance, the dreadful rev of an engine broke the eerie silence. They were moving, which meant they weren't ahead of her. Not yet.

The sight of the derelict building almost made her cry with relief. But it was nothing like the log cottage. There was no sign of life here. The woodland wasn't as dense and the space around it felt exposed. Breathing hard, she gazed up at the sagging roof which was bowed by a fallen tree now covered in moss. There was a menacing quality to the building, and as she took in the smashed windowpanes, she wasn't sure if she wanted to go inside. Her mind raced with thoughts of booby traps, and she cautiously negotiated the path as she approached the doorless front entrance. Glass, leaves, and debris lined each floor of the narrow bungalow. The air was cold and sharp against her skin. There was nothing she could use as a weapon. Nothing that would protect her from a gun. She spun around as movement rose behind her. But the person behind her wasn't Damien or Lucy. It was Lillian.

'What...what are you doing here?' She could barely catch her breath to speak to her biological mother. She curled her hands into fists, ready to fight her way out.

'Steady now, take it easy.' Lillian's eyes were as big as saucers as she took Amy's form in. 'I'm here to help.'

'Have you called the police?' But Amy knew as soon as she'd had blurted the words there was no chance of that.

'And get Damien nicked? Don't be daft.' Lillian looked Amy up and down.

Amy didn't trust this woman. 'Then what are you doing here?'

'To put a stop to this, of course. Damien's gone too far.' Her gaze trailed to Amy's stomach. 'I'm not completely heartless, you know.'

So Lillian was aware of her pregnancy.

'Jesus. What have they done to you?' Lillian slipped her jacket off. She handed Amy the red coat and rested it over her shoulders.

Amy pushed her arms into the sleeves. It was a small gesture of kindness. One of few she had witnessed from the woman before her. 'Please tell me you're parked nearby.' Amy's teeth involuntarily chattered from the cold.

'I'm parked a mile down the road,' Lillian said. 'It wasn't easy, finding a way into this place without being seen.'

'We need to go.' A stitch burned in Amy's side. At least, she hoped it was a stitch. She hadn't felt any movement from her baby in a while. 'Have you got a phone?'

Lillian smiled derisively. 'If I had, I certainly wouldn't give it to you. I'll get you to my car but on my terms. Agreed?'

Amy nodded, too weary to disagree. Right now, Lillian Grimes was all she had.

'Stay here. I'll see if the coast is clear. I've tried calling Damien, but he's not picking up.'

Amy could have cried in relief. She was almost safe. With Lillian on her side, Damien may see sense. That's if he didn't escape with Lucy first. All this time, and she'd been just a mile from a road. She dared to imagine safety. Of seeing Donovan again. Of one day holding their baby. But as Lillian went to the front of the cottage, Amy watched her movement, and a sudden thought struck. Her height, her hair, her black trousers, and white blouse. Amy looked down at her clothes. From a distance, Lillian appeared just like her. She had been dressing to annoy her, filling her wardrobe with identical clothes and even the same haircut. But now it may just cost Lillian her life. She opened her mouth to call out. To tell her to exercise caution. But as she took a breath to shout, a shot rang through the air. It was followed by a deadened thump, and from the distance, a joyous scream. Oh no.

CHAPTER FIFTY-SIX

Lucy whooped before Damien as he sped to the cottage. Someone would have heard the shot as it cracked through the air, sending wildlife into an explosion of panic. She didn't have time to gloat. But Damien could not leave without checking the body. Was his sister really dead? There was a blackness in his heart at the sudden sense of finality. It felt as if someone had shoved their fist down his throat and was squeezing hard. He pulled up next to the cottage, almost coming off the bike, his legs like rubber bands. Stumbling to the front of the cottage, he collapsed next to the lifeless body, which was facedown in the mud. Damien dug his fingers into the soil, which was wet with blood and brain.

Lucy stood over him, a gruesome smile on her face. 'Good shot, if I say so myself.'

Damien ground his back teeth. The bitch had planned this from the beginning. He should go. Take his mother's warning and leave, while there was still time. But there was something about this scene that was out of kilter. He cast an eye over the corpse's red nails and the aging, bloodstained hands. He placed a hand on her cold wrinkled skin, now slick with blood. He had to see for himself, because he wouldn't believe it. Not until he saw her face.

Grappling with the deadened weight, he turned the body over and took in what was left of her face. It wasn't Amy. It was Lillian. His mother was dead. Tears welled in his eyes as he called her name and the bottom fell out of his world. 'Mum!' He began to sob. 'Mum!' But she was gone.

'Don't waste your tears on her. She had it coming,' Lucy sneered. 'And the game's not over yet.' She marched into the derelict cottage, kicking debris out of her way.

Damien wiped his face with the back of his hand, the air thick with the smell of blood, sulphur, and the trail Lucy's perfume. He couldn't comprehend what had just happened. Lucy, the first woman he had opened up to about his family, had just shot his mother in cold blood. But there was no undoing what had happened.

Lucy held her rifle with confidence as she swaggered into the cottage. 'Amyyyyy,' she sang. 'Come out, come out, wherever you are!' She was relishing every second as she entered the derelict cottage, proudly declaring that she was the woman who killed Lillian Grimes. It had not been a case of mistaken identity. She'd meant to finish his mother off. Now she had Amy in her sights.

'You didn't tell us you were pregnant.' Lucy's smug voice rose from inside the building. 'Hey babe,' she shouted from within. 'I get two for the price of one!'

Damien took a sudden breath before getting to his feet. Taking his pistol from the back of his jeans, he followed Lucy inside. She was right. This ended now. Damien's footsteps were heavy, his thoughts dark.

Amy was not cowering in the corner. She was standing in front of Lucy, her fists in the air. 'At least drop your weapon,'

Amy reasoned. 'Make it a fair fight. Unless you think you're going to lose.'

But Lucy continued to cackle. 'As much as I'd love to do the honours, it's not my turn. It's Damo's. Hey, babe, have you seen...?' Her smile faded as Damien approached.

'You murdered my mother.' His words were dead, his tone flat, as if a part of him had retreated into itself.

Amy stepped backwards.

Lucy blurted a nervous laugh. 'Aw, babe, I didn't mean to. How was I supposed to know she'd come running out of here in the same clothes? C'mon. Let's finish this off. Right here. Right now.' Her gaze returned to Amy as she handed Damien the gun. 'Shoot the bitch.'

'Yeah.' Damien raised the pistol, feeling numb inside. 'It's my turn.' He closed one eye, took aim and pulled the trigger.

CHAPTER FIFTY-SEVEN

TEN MINUTES EARLIER

Amy stared at Lillian's lifeless body, unable to take it in. A crack had rung out, splitting Lillian's forehead. She was dead. Pain rippled through Amy's body, and she backed up against the wall as it took her breath away. No. She was only five months gone.

'Please, no,' she whispered, clutching her belly. *Not when we've come this far.* Because there was no doubt left in her mind. She wanted this baby more than anything in the world. But now she was weak as pain rippled through her body. Her gaze darted around the room as the sound of Damien's scrambler tainted the air. She wasn't physically able to run. There must be something she could use as a weapon. But there was nothing but her fists. The sound of Lucy's mocking tone filled her with dread. 'Good shot, if I say so myself,' she said, without remorse.

Amy looked out the window as Damien's cries filled the air. He was hunched over their mother's body, and now Lucy was strolling in. Damien wasn't watching Lucy or listening to what she had to say. His head bowed, he was completely focused on Lillian's remains.

'Amyyyyy, come out, come out, wherever you are!' Lucy laughed as she found Amy, hunched on the floor. 'Ding-dong, the wicked witch is dead! Bet you didn't think I had it in me, did ya?' Her face was locked in a terrifying grin. 'I'm the woman who killed Lillian Grimes.'

A bolt of laughter left her lips. She had clearly lost the plot. She was walking with the swagger of someone who believed she was a god. That's what this was all about. The power had gone to her head. Without a matriarch in her family, Lucy had veered out of control. There was no sympathy from her father, who deemed her an utter disappointment. She had nowhere to turn because her friends were false. Using a cocktail of drugs, she abandoned herself to the darkest of thrills. Anything to feel different. Anything to feel alive. Because as much as Amy hated her, she understood her, too. Her mother was exactly the same. But now she was lying dead, having gone outside to check that the coast was clear. Her final act in this world would never make up for the devastation she'd caused, but it was an honourable one.

Amy breathed through the pain, one hand on her stomach as she got to her feet.

Lucy tilted her head to one side as she took in her form. 'You didn't tell us you were pregnant.' She glanced back out through the broken window pane, her voice rising an octave as she shouted to Damien, 'Hey, babe, I get two for the price of one!'

Her laughter filled the derelict room in a manic symphony, and Amy raised her fists in the air.

'At least drop your weapon. Make it a fair fight. Unless you think you're going to lose'

But Lucy continued to laugh. 'As much as I'd love to do the honours, it's not my turn. It's Damo's. Hey, hun, have you seen...?' The words died on her lips as she saw the look on his face.

His cheeks were wet with tears. His eyes narrowed, spittle gathering in the corners of his lips. A daub of Lillian's blood streaked his skin from where he had wiped away his face.

'You murdered my mother.' His words were dead, his tone flat, as if a part of him had retreated into itself.

Amy stepped backwards as she watched the exchange.

'Aw, babe, I didn't mean to. How was I supposed to know she'd come running out of here? C'mon. Let's finish this off. Right here. Right now.' Her attention returned to Amy before she gave Damien the gun. 'Shoot the bitch.'

Nodding, Damien raised the pistol and aimed it in Amy's direction. She was backed into a corner. There was nowhere to go.

'Please,' she whispered. 'Don't hurt my baby.' She wanted to tell him about Lillian. To say she'd come here to stop them both. But time didn't allow it, and now all she could think about were the people she was leaving behind. She squeezed her eyes shut as Damien's finger tightened around the trigger and pulled.

CHAPTER FIFTY-EIGHT

Amy crouched in the foetal position, her hands over her ears as the thunderous blast of gunshot filled the air. She ran a hand over her head, expecting to see blood. Had Damien missed the shot? Did she not feel the pain? But there was nothing, apart from the ache in her stomach that was now ebbing away. She rubbed her eyes to clear her vision and saw Damien standing over Lucy, who was now lying on the floor. Her blonde hair was matted with blood, her limbs sprawled in unnatural positions. With shaking hands, he pointed at Lucy's remains. The pool of blood beneath her body flowed outwards until it touched his shoes.

'She killed Mum.' He stood, wide-legged, as he stared at Lucy's body. 'She killed her.'

Amy exhaled a shuddering breath. She wasn't safe yet. Damien was a loose cannon. She couldn't predict his next move.

He looked Amy up and down. 'I was going to let you live. It was what Mum wanted. Until she...oh GOD!' He lurched towards the corner of the room, dropping his gun as he puked.

The loss of his mother was clearly too much for him to bear. Amy sat, immobile, feeling totally numb. She was Poppy Grimes again, hiding behind the floor length curtains because her mummy and daddy had done something bad. She shivered involuntarily, and the sound of a car engine rose in the distance as she returned to a reality she was not strong enough to face.

Someone's coming, she thought vaguely. She should grab the gun from the floor, take control of the situation, but yet movement would still not come. She was rooted to the spot. 'Go,' she whispered to Damien. 'Run!'

He lingered only for a second as they exchanged a glance. A moment of understanding passed between them. She was living up to her word, because that's what Grimes' family members did. Was she telling Damien to run because he was family or because it would get him away from her? The truth was, she didn't know. She just needed him gone. The car was approaching at speed. But who was inside?

She closed her eyes for a moment, and when she opened them again, Damien had gone, along with the gun. She buried her head in her knees, whispering a silent prayer to her baby as a ripple of pain took hold. The car pulled up outside and a door slammed with force. She should go outside, make herself known. She should do a lot of things. She breathed through the cramps. She couldn't lose her baby. Not now. But neither could she bring herself to leave the windswept room. Because Lillian was outside, lying dead on the grass, the brain that harboured so many dark ideas now exposed to the open air. Another killer lay before her, remorseless to her last breath. Two women the world was better off without. Amy didn't know how long she had been sitting there when Donovan's form filled the doorway, and he exhaled a cry of relief.

CHAPTER FIFTY-NINE

The journey to Amy's suspected location had been hell on earth. Donovan hadn't just planted a recording device in Lillian's hotel room, he'd placed a tracker in her bag, too. If it was good enough for Damien Grimes, then it was good enough for him. This was one of the few times in his career that he'd worked without the necessary permissions in place. Lillian had barely moved from her flat since their rendezvous, and it was with immense relief that he'd discovered she had left London to drive to the privately owned woodlands in Little Dunmow in Essex. Something told him it wasn't to have a picnic. But then Lillian had abandoned her car a mile up the road and hidden her bag beneath the front seat. The woodlands were so dense with vegetation that Donovan had briefly lost track of her. Then he'd heard the scramblers and the jarring sound of gunshot. Before, there was hope. But then there was the knowing – the awful, dreadful knowing that good or bad, it was over. They had run out of road. This was it. His gut had twisted as a sense of finality told him there was nothing more he could do.

Lillian was too late. He could not contemplate a life without Amy. He'd forced himself to focus as he abandoned his car and raced to the scene. Too late. They were too late. The words taunted him, repeating in a loop in his brain. He couldn't breathe as he took in the scene. The body on the ground. Black hair. White top. Blood bloomed under their head, seeping into the soil. Her face...it was gone.

'Jesus!' he'd cried, trying to keep his balance as he faltered on the torn-up ground. He wasn't thinking about Damien or the danger he could be in. This was a firearms incident. Procedure deemed that he waited for police firearms backup because there were armed suspects involved. But Donovan had ran blindly towards the body, calling Amy's name. His eyes blurred with grief-stricken tears, he knelt beside her. But it wasn't Amy. It was Lillian. He'd taken in a sudden, icy breath. It was Lillian lying before him, dressed in similar clothes. There had only been one gunshot. Amy had to be alive. But he had not lost sight of the fact that she could still be in danger. Lucy could have beaten him there.

He'd focused on the cottage, taking slow, steady steps towards it as he listened for every sound. His heart had faltered as he saw the second body. But his gaze did not linger there for long. It was drawn to the figure in the corner. He exhaled in monumental relief.

'Amy?' he'd said softly. Because it didn't feel like her. She sat in stunned silence, her knees drawn up to her chest. He cast one more glance over Lucy, who had been shot in the head. She wasn't getting up from that. And now he was standing before Amy, asking if she was hurt. He summoned an ambulance and updated control when she failed to respond. 'Amy?' he said again, touching her windswept hair.

'I'm cramping,' she said. 'I'm not moving until the ambulance gets here.'

'Oh, sweetheart.' Donovan kissed the top of her head. 'I thought you were dead.'

Amy's gaze turned to Lucy, her grey eyes devoid of sympathy. 'She…she shot Lillian. Then Damien shot her. He wanted to let me go.'

'But you're OK?' He looked Amy up and down. There were bruises, cuts, old injuries, but no blood on the floor.

'The baby…' she said. Donovan realised from the vacancy in her eyes that she was in shock.

'Shh, it's OK,' he said, opening his arms to hold her close. She felt thinner, and freezing cold. She was wearing Lillian's jacket, and trembled beneath his touch. 'You're safe. You both are. We're going to get you into hospital now.'

His world was reforming, the ground settling beneath his feet. He realized he'd been crying tears of relief and wiped them from his face.

CHAPTER SIXTY

Paddy was a pessimist by nature. Experience taught him that hope was a dangerous thing. He knew what they were dealing with when it came to Damien Grimes. Lillian may not have taken Amy, but she was certainly pulling his strings, and that was a very dangerous thing.

When Donovan's call came in to the office, Paddy was ill-prepared.

'I'm with Amy,' Donovan spoke in short gasps as he relayed the news. He seemed overcome by emotion, happy beyond belief as he explained that they were on their way to the hospital. 'She's injured but in one piece. Damien's taken off. Lucy and Lillian are dead.'

'Jesus, Mary and Joseph!' Paddy blurted, another one of his mother's old sayings, reserved for the most extraordinary news. 'Where the feck are ya?'

'Great Dunmow, in Essex,' Donovan replied. He gave him a brief low down of the situation before explaining that he had to go. So that was why it hadn't come in over their police channels. It was in the hands of a different force.

'Leave it with me,' Paddy said, hardly able to believe it. 'I'll tell Craig and the team, then I'll speak to Sally-Ann.' He couldn't wait to share the good news, but how would Sally-Ann take the news of Lillian's demise? A whoop rose from the main office. Molly was bouncing in delight as she hung up the phone. News had obviously filtered through.

'That was Essex Police. They've found her!' she exclaimed. One by one, her colleagues dropped what they were doing to take in the news. 'She's in Great Dunmow,' Molly continued, her cheeks flushed with excitement. 'We were right. It was Damien and Lucy all along.'

Paddy could have shared in their celebrations, but he needed to be with Sally-Ann before she heard the news second hand. DI Craig Winter walked in. He approached Paddy, his expression relaying that he had also heard the news. 'So you've heard then? I've just updated mum. She's over the moon.'

'It's great news,' Paddy smiled, knowing that if Amy were here, she'd have a go at Craig for not telling Flora in person. At least Flora had the support of the FLO who would answer any follow up questions and organise a visit to the hospital.

'Boss, do you mind if I take off?' Paddy asked. 'I don't like to leave the team short-handed, but I need to break the news to Sally-Ann. She'll need to know about her mum, too.'

'What?' Craig said, distracted, as Molly and her team chatted amongst themselves. They were reading the on-screen updates aloud as they filtered through from control. 'Oh, yes, of course,' he added. 'Lillian. I can't say I'm sorry she's gone, but Sally-Ann needs to hear it from you. Denny can act up in your absence. Take the rest of the day off.' Denny had covered as acting sergeant before and was capable of covering his absence. The rest of the investigation would need to be tied up, and a debriefing would follow soon, but right now, Sally-Ann was Paddy's priority. He needed to tell her in person. He didn't know how she would react. Paddy was fine as he made his way down the police station corridor. He kept it together as he got outside. It wasn't until he sat behind the steering wheel of his Jaguar that his shoulders began to shake and he cried tears of relief. Despite all his platitudes to Sally-Ann, he hadn't dared hope that he'd see Amy alive again. He reached into his pocket for a tissue, and his fingers brushed against the engagement ring box. Amy was alive. They were waiting for news on her baby, and Lillian would never cause havoc in the world again. Perhaps now was a better time than any to let Sally-Ann know how much she was loved.

This time, Paddy was happy to shove his key in the Yale lock of his front door. Sally-Ann was upon him in minutes, her face tearful and expectant. 'They've found her,' he said, still tearful himself. 'And she's OK.'

Sally-Ann responded with cry, too choked up to articulate her words. He hugged her tightly. The house was cold due to the dip in the temperature outside. Soon he would turn up the heat and breathe some warmth into the place. Everything would be better, now Amy had been found. He waited for Sally-Ann to part before sharing the rest of the news.

'There's something else, isn't there?' There was concern in her voice as she studied his face. 'What is it? Has she lost the baby? Are you sure she's OK?'

'It's Lillian,' Paddy said quickly, wanting to get it over with. 'She went to find Amy. She tried to help her escape.'

'But?' Sally-Ann replied, wiping away her tears.

Paddy led her into the kitchen and they sat at the table

where they had plotted and planned over the last few days. For once the kettle was cold. There was no food cooking in the oven or bubbling on the stove.

'Lucy and Damien were on a hunt. Lucy saw your mother in the distance. She was dressed the same as Amy. I'm sorry...' he shook his head. 'But she's gone. Lucy shot her in the head.'

Sally-Ann's hand rose to her mouth. 'Oh. And she's dead?'

Paddy nodded. 'Damien turned the gun on Lucy for killing your mother.'

'He...he murdered her? His own girlfriend? Are you sure?' She stared at Paddy in disbelief.

'Aye, and Damien's on the run.' He monitored her expression as he rested a hand on her back. 'Can I get you anything?'

'I'm fine.' Sally-Ann took a couple of deep breaths. 'I should feel bad, but I don't. Because I have you and Amy and everything's going to be OK... isn't it?'

In the last few weeks Paddy had agonised over how he was going to propose to Sally-Ann. He'd thought about hot air balloon rides, flash mobs in London, or hiding the ring in a cake. But now, more than ever, he wanted to reassure her that she was right. He took the box from his pocket and slid it across the table. 'Till death do us part. We'll take whatever life throws at us and more. What do ya think?' It wasn't the most romantic proposal, but it was from the heart.

Sally-Ann offered up a knowing smile. It was the expression of someone who had been waiting for him to propose all along. Had she found the ring in his pocket? Known what he was trying to say? None of that mattered now, because she was sliding the ring on her finger and rising from her chair to give him a tearful kiss. 'I thought you'd never ask,' she simply said.

CHAPTER SIXTY-ONE

Amy slid a hand over the swell of her stomach as she opened her eyes. The light stung her irises, and she groaned in response. Something was connected to her wrist, and she tried to shake it off. For a split second, she thought she was back in the cottage, her wrist shackled to the bed.

'Amy, it's alright. You're in hospital.' The voice was rich and soothing. Donovan. A warm hand gently guided hers back down to her bed. 'It's your drip, don't pull it out.'

Every time she fell asleep, she awoke with a start. Her thoughts went to their unborn baby. Were they still OK?

Of course, she thought, eventually taking in Donovan's words. She was on a drip. She had been dehydrated and starved over the last few days. 'The baby...' she said, but immediately, her question was answered by a dart of movement. Then she remembered: the pains she had experienced had been hunger cramps and nothing more.

'They scanned you, remember? He's fine.' Donovan squeezed her hand. 'Take it easy. You've been through a lot.'

Amy rested her head against the pillow. It smelled crisp and clean. No lingering stench of cannabis or smoke filtered through. She wanted to ask another question but couldn't bring herself to say the words.

Donovan leaned over to kiss her on the forehead. 'I almost lost you. I'm never letting you out of my sight again.'

'Lillian...is she?' Amy gave in to the question stubbornly resting on her lips.

'Dead.' Donovan slowly nodded. 'Yes.' Another squeeze of her hand. He looked tired, but smelt good as he leaned in to kiss her forehead.

'Can I?' he said, his hand hovering over her bump.

'Of course you can touch me, you numpty.' Amy forced a smile. She knew why he had asked. Victims who'd had all their rights taken away needed to be treated with care. 'I'm not a victim,' she said, keen to ascertain herself. 'I knew you'd find me in the end.'

But Donovan didn't appear convinced. 'Then you knew more than me. If it wasn't for Lillian... Sorry,' he added with a sigh. 'It's too soon, isn't it? You don't want to think about her.'

'No, it's fine,' Amy said. 'I'm OK.' She touched her stomach. 'We're OK.' Laughter escaped her lips. Small at first, then growing louder. 'I'm free. I'm finally free of her.' Another wild giggle which turned into a sob. Her emotions were running wild. She didn't know how to feel. But she was alive, and so was her baby. She would focus on that for now.

'Are you sure you're alright?' Donovan looked at her quizzically. 'Do you want me to get someone?'

'I'm fine.' Amy took a breath and composed herself. She glanced around the room, noticing the flowers and 'get well soon' cards. 'How's Sally-Ann?'

'She's on her way. She's been relentless, Amy. Your sister has done you proud.' Silence passed between them. 'How are you feeling?'

'Nothing a saline drip and a good meal won't fix,' Amy said

softly, although deep down, she knew she wouldn't just bounce back from this. She shifted her arm, which was heavily bandaged. 'Any permanent damage?'

'The doctor said you were lucky. But you'll have scars and will need physiotherapy before you can get back on your feet properly.'

Her eyes flicked to the glass on her bedstead, and Donovan filled it before handing it over. At least they were in a private room.

'Are you in pain? I can call the doctor...'

Amy was in pain, but she was in no rush to blur the time between them with drugs. 'Just sit with me. Please. This is all I want. You here beside me, and our baby, safe.'

'Then you have me. Always.' His eyes were clear but sombre.

'Do you mean that?' Amy said. 'Always?'

Donovan seemed to view her with a new appreciation. 'Always.'

'Then let's make it official.'

'Seriously?' Donovan said, his eyes twinkling. 'Because I've got the ring right here.'

'I bet you have.' Amy chuckled.

He plucked a small red velvet heart-shaped box from his jacket pocket. 'Or is it too soon? I mean, I don't want to take advantage.'

'Seriously?' Amy stared in disbelief. 'All this time you've been proposing to me, and now that I suggest it, you're getting cold feet?'

'There's nothing in the world I'd like more.' He smiled, a world of warmth and affection behind his eyes. 'Winter, will you marry me?'

'Of course I will.' From the moment the ring slid on her finger, it felt like she had come home. Clapping erupted from the corridor. Sally-Ann and Paddy had been watching.

'We're engagement twins!' Sally-Ann showed off her own sparkling ring.

'Congratulations.' Amy beamed, wincing as her sister took her in for a hug. Her bruises may have been painful, but she never imagined the world would feel so good again.

CHAPTER SIXTY-TWO

Damien sat in his secret bunker, listening to movement overhead. He had enough supplies to keep him going for as long as a month or more. The bunker wasn't on the plans of the house, and the cops would never find him here. He knew this job was a risky one, but he had never imagined he would be hiding out here alone. At the very least, he'd expected to have his mother, who had vowed to get him out of the country safely – to Spain where he would meet up with her network of friends. But now, Lillian was lying in a morgue with a tag on her toe, and Lucy was most likely in the drawer next to her. When it came to family loyalties, Lucy shouldn't have tested him.

It was meant to be a game. It had ended with the loss of her life. He hadn't hesitated for a second as he'd pulled the trigger on her. Something primal had taken hold of him. She had killed his mother. She would not end his sister and unborn baby, too. Damien knew it was skewed thinking, after everything they had done, but he had never intended to kill Amy at the end. After all the time they'd spent together, he understood her a little more. She wasn't that much different to him after all. He had imagined him and Lucy, hiding out here for a month, while Amy and her team furiously tried to find them.

He had fantasised about the satisfaction he'd feel when he finally got away. But then he'd discovered Lucy had no intention of going anywhere with him. He'd heard her on the phone to her father as he'd pleaded with her to come home. He'd spoken about how he'd get the best lawyers. How they could pin it all on her boyfriend. But the problem with that was there were two witnesses who would say otherwise. With Amy and Lillian gone, Lucy could blame the whole thing on him. He'd thought about nothing else, imagining her laughing at him. Had he done the right thing? At least now he could get away. Start again. True to her word, Amy had given him enough time to run. But would the itch to kill return? It was only a matter of time before someone pissed him off. Or some woman needed to be taught a lesson or two. He licked his lips. He would have to be more careful next time. He closed his eyes as tiredness closed in from every side.

He was awoken by a shaft of light. He sprang to his feet, grabbing for his gun. But it was too late. His movements slowed because two red dots were trained on his chest. The next thing he knew, his face was being ground into the floor as the police took control.

'How?' he asked, because he had to know. 'How did you find me?' He put the question to Donovan as armed officers marched him to the awaiting police van.

'We re-enacted a hunt in the forest, and it's been on my mind ever since,' Donovan replied.

He seemed a different man today. Damien didn't need to ask how his sister was doing. He knew she would be just fine.

Donovan was still explaining, a bounce to his step. 'I realised that when animals are being hunted, it's in their instincts to do one thing...'

They exchanged a glance.
'They go underground.'

A LETTER FROM CAROLINE

My Dear Reader

I would like to thank you for taking the time to pick up my book. I hope you've enjoyed Amy Winter's journey in this latest episode. There are four previous books in this series if you haven't read them already, and I recommend beginning with Truth And Lies.

As always, I am hugely grateful to my readers and book bloggers for spreading the word. Recommendations are the lifeblood of any series, and it's heartening to know that many of you are keen to continue with Amy's journey. I've enjoyed writing In Cold Blood and I hope there will be more to come.

If you've enjoyed this book, I would be grateful if you could write me an Amazon review, even a one liner is enough to help my book stay visible in the charts. I love to hear from my readers and you can follow my author page on Facebook, Twitter and more.

Thank you again for your support. It's a dream come true to be able to write for a living and I couldn't have done it without you.

Caroline x

ACKNOWLEDGMENTS

Thank you to everyone who has brought this latest book in the Amy Winter series to fruition. Without the enthusiasm of my readers and bloggers, she would not be out there, solving crimes and getting herself into scrapes.

I hope my police colleagues forgive my use of creative licence when it comes to the amount of freedom my characters are allowed, and the paperwork that always seems to get done on time. Writing about crime is a lot more fun than the real-life graft of trying to solve it, and I have the utmost respect for those still in the job. You are the real life heroes.

While my time living on the coast of Essex will always stay with me, I've recently moved to Lincoln and I'm looking forward to getting to know the friends I have yet to meet. As readers of In Cold Blood will see, I've already found the nearby woodlands to be an inspirational setting for my books.

As always, I'd like to thank my family, friends, bloggers and fellow authors who provide me inspiration on a daily basis. In particular, Angie Marsons, her partner in crime Julie, and my bestie Mel Sherratt have been a huge inspiration to me along the way. If you haven't yet read an Angela Marsons or Mel Sherratt book then I highly recommend you do.

Finally, I'd like to thank the people who have helped shape this book up. To The Cover Collection for the cover image, and to Emmy Ellis of Studioenp for her editing services.

ABOUT THE AUTHOR

Caroline Mitchell is a New York Times, USA Today, Washington Post and International #1 Bestselling Author. Shortlisted for the International Thriller Awards for the best ebook 2017 and the Killer Nashville Best Police Procedural 2018. Over 1.5 million books sold with numerous editions translated worldwide.

Originating from Ireland, Caroline now lives with her family in a pretty woodland village outside Lincoln. A former police detective, she has worked in CID and specialised in roles dealing with vulnerable victims, high-risk victims of domestic abuse, stalking and serious sexual offences. She draws inspiration from the courage shown by survivors she safeguarded, combining it with her knowledge of police procedure to write crime thrillers full time. This is her eighteenth book.

To download a free short story and be kept updated of new releases, join her reader's club at www.caroline-writes.com

facebook.com/CMitchellAuthor
twitter.com/Caroline_writes
instagram.com/caroline_writes

Printed in Great Britain
by Amazon